SCENARIO F

Klein turned completely around, surveying the scene in its entirety. Bodies were spread-eagled on their backs everywhere amid the tall blue flowering weeds that rippled lazily in the breeze. Severed hands, bloody ears, legs, arms and internal organs that had been ripped from bodies mingled with piles of tortured silver metal, twisted hydraulic pipes, wing flaps and pages of that morning's edition of the Chicago *Tribune*. A little distance away two Catholic priests had appeared from nowhere, administering last rites, moving from body to body, divining in some way which of the dead passengers who didn't wear crucifixes belonged to their own faith.

Klein stepped aside to avoid the corpse of a stout, middle-aged woman, naked except for tattered pantyhose, a shaft of the steel frame of the seat in which she had been sitting speared through her back and sticking out of her belly, which even now was disgorging entrails in spasmodic jerks as rigor mortis set in . . .

Also by Basil Jackson in Sphere Books:

SUPERSONIC
SPILL!
THE NIGHT MANHATTAN BURNED

FLAMEOUT

BASIL JACKSON

SPHERE BOOKS LIMITED
30/32 Gray's Inn Road, London WC1X 8JL

First published in Great Britain by Robert Hale Ltd 1977

First Sphere Books edition 1978
Reprinted 1979 (twice), 1983 (twice)

TRADE
MARK

Flameout is a work of fiction. None of the events described is alleged to have taken place in fact, and many of the names of manufacturers and operators of aircraft equipment have been changed to emphasise the fictional nature of this work.

Set in Intertype Times

Printed in Great Britain by
Hunt Barnard Printing Ltd.,
Aylesbury, Bucks.

To Sherry Huber,
editor, mentor, and friend,
with gratitude

An air accident investigator must have an inquisitive nature, be dedicated to his work, be diligent and patient . . . humility, integrity and respect for human dignity must be his guiding rules.

– From *Manual of Aircraft Accident Investigation*,
International Civil Aviation Organization

CONTENTS

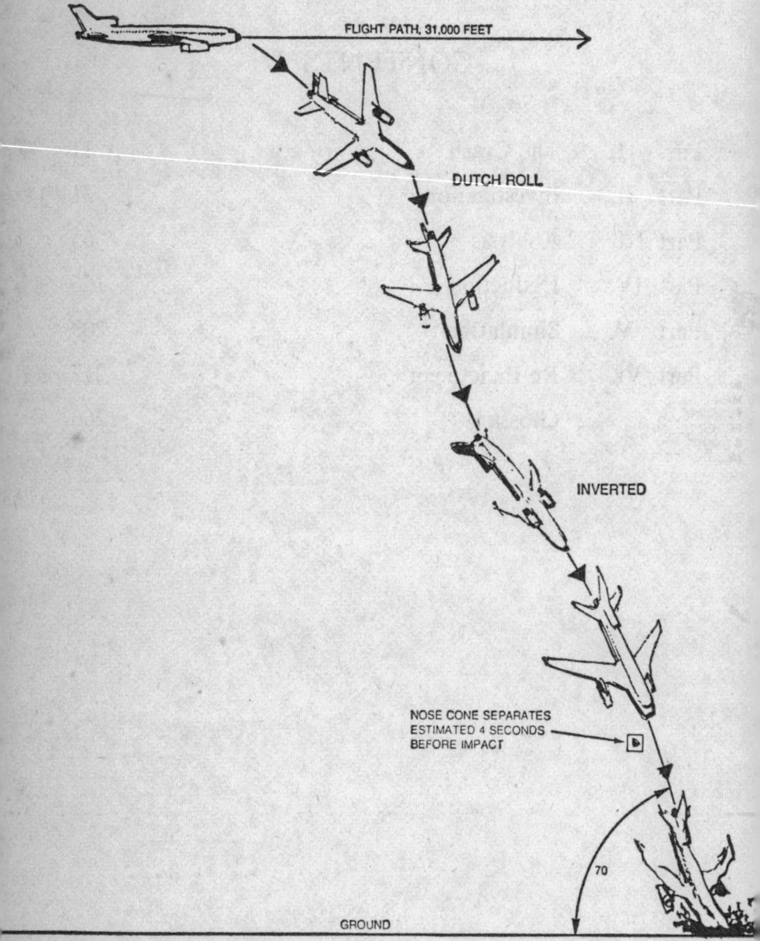

ESTIMATED MOTIONS OF CA-100 CARAVAN DURING LAST 69 SECONDS

Air Accident Report No. DCA 77-A-22

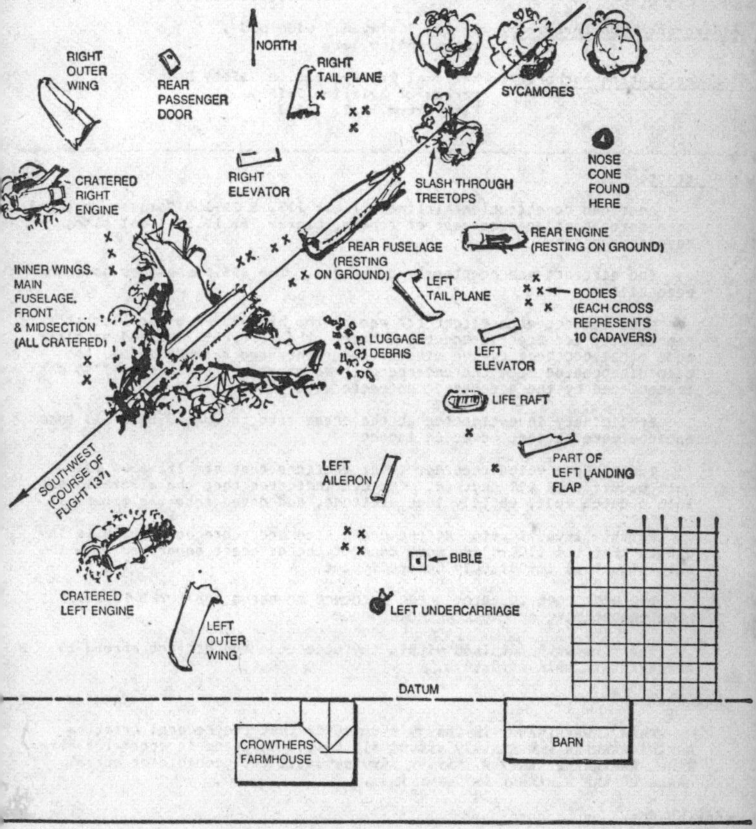

WRECKAGE DISTRIBUTION CHART
Air Accident Report No. DCA 77-A-22
CA-100 CARAVAN AIRCRAFT
—PREPARED BY MS. HELEN DIMITRY,
DRAFTING & SURVEY SECTION.

Security Classification of This Document:	RESTRICTED - NOT FOR PUBLICATION
Title of Document:	Air Accident Report No. DCA 77-A-22 (Preliminary)
Author of Document:	Steven L. Klein, Investigator-in-Charge
Aircraft Type Involved:	CA-100 "Caravan," wide-body, three-engine jet
Investigation Authority:	National Transportation Safety Board Bureau of Aviation Safety Washington, D.C. 20594

Abstract:

American Constitution Airlines Flight 137, a CA-100 Caravan, crashed on a farm 30 miles southwest of Topeka, Kansas, at 10.53 local time, May 16.

The aircraft was completely destroyed. The 406 passengers and crew were killed.

Last contact with Flight 137 was by the high-level controller at Kansas City Air Traffic Control Center. The aircraft reported an altitude of 31,000 feet twelve minutes and twenty-two seconds before the blip disappeared from the radarscope. No emergency radar code 7700 was transmitted by the aircraft. No radio Mayday was called.

Preliminary investigation at the crash site indicated that all three engines were at zero power on impact.

The cockpit voice recorder (CVR) confirms that simultaneous flameouts occurred on all engines. The CVR indicates that the aircraft went into a dutch roll, rapidly lost altitude, and dived into the ground.

Further investigation at the crash site and subsequent analysis indicate that the fiberglass nose cone of the aircraft separated from the main structure immediately before impact.

THE NOSE CONE INTERIOR SHOWS EVIDENCE OF BEING SUBJECTED TO EXTREME HIGH TEMPERATURE OF CAUSE UNKNOWN.

The fire was contained within the nose cone and did not spread to the aircraft main structure.

Action:

This Investigator-in-Charge recommends that the Federal Aviation Administration immediately ground all CA-100 Caravans in worldwide airline, freighter, and/or charter service until the probable or actual cause of the accident is determined.

Key Words:

Flameout, nose cone, fire - CAUSE UNKNOWN.

NTSB Form 1765.2

Part I
The Crash

ONE

Steven Klein lay in the middle of his office floor and swung his legs high into the air until his stubby body was in a perfect yoga Shoulder Stand. Mentally shutting out his surroundings, keeping his awareness within, he stayed in the pose for three minutes before allowing trunk and legs to descend to the carpet under abdominal muscle control.

He raised himself to the cross-legged Lotus position, took deep yogic breaths, loudly hummed a long, resonant 'OM . . . OM . . . OM . . . ,' and finished by softly singing, 'Shanti . . . peace . . . shalom . . . '

Lena Shaw, sitting at her desk outside, waited for the last syllable to die away before uncoiling her willowy five-foot-ten body from the chair. She entered his office, a cigarette burning in a slender ivory holder balanced between her fingers.

'It's sure good to hear you OM-ing and shalom-ing again, Steve.'

Shaw's never said that to me before, he thought, slowly rising to his feet and studying her face. Her usually placid eyes were troubled. 'What's up, Shaw? You always run this office like clockwork when I'm away.'

'It's Legal Department, Steve. They've rejected the Avianjet report you sent up before you went on vacation.' She blew a stream of smoke towards the ceiling. 'Ah – Legal, what do *they* know about the sweat you poured into that one?'

Klein smiled and made a sweeping gesture with his

left arm. 'The way I feel this morning, that can wait a minute.' He crossed to the coat rack and felt in his jacket pocket with his left hand. The action emphasised the flash of a chunky signet ring and the glint of gold cuff-links. His right arm hung loosely at his side, the result of a flying accident.

'Sarah helped me choose this. Got it in the best jewellery shop in Bermuda. Hope you like it, Shaw.' He handed her a small package and stood back expectantly.

Her face cleared, and she flashed her marvellously warm smile, stuck the cigarette holder between her lips at a jaunty angle, and untied the package. 'It's beautiful,' she said, withdrawing a bracelet of polished coral beads.

She slipped it over her wrist next to the two colourful bangles she already wore, the pink gleaming vividly against her black skin. 'Fits perfectly, Steve. Tell Sarah she's got good taste, just like you.' She bent over and planted a kiss on his cheek.

'Now, what about the Avianjet case?' Klein asked, sitting behind his desk.

'You remember your argument proving it wasn't the pilot's fault – that he didn't stand a chance?'

'Sure.'

'Legal's tossed it out.' Her face grew serious again. 'They imply he'd been drinking. They're trying to malign the character of a dead man, Steve.'

'Let's see it.'

She went to her desk and returned with a blue-bound report, handed it to Klein, and sat in the opposite chair.

Klein turned the pages, refreshing his memory. The little twin-jet executive aeroplane had taken off with one engine in reverse, due to the negligence of a mechanic who had reversed an electrical connection. Seven people, including the pilot and co-pilot, had been killed when the aircraft stalled, crashed, and burst into flames.

The crew was properly certificated, and there was no evidence of crew incapacitation, he had written. Someone had scrawled a big red question mark against the word 'incapacitation'.

His dark eyes raced down the page to a red hand-written note near another of his statements. *Too redeeming of what apparently was gross flying error,* it said.

'For God's sake,' he said, looking up at Shaw ' "Too redeeming of what apparently was gross flying error!" Why the hell don't they come right out and call it pilot error? It *wasn't* pilot error and the guy hadn't been drinking. The autopsy proved that.'

'Cool it, Steve. You'll lose the benefit of your holiday. Not to mention yoga.'

'But this is too much, Shaw!' he exclaimed indignantly. 'I'm going to take it up with Ray Malik.'

'What can the general manager do against all the weasel minds in Legal?'

'He's the highest I can appeal to in the investigation branch. I'll get him to argue the case with Legal's top man.'

He read other sections of the report. Shaw leaned back, puffing smoke, studying his pensive face. Working with him, as she had, over the past eleven years, she knew where the signs of frustration first showed: tightening muscles around the soft, kind eyes, and the pulling together of the bushy grey eyebrows. He had full lips, and a firm jawline, and she noticed that the suntan emphasised the lines on his forehead, up to the receding hairline. She thought again of the act of fate that had guided him into becoming an air accident investigator with the National Transportation Safety Board's Bureau of Aviation Safety. He'd been first officer of a DC-8 vectored over Newark when a Constellation had collided with the jet. The Connie's propeller blades had sliced through Klein's arm, and thirty-eight people, including the Connie's crew, had perished. The DC-8 had landed safely, with Klein the only casualty. She wondered what Klein would have been today if he had not been grounded: probably captain of a Boeing 747 or Lockheed TriStar. She waited for him to finish re-reading what he'd written, and she had typed, about the Avianjet's dead pilot.

'Listen to what I said,' he remarked, as if their minds worked together. *'There are three possible explanations for the catastrophe resulting from one of the engines being in reverse thrust at take-off. One, the pilot could not determine what the problem was; two, the pilot determined the problem but could not get the emergency system to work to correct the unwanted reverse thrust; and three, the pilot determined the problem but used an improper emergency procedure. This investigator is of the opinion that the latter possibility does not apply for reasons given later in this report.'*

He threw the report on the desk and looked at Shaw with a scowl on his face. 'I still hold that opinion, you gotta believe. Too redeeming – that's what you get for trying to protect a dead man's reputation in a case where he was blameless. I wish I could drag some of those desk-bound Legal types out to a wreckage site someday.'

'Once was enough for me.'

'You're right, Shaw. I shouldn't wish it on them.' He sighed, and pushed the report away. 'I'll read it again thoroughly and take it up with Malik.' He glanced at the stack of paperwork in his in-tray. 'First thing tomorrow. Who's on with me?' he inquired, looking at a sheet of paper Shaw had pinned at the exact centre of a notice board on the wall alongside his desk.

'Your old pal Bill Houston and a lot of other familiar names.'

He studied the list. It was headed GO-TEAM CATASTROPHIC ACCIDENTS – NOTIFY. Below, Shaw had typed: 'For week beginning May 16.' Klein's name was at the top as Investigator-in-Charge. Directly below was Duty Officer Earl Derrigan and his backup Harvey Foxe. Bill Houston was down under Powerplants, Jeffrey Liss for Systems, and Howard Bradley for Structures. Bradley was solid and so was Liss, who headed the group responsible for electronics, hydraulics, and flight controls, and for finding the all-important data recorder when an aircraft crashed, the so-called 'black-box'.

Shaw stood up: 'I've got things to clear off my desk, Steve. Let's pray it'll be another quiet week, eh?'

'I'm not religious, Shaw. You know that.'

'You'll go to hell.'

She laughed and waved her cigarette holder through the air as she slipped out of his office.

Klein continued down the list, wondering if Houston was going to be a father again: he hadn't seen the aero-engine expert for months. The seven-days-a-week, twenty-four-hour duty rosters shuffled investigators' working times unpredictably, depending on how many were already at accident scenes. Ah, George Downey was listed for Human Factors. He thought about the prematurely aged, silent man who was dedicated to the recovery of mangled and burned bodies and dealing with distraught relatives, and made a mental note to drop into his office later to say hello. Don Ackerman was down for Flight Operations, Dave Jacobs for Air Traffic Control, and Len Davies for Weather. Charlie Reynolds, Office of Public Affairs, was there as usual. His name was on every list. Poor bastard: he was the guy who had to explain to newsmen what the Go-Team discovered at a wreckage site.

One of the occupational peculiarities of being an air accident investigator was that there were often long periods of inactivity. Men occupied their time in different ways, depending on their individual interests: Liss built model aeroplanes; Houston, a devoted family man, spent a great deal of time at home; Downey, Klein understood, studied latest developments in pathology; and Bradley would likely be out on the golf course. They all wore Bellboy radio receivers in their shirt pockets, in case they could not be reached by telephone if the duty officer had to contact them. The rule was: airborne to an accident scene within two hours and if the Grumman Gulfstream or the Learjet in the Federal

Aviation Administration's Hangar Six were filled, or unavailable, everybody carried authority to fly the jump seat on the flight deck of any commercial airliner, domestic or foreign, to any place in the world.

Klein used his waiting time reading, and he surveyed the books on the shelf at his side, his eyes passing over some of his favourite volumes: *Out of My Life and Thought*, by Albert Schweitzer; *Wind, Sand and Stars*, by Antoine de Saint-Exupéry; *Night Flight*, by the same author, and, tucked away at the opposite end of a row of books on modern philosophy, a slim volume of Carl Sandburg's collected verse.

He turned from his books, restless and fidgety. Shaw's news had disturbed him. He consulted his 'Investigations-in-Progress' chart, consisting of horizontal strips of coloured plastic of varying lengths, the length denoting the stage of each case. He checked the number allocated to the Avianjet and traced the red strip backward from Draft Report Ready, through Simulated Test Flight, Lab Tests, Field Operations, Review Board, and First Meeting, to the date of the crash. It had already taken three months to get to this stage, and now God only knew how much longer Legal would argue and delay his writing of the final report.

He noticed a ladybug on the edge of the chart. Taking a letter opener from the desk, he manoeuvred the insect on to it and crossed to the window. His office was in the old wing of the building, where windows could still be opened. He gave the window a shove.

'Cleared for take-off, little lady. Contact tower on one-zero-two at ten thousand feet,' he said.

The insect remained motionless on the tip of the letter opener. 'Tower to ladybug. You are cleared for take-off,' he repeated, examining the red, black-speckled roundness of the beetle. 'Go, lady, go. Open up those throttles.'

Two translucent wings spread in flight as the ladybug suddenly soared upwards to freedom. Grinning widely, he watched it disappear over the rooftops in the direction of the Capitol, and left the window open, tapping the letter opener on the sill, indulging in an old pilot's habit, studying the sky. It was CAVU, pilot's shorthand for ceiling and visibility unlimited, one of those crystal days of May when the sun lit up the buildings in hard planes of light and shade, and he was suddenly transported in thought to a Bermuda beach, stretched out alongside Sarah, the sun warm on his body.

The ringing telephone jarred him back to reality. He scooped up the receiver with a practised movement of his left hand.

'Klein, IIC.'

'Duty Officer Derrigan reporting a Major, sir.'

Klein supported the telephone between his jawbone and shoulder, to leave his left hand free for the belaboured writing he would have to do with it. His heart pounded.

'A CA-100 Caravan, approximately thirty miles south-west of Topeka, Kansas, near a village called Little Cedars. American Constitution Airlines Flight One-Three-Seven en route from Chicago O'Hare to Los Angeles International.'

Klein read it back. 'Roger,' Derrigan said. "I'm confirming we're calling out the Go-Team now. Hold the line, sir.' Derrigan had a reputation for announcing the most calamitous news in a dull, unshakable voice when the red telephone rang in his duty room. Klein squeezed the receiver tighter to his ear. There was another voice in the background. That would be Foxe calling up top-echelon brass and making Bellboy calls to Go-Team members who hadn't answered their telephones. Derrigan's monotonous voice droned on.

'Kansas state police phoned Regional to report a farmer's son saw it go down on the farm and says it's a complete wipeout. That's only what the boy says,' Derrigan added cautiously to cover himself. 'Just a moment, sir. Here's a tele-type just in from Regional. American

Constitution says the passenger and crew manifest totalled four hundred and six people.'

'God almighty – ' Klein muttered.

Click. Derrigan rang off to dial the next number on his copy of the Go-Team list.

TWO

Bill Houston reached under the bedsheets and encircled his wife's warm, plump body.

'Hmmm . . . ' she murmured, coming slowly awake.

'Hi, lazybones,' Houston chided. 'I've seen the kids off to school an hour ago, put the cat out, made your breakfast, come back to bed, read the latest report on why engines fail – to the accompaniment of your jet-propelled snores – and you still deny your loving husband of, how many years now? – well, a hell of a longtime husband – his conjugal rights by dropping off to sleep.'

'Hrmmm . . . ah.' Bette Houston rolled over on her back. 'Such a pretty little speech, dear.' She yawned and put her hands around his waist. 'I hope you spell that r-i-t-e-s. Such a loving, considerate husband to do all those things. And on his day off.'

'I'm still on duty, although I'm home, remember.'

She stroked his big belly. 'You did yourself a nice breakfast, dear. What did you have?'

'Only a snack. Double portion of bacon and eggs, toast and jam, cornflakes with sliced banana and grapefruit, and coffee, of course.'

'That explains why this is getting bigger,' Bette Houston said, pressing his stomach. 'What time is it?'

He glanced at the clock radio beside the telephone on the bedside table. 'Five after eleven. The kids'll be home for lunch in an hour,' he said, moving his huge hands gently over her body, stroking the most tender places. He kissed her, and sucked in a deep breath against her neck, inhaling her sweet fragrance.

She disengaged herself and slipped out of her black

nightie. Houston fondled her breasts and kissed her nipples.

'Oh, darling. You're *so* good. I can never tell you that enough.'

'That's because you're so easy to be good to, honey, and because I love you.'

He felt the swaying of her hips against his, arousing his passion. She put her hands behind his neck, pulling him closer. He was responding to her mounting excitement when the telephone rang shrilly. Her body stiffened. Houston reached out, grabbed the phone, and clamped it to his ear.

'Hello! ' he barked.

'Is that Bill Houston?'

'Yes.'

'It's Backup Duty Officer Foxe reporting a Major thirty miles south-west of Topeka . . . '

'I'll be right over.'

Houston clamped the receiver on its cradle and looked down at his wife. The flicker of resentment that danced behind her hazel eyes slowly turned to a soft lovingness.

'You have to go *now*,' she said quietly. 'It was half question, half a statement of fact.

Houston nodded. Without a word he gathered her up in his arms, kissed her, and swung out of bed.

Jeff Liss throttled back and adjusted the mixture control until the engine settled into a steady thrum. He pulled the goggles over his face, brushed an imaginary thread from his kapok flying suit, looked along each wing, and checked that the runway was clear.

'Chocks away, corporal,' he called.

Unwinding his six-foot frame from where he had been bending over the model aeroplane, he strode to the radio-control box on the ground near his car a dozen paces away. Extending the antenna on the box, he moved a switch, pushed a lever, and watched the eight-foot red plane move forward. It picked up speed on the runway of the disused airfield, the tail rising. Skilfully moving the rudder control to compensate for the cross-wind, he advanced the throttle. The plane skimmed above the concrete and soared into the air. At fifty feet Liss levelled off. The airspeed indicator he had installed on the panel of the box showed thirty knots. His thin features broke into a grin.

'Follow me, men.'

He manoeuvred the miniature control column and the rudder lever. The model spun around in a graceful bank, wings glinting in the sun.

'Keep alert for the enemy.'

The nose pointed up, the engine roaring as the model climbed. He squinted, searching for it in the sun's glare. A second later the wings appeared a hundred yards away as the machine swooped towards the ground. Effortlessly it gathered speed and pointed skyward. He climbed it at a steep angle and at three hundred feet pulled back the throttle. The aeroplane hung on the propeller, stalled, and the nose came over. He put the plane into a vertical dive, and with judgement born of long experience pulled it out of its self-destructive manoeuvre with two feet to spare above the cracked concrete.

'Maintain close formation, men.'

He adjusted a lever, and flaps under the wings' trailing edges dropped thirty degrees. The aeroplane bounced upwards as it responded to the extra lift.

He moved the flap control, and the model continued to climb with added power from the throttle lever. He watched it dash to the far side of the airfield. Grabbing binoculars from the car roof, he peered at the dot over the ruined hangar a half mile away. By deftly manipulating the controls, he cork-screwed the plane through the air until it was a hundred yards away. Putting down the binoculars, he levelled the wings, shoved the column forward to gain speed, and flicked the aeroplane into a roll on top of a loop, followed by an Immelmann turn and a dutch roll.

'Cruising flight. Straight and level.'

He pressed a button; the plane roared overhead, wings dipping before settling into level flight a hundred feet above the runway, held in the firm grip of automatic control. As he'd explained it to a fellow member of the Silver Spring Model Aeroplane Club, 'Simple. I put electronic sensors on the wing tips and tail to respond to phugoid oscillations and dampen yaw. The control servos respond to the inputs from the sensors.'

The plane sped to the end of the runway, held on course against the crosswind. Overriding the auto control, he flew it around in a steep bank, engine roaring. He was aware of the clear sky beyond; ideal weather for a full morning's flying. The engine suddenly spluttered and stopped.

He gripped the control column and manoeuvred the plane into the wind. Adjust for the wind vector, steady, not too jerky. He brought the craft towards the ground, the wheels touched, and it rolled to a stop at his feet. He bent over the engine. At that precise moment an insistent beeping sound came from the pocket of his flying suit. He dashed to the car and lifted the receiver from the mobile telephone.

'Colonel – uh, I mean, Jeff Liss here.'

'Duty Officer Derrigan reporting a Major.' Liss repeated the message, adding, 'I'll be at Hangar Six in thirty minutes.'

In the space of five minutes he had dismantled the model, stowed it in the trunk of his car, and donned a tweed jacket. Then he drove through the tumbledown gate of the old airfield and headed west in a hurry.

Madge Harrilyn reached for her glasses and turned back to the desk in the middle of her apartment living room. She stubbed out the cigarette in the ashtray, and absent-mindedly opened another package as she searched for a report amid the stack in the centre of the desk. Before picking up the blue volume, she lit the cigarette and sent a cloud of smoke towards the ceiling. She reread the title: 'Aircraft Accident Report, Pan American World Airways, Inc., Boeing 707-321C, N458PA, Boston, Massachusetts.' She flipped to page 120, where her name appeared with the four other NTSB board members. She wasn't checking her name; she'd been a board member long enough now for the printers to take care to spell her name right; it hadn't always been that way. Once a typist had spelled it 'Harrilin', and the blooper had gone through three proof readers and not been discovered, and she had felt slighted, possibly with reason, but had not pointed it out. She read the title of the section above, headed 'Safety Recommendations', and smiled when she read the name below.

'But he'll probably never notice,' she said aloud to the Persian cat in the armchair. The Safety Recommendations at the back of every report were addressed to 'the Honourable Christopher M. Grewson, Administrator, Federal Aviation Administration,' whose job it was to consider and, if thought necessary, implement the recommendations made by the NTSB. The word 'Honorable' was spelled 'Honourable': probably by one of those new English typists the Bureau had recently hired, she thought. Well, he'll have something to blow his top about now, the fussy old bureaucrat. Lately the Federal Aviation Administration and the NTSB had not been getting on well; not since the NTSB had been granted the right by the Senate to file comments on new rules proposed by the FAA, which was the organisation responsible for granting Certificates of Airworthiness to aircraft, and ran the Air Traffic Control system in the United States.

She put down the report and went into the kitchen to plug in the coffee percolator. As she passed the mirror, she stopped and patted her brown hair into position, a soft smile dimpling her cheeks, mentally arranging her day. After midmorning coffee she'd drive over to the Library of Congress and pick up the files dealing with the president's report on transportation, eat lunch with Senator MacDonald to discuss next week's agenda for the Greater Washington Traffic Safety Committee, and, if there was time, join the crowds in the visitors' gallery in the House to listen to what they were saying about the bill recently introduced to improve airport security.

The coffee was beginning to bubble when the telephone rang. She hurried to her desk to answer it.

'Mrs Harrilyn?' a voice asked.

'This is she.'

'It's Backup Duty Officer Foxe reporting a Major . . . '

She listened while Foxe gave her the details, lighting another cigarette to stop the flutter in her heart.

'I've got it. I'll be right over.'

She crushed out the cigarette, pulled out the percolator plug, replenished the cat's food dish, and checked her handbag for car keys before slamming out of the door.

'If you buy this one, you save thirty-seven cents, Mother.'

Howard Bradley pointed to the can of peaches on the supermarket shelf and looked down at the slide rule in his hand. 'The big economy size *is* cheaper.' He manipulated the rule to check his calculations.

'All right, dear, I'm convinced.' Mrs Bradley adjusted the steel-rimmed glasses on the end of her nose and squinted across the aisle at the vegetable counter. 'We need some tomatoes and lettuce, Howie.' She inspected the vegetables as Bradley impatiently pushed the buggy ahead. 'Look at these,' she said, her voice quavering with indignation. 'And the price!'

'What about a cabbage instead, Mother? Here's a nice one.' He held up a big cabbage.

'That looks better. Put it in the buggy.'

'Anything else?' He glanced at his watch. Half the morning already shot. The golf course would soon be crowded with business executives purposely losing to their clients at their midweek games. He could only spare today away from the Bureau office because he had a report to write, and Met had forecast rain by week-end.

'A few odds and ends at the grocery counter.'

Bradley suppressed a sigh and swung the buggy around on one wheel. It wasn't often that his mother, who was seventy, asked him to drive her to the supermarket: usually she ordered by telephone and the store delivered. But prices had rocketed in the past few months, and the manager had taken advantage of his telephone customers to get rid of some of the more elderly fruits and vegetables.

'What about these soap flakes, Howie?' she asked, pointing to a large gaily coloured box.

Bradley checked the price of several nearby boxes, and worked the slide rule. 'If you buy two smaller packages, you get more for twenty-four cents less.'

'Such dishonest merchandising,' his mother said disgustedly. 'Mollie doesn't know how lucky she is to have you to go shopping with.'

'Sure, Mother.' He nearly added, 'Except I'm usually at home because someone has to baby-sit,' but thought better of it.

Mrs Bradley moved on. 'Reach me one of those packages of coffee please.'

'Anything else?'

She held the list under her nose and peered at it. 'A loaf of dark bread and then we're through.'

There was a short line at the checkout counter. Bradley waited for the woman ahead to put her groceries on the conveyor belt, and glanced at the clock: seven minutes past eleven. He watched the cashier tap the keys of the cash register while instinctively working on the slide rule. With a few swift shuffles of the slide he could do all the extensions of the grocery prices and total them quicker than the electric machine.

During his career as stress analyst with Lockheed Aircraft and, later, doing research on the strength of experimental supersonic structures at the Wright-

Patterson wind tunnels in Dayton, Ohio, Bradley had worn out a succession of slide rules. He claimed that he could do complex calculations faster on his slide rules than an expert on the latest pocket electronic calculators, a claim that had once been put to the test in a fifty-dollar bet. He still relied on the older unwieldy mathematical time-savers, and his collection of slide rules was unique. At his Bureau of Aviation Safety office they dominated the windowsill. Flat rules ten inches long made of Japanese bamboo; five-inch pocket slide rules of polished aluminium; flat circular plastic rules that slipped into a vest pocket; and his *pièce de résistance*, a barrel-shaped slide rule consisting of three interlocking concentric barrels that rotated independently .

'It has an accuracy,' Bradley never tired of informing the curious inquirer, 'equivalent to a slide rule twenty feet in length.'

The cash register tinkled and paper unrolled from the top. 'That's thirty dollars, sixty-nine cents,' announced the cashier, tearing off the paper strip.

The woman stared down at the dozen items the girl was shoving into a paper bag. 'Thirty bucks for *that?*' She shook her head.

Mrs Bradley made a sympathetic gesture.

'And nothing tastes like *real* food any more,' the woman added. 'All that artificial gunk they put in.'

Bradley took the things out of the buggy and arranged them in orderly files on the conveyor. He put the bread on last, to make sure that the girl packed it on top of the hard goods. As he pushed the buggy away, he wondered how he could manage to pay for the groceries without damaging his mother's pride. His thoughts were interrupted by a continuous beep-beep-beep from his shirt pocket.

Feeling for the loose change he always kept in his hip pocket, he swiftly located the public telephone. He spun out 726-3944. The receiver at the other end was picked up immediately.

'Earl Derrigan, Duty Officer,' said a voice.

'It's Bradley. What's up?' After the message, he groaned. 'Christ, a Caravan! That's a first. I'll be at Hangar Six in twenty minutes.' He hurried back to the checkout counter and quietly explained. 'It's an emergency, Mother. I've got to go right away.' He fished in his pocket and produced two twenty-dollar bills. 'This'll handle everything, and here's a couple of dimes to phone for a cab.'

He leaned over and planted a kiss on his mother's mouth. Before the startled lady could say anything, he was through the swinging doors, headed for the car park.

'That's everybody,' Derrigan said, putting a check mark against the last name on the list, Richard Demsar, the man who would investigate American Constitution's maintenance records. He looked at Harvey Foxe. 'What about you?'

'All contacted,' he said, rechecking his copy of the list.

'Did you get the board member listed?'

'Out of town. I got Mrs Harrilyn.'

Derrigan shrugged. 'Call Congressional Liaison, Harv. I've a feeling there's going to be a bust-up on Capitol Hill. Or at the very least a run-in with the FAA.'

While Foxe phoned, Derrigan took a list of alternate Go-Team members and pinned it to the wall. If another accident occurred while the current Go-Team was at the CA-100 Caravan site, it would be Derrigan's and Foxe's job to call the members of the alternate list into action.

Derrigan picked up the current Go-Team list and looked at the last line where Shaw had typed: 'Next accident number DCA 78-A-22.' He took a blank form from the shelf above his desk and with a deliberate hand copied the letters and digits. Then he wrote the next higher number at the bottom of the alternate Go-Team list.

Foxe put down his phone, picked up a partly eaten ham sandwich, and tossed it into the wastepaper container.

'Suddenly lost my appetite,' he said, and turned to stare out of the window.

Part II
Investigation

THREE

The Gulfstream touched down at Kansas City Airport at 2.50 p.m. One of the NTSB's regional offices was located at Kansas City, and Robert Armstrong, who headed it, had hired cars for the Go-Team, then gone ahead with his own experts to the crash site in the equipment truck. A half hour after their arrival at Kansas City the car carrying Klein bounced down the potholed drive of a farm. He craned forward, trying to see past the crowd of people who had come from miles around.

His gut tightened into a hard knot at his first glimpse of the pulverised hunks of aluminium and steel debris and the grotesque attitudes of the bodies scattered about. Despite his many years as an air accident investigator he'd never been able to subdue the stab of despair at the first sight of a crashed aeroplane, scenes that over the past few years had grown more devastating. In the early days the crashed DC-4s and Constellations were wrecks *on* the ground. But since the era of high-flying jets that cruised in excess of six hundred miles an hour, crash scenes were like bloodied battlefields. The huge wide-body birds weighed three hundred and fifty tons fully loaded with passengers and cargo. When they slammed into the ground, they bored deep into the earth, gouging craters thirty feet deep, scattering bits of metal for hundreds of yards. Aircraft that suffered cabin depressurisation, and particularly those that had been sabotaged, hurled debris over several square miles of countryside, making it necessary to recover as many of the thousands of fragments as was humanly possible before even a preliminary investigation could begin. Worse, casualty lists had become longer as the wide-body jets, the so-called 'jumbos, had taken to the airways. He turned to Houston. 'No fire.'

Houston grunted as the car braked next to a fire truck with 'Little Cedars Volunteer Fire Department' hand-painted in gold letters on the sides. The firemen, dressed in an odd collection of dungarees and blue jeans, wearing helmets, stood around in little groups, talking in quiet voices. State police cruisers, and two ambulances, were parked nearby.

Klein got out of the car, a small figure that moved with a trim agility despite the bulky coveralls that were standard dress for the Go-Team, and hurried towards the area the police were still roping off. Several members of the Go-Team rushed past, carrying equipment. Houston lugged a short telescopic aluminium ladder and Downey had a satchel slung over his shoulder that Klein knew contained test tubes with tightly fitting stoppers for collecting blood and tissues for pathological analysis. They all carried clipboards, except Klein, who could not write with his right hand. He felt in his coveralls pocket for a small tape recorder, checked his watch, and spoke into the microphone. 'Arrived on site, fifteen-twenty central time.' At that moment a burly man with a distressed look on his face hurried up, shaking his head. It was Armstrong.

'The first report's true.'

'All dead?' Klein demanded.

'I wish to God I was wrong, Steve.' He waved his arm. 'My men have checked all over. Everybody thrown out is dead and those still inside didn't have a chance in hell.'

Klein scanned the site. Most of the wreckage was in a large uncultivated field at the back of the farm, but smaller heaps of debris lay strewn over an area of several hundred square yards. Members of the Go-Team were spreading out, joining investigators from Armstrong's group.

'Witnesses?' Klein asked. It was Regional's responsibility to head up the Witness Group.

'Only the farmer and his teenage kid so far.' Armstrong looked at the Statement of Witness form on the clipboard he carried. 'George and Andrew Crowthers.' He screwed up his face critically as he studied the form. 'Neither says much. Basically that the aircraft suddenly appeared in a dive and piled straight in. The kid says he saw a flash like an explosion as it dived, but that could've been sunlight reflection. His father was damned lucky. He was driving his tractor down the side road only a few hundred yards away from where it ploughed in. Scared him like hell.'

Klein looked at the state troopers and the line of stakes they were driving into the ground. 'Any soot or ice?' he asked, striding with Armstrong towards the field.

'What's left of the wing leading edges are buried, so I couldn't check if there was any ice build-up on them. It went in at a high impact angle, as you can see. Both wing engines are cratered, but the rear engine's on the ground and the intake's covered with fuselage debris.'

'Better tell Len Davies. He's heading up the Weather Group.' Soot indicated on-board fire; ice on wing leading edges affected lift and in engine intakes restricted the airflow through them and reduced engine power. Even on a clear summer day ice could form on aircraft at high altitude. He looked towards the far side of the wreckage site. 'Hey, get those kids away, officer!' he yelled, pointing to the far side of Crowthers' farm where children trampled through debris.

Souvenir hunters were a menace to his team's work, stealing bits of metal that could, if left in position, help determine the cause of the crash. But souvenir hunters weren't the only reason why the area had to be quickly cordoned off. Ghoulish scavengers prowled among major aircraft wrecks looking for passengers' valuable possessions: credit cards, money in billfolds and purses. Klein recalled with a shudder the several times he'd found a body, usually a woman's, with the fingers chopped off with a knife or even an axe, where someone had stolen diamond rings with cool efficiency.

A man hefting a videotape camera on his shoulder brushed past, focusing his camera for another long shot before his close-in-walkaround of the crash site.

'What about the still photos?' Klein asked.

'I've got three men on it,' Armstrong replied.

'Ordered up a helicopter for the aerial shots?'

'Before I left Kansas City.' He looked at the distant sky. 'It should be here soon.'

'And the cargo?' Klein asked as they walked through the police line, where newspaper reporters fought for the best positions to point their cameras.

'Hey, Mr Klein!' a man shouted. Klein turned and recognised a reporter from the Kansas City *Star* who'd been at an accident site several months ago. 'What about it, sir?'

Klein considered when to allow the reporters on the site: it was a standing rule that the press be allowed one official survey before being shooed back across the police lines.

'After our preliminary examination,' he replied. 'I'll give the word to Mr Reynolds, the public affairs officer.'

'Are you gonna hold a press conference, sir?' another newsman asked.

'When we have something to say,' Klein said curtly, striding past. Armstrong gave instructions to a policeman and hurried after Klein.

'What about the cargo, Bob?' Klein repeated.

'The airline says it's clean; no explosives.'

'We'll see about that.'

He looked up at the trees that fringed the area, noting that the tops of the sycamores to the north had been sliced off. Bits of the tail section of the aircraft lay at the foot of the trees, the tail plane and elevators shattered but the fin on the rear fuselage seemingly in one piece, with deep, irregular corrugations in the aluminium alloy skin. It was clear that the aeroplane had gone in steeply. He stepped around chunks of debris and came to the place where the main part of the wreckage lay. The forward section of the fuselage was embedded in a crater more than thirty feet deep, leaving circling mounds of soft earth and upturned sod where the tons of metal had plunged into the uncultivated ground. Bits of outer wings, and shattered flaps and ailerons, had sheared off and lay some distance away, deep furrows showing the path they had ploughed. The rear fuselage, broken from the remnants of the main fuselage by the tremendously high gravitational forces, had been hurled off, cutting a swath through the weeds, churning up surface stones and underlying gravel in its wake. It lay like a huge squashed silver-plated concertina near a clump of bushes, trailing a spaghetti-like confusion of tangled control cables, twisted hydraulic pipes, and electrical wires, a snare for unwary feet. Klein pointed with his good arm beyond the immediate area.

'Make sure the photographers get all that outlying debris, Bob.'

Armstrong nodded and hurried away. Klein, his jaw set tight, walked towards the mass of metal fragments that reflected the sunlight a hundred yards away.

He took a quick look around the field, checking the groups of men sifting through debris. Occasionally one would carry a battered piece of metal to a central area and carefully lay it on the ground, tag it, and have it photographed by one of the cameramen. From time to time one of Downey's helpers held a piece of jewellery high in the air, so they would not be suspected of thievery, before tagging it and placing it in a plastic bag attached to a body . . .

Klein checked his watch. They'd been on the site for an hour and still Christopher M. Grewson hadn't arrived. More cars had driven up and been hastily parked near the police line, and he recognised officials from American Constitution Airlines and two men from the engine manufacturers, General Powerdyne Corporation. In the distance he could make out the tall figure of Ben Rexford, chairman of the Air Line Pilots Association's own accident investigation committee, with a man who was attached to Liss's Systems Group. The preliminary investigation, although a seemingly slow business, was in actual fact a fast-moving anthill of activity as the different experts quickly went to work. But he wished the Air Force pathologists would get here soon. Downey, in charge of the Human Factors Group, badly needed help.

Klein's job on the site was to co-ordinate the various groups' activities, but if the right people didn't get here on time . . . He turned completely around, surveying the scene in its entirety. Bodies were spread-eagled on their backs everywhere amid the tall blue flowering weeds that rippled lazily in the breeze. Severed hands, bloody ears, legs, arms, and internal organs that had been ripped from bodies mingled with piles of tortured silver metal, twisted hydraulic pipes, wing flaps, and pages of that morning's edition of the Chicago *Tribune.* A little distance away two Catholic priests had appeared from nowhere, administering last rites, moving from body to body, divining in some mysterious way which of the dead passengers who didn't wear crucifixes belonged to their faith.

He stepped aside to avoid treading on the corpse of a stout middle-aged woman, naked except for tattered pantyhose, a shaft of the steel frame of the seat in which she had been sitting speared through her back and sticking out of her belly, which even now was disgorging entrails in spasmodic jerks as rigor mortis set in.

For the thousandth time he wondered what inner compulsion had attracted him to air accident investigation. Was it because of a deep conviction about the humanitarian factor, the need to find out why an aircraft crashed so that the cause could be eliminated and lives saved in future? Perhaps subconsciously he *liked* being amid scenes of devastation, injury, and death? He'd heard war veterans say how they felt gloriously elated when they charged the enemy's hideout, the rush of adrenalin through the bloodstream, the feeling of power. He shook his head wearily. It sure as God had more to do with his reading of the accident report about the Connie crash he was involved in. Subsequently he had applied to train as an investigator at the National Aircraft Accident Investigators School, just starting up in a secluded corner of Dulles International Airport in Washington. It also had something to do with his regard for all living creatures, even insects. He could vividly remember waiting at a bus stop when he was a schoolboy. A big, black beetle scuttled across the sidewalk, scrambling for safety towards the grass on a nearby lawn. A businessman in the commuter crowd had deliberately stepped out of line and crushed the helpless insect under his shoe, leaving a smear of oozing goo on the sidewalk. Steve had been shocked and upset. As a child he would sit on the floor of his father's fruit and vegetable store on the lower East Side and pick bugs out of the cabbages, setting them free in the backyard weeds. His mind wandered on, thinking of the hours he'd spent in the old shop, and how disappointed his father was when Steve told him he didn't want to go into the business, because he was crazy about flying.

In his spare time he built model aeroplanes and read all the aviation magazines, buying them with the money his father gave him for helping in the store. His father paid little attention to Steve's aeronautical ambitions – until his bar mitzvah day. On that auspicious occasion, anxious to impress his out-of-town cousins, Steve flew a six-foot wingspan, gasoline-engined model from the school yard across the street. The aeroplane zoomed out of sight and entangled itself a quarter mile away in the steel bracing of a factory water tower. The first indication of where it had landed reached the shocked adult guests in the form of the screaming siren of the local fire engine, called out to remove the mess on the tower. His father grounded his model flying for a month.

Dreams of a flying career ended abruptly when his

father died and he had to work long hours in the store to pay his father's debts. When his mother, a quiet woman of great forbearance, from whom he had inherited an infinite patience, died two years later, he sold the business. He was twenty-two, physically fit, keen to learn to fly and study aeronautical engineering, but with insufficient funds to do both. A chance encounter with a former school pal decided his course of action.

'Plenty of good flying schools in California, and they're reasonable. I've been on the Coast two years now, flying for a living.'

'How long to get your licence?'

'Thirty-five hours to solo, if you're good.'

'You make it sound easy.'

'I'm second pilot with an air taxi business. Not bad, eh?' His friend displayed gold cuff links and a custom-made suit and pointed to a new Buick at the kerb.

Klein asked, 'When're you leaving for the Coast, Sam?'

'Day after tomorrow. Pick you up seven-thirty in the morning.'

Two weeks later Klein drew up a chair at a desk at West Coast Flying School for his first lessons in theory of flight and elementary navigation. Three weeks later he soloed. A year later he won his commercial licence, later qualified on twin-engine aircraft, and got a part-time job as a co-pilot in DC-3s flying oil-drilling equipment under charter for the early explorations in Alaska. As his flying hours piled up, he took conversion courses to fly as captain of DC-4s, and several years later qualified as a first officer on DC-8s. The mid-air with the Connie and the arm injury that ended his career as a pilot flickered in the back of his memory, and he shook off the feeling of depression with difficulty.

He found himself staring at a woman's shoe in the rough grass. Near it was a torn handbag, resting on a mound of cattle dung, that had disgorged a lipstick, a circular birth-control pill dispenser, and a cigarette package. Pages of a book fluttering in the thicket a few feet away caught his attention. He walked over, picked it up, and read the title: *Good Times in Los Angeles: A Young Person's Guide.* He turned to the inside back cover by flipping the pages against his coveralls. The book had been checked out of the Evanston Public Library the day before. The library would confirm the name and address of the borrower, and Downey would cross-check the passenger manifest. But he'd have to match the book to the body, a more difficult job. He replaced the book and saw a woman's brassiere waving in the breeze where it had snagged on the other side of the thicket. Lying on the ground directly below, half hidden by sturdy sprouts of new spring grass, was the dark green cover of a United States passport. He noted its position, picked it up, opened the cover, and found himself looking into the face of a black girl, lips drawn slightly upwards in a shy smile, intense eyes filled with the frankness of youth. He turned the page and read her name: Olive Patricia Williams. Her date of birth showed that she would have been nineteen next month. 'Oh, God,' he sighed softly, carefully replacing the passport in the grass.

'Excuse me, sir.'

A man from Regional, accompanied by his assistant, who held a transit on a tripod, had come up unnoticed.

'We need to put in a stake about here, sir.'

'Be careful not to disturb that,' Klein said, pointing to the passport and other personal possessions of the dead passengers.

He watched the man drive a stake into the ground, and looked around, mouth twisted, checking the lines of stakes they had already hammered into the earth. They had chosen as their base line a point between the barn and the farmhouse; a good datum. With the latitude and longitude of the site, the wreckage distribution chart built up from the survey teams' work and the photographic group's records would provide a permanent pictorial record that could be referred to after the wreckage had been carted away. The chart would be used to help determine the sequence of the aircraft's breakup when it impacted.

In the distance he saw Reynolds, engaged in a heated argument with the newsmen. The photographic helicopter that had buzzed the site moved towards a rise on the north side of the farm. A cloud of dust indicated a convoy of cars speeding along the back road, probably the officials he was expecting, representatives of 'the interested parties'. Houston and two men were holding an earnest conversation around one of the cratered engines, and Armstrong's survey team and several other experts picked their way through the mounds of metal. Don Ackerman, in charge of Operations, and Dave Jacobs, heading up the Air Traffic Control Group, would be well into their investigations at Chicago's O'Hare International Airport. He wouldn't consult with them until he returned to Washington.

In the middle of the site, Len Davies, Weather Group, was chattering with meteorologists from Regional, one foot resting on a case of recording instruments. Two FAA dog handlers led their charges towards the piles of debris. Trained to sniff out explosives, the animals had become a familiar sight at air crash scenes since the era of Arab terrorism. He saw George Downey and his assistants move towards the rubble that was the fuselage and wing centre section, with the photographers positioning their equipment nearby. Until they finished, it was impossible to start digging into the crater, widening it to permit a mobile crane to move in and hoist the remains out. To get an even better view, he strode towards a rise in the terrain, noting that there was less wreckage on the higher ground. He stopped, chewing on his lip, getting an over-all view of the scene before checking on Liss's search for the all-important flight data recorder. With his left hand he caressed his chin, looking down. A dozen paces away, partly hidden by weeds, was a smooth black conical shape, like a four-foot-diameter mushroom.

'Hey, Bradley!' he shouted, running towards it.

The trio of men around the engine crater looked up.

'Bradley. Where's Howard Bradley?'

Houston pointed towards the rear fuselage and bellowed Bradley's name.

'Coming!' Bradley emerged from the wreck. Seeing Klein wildly waving, he ran up the slope, puffing, and stared at the shape in the weeds.

'What in hell is the nose cone doing here when the fuselage's buried two hundred yards away?' Klein asked incredulously.

FOUR

Bradley examined the nose cone. Grass was stuck to the surface, but it appeared to be in perfect condition, a tribute to the reinforced fibreglass maker's art. He shook his head. 'Jesus, it beats me,' he muttered.

Klein knelt beside Bradley and peered at the black surface. 'Look at this,' he said, his voice going high and squeaky as he pointed to the recessed hinge fitting that had secured the nose cone to the front of the fuselage. 'Snapped clean off.' He whipped out a magnifying glass and focused it on the break. After a few seconds he turned to Bradley. 'Look at *that*.'

Bradley bit his lower lip as he peered at the fracture. 'Looks like it's been subjected to intense heat,' he said guardedly.

'You gotta believe it.'

'Now, how would – ?' The arrival of the photographic team interrupted his question.

'Did you shoot this?' Klein asked the cameraman.

'No, sir. We've been concentrating on the main – '

'Get a distant shot to show the location. Then close-ups. Really close. Especially on the hinge fitting.'

'Yes, sir.'

The photographers went about their business, moving skilfully.

'Do you want shots from other angles, Mr Klein?'

'That'll do for the exterior,' he said, and to Bradley. 'Help me turn it over.' He waited for him to position himself opposite, and stuck his left hand under the cone's edge. 'Together, easy . . . over she goes.'

'Get a load of that!' Bradley exclaimed.

Klein stared at the burned inside surface of the upturned cone. 'Never seen anything like this in my whole goddamned life,' he said. They continued to peer at the interior of the nose cone, with frankly puzzled expressions. The laminae of tough fibreglass had buckled and separated from the heat. Klein turned to the cameraman.

'Make sure you get these laminae from every angle,' he said, standing.

'Yes, sir.'

'It would take a temperature of about four hundred degrees centigrade to buckle reinforced synthetic resin like that, Howard.'

'Perhaps higher,' Bradley said. 'Between four and five hundred degrees. It's the new high-density material that recently passed high-strength tests at the Ames labs. The Air Force use it on the supersonic F-16s.' He paused and scratched his head. 'What the hell would cause a fire in the nose cone?'

'Equipment in the systems group?'

'Systems?'

'Yes,' Klein said. 'Systems. Maybe weather radar.' He looked around for Liss, hoping he'd appear with the welcome news that the flight data recorder had been found, which might show if the weather radar had developed a fault, such as a short circuit.

'Take another shot to show the other side,' Klein told the photographer. He held out his hand. 'From this angle.'

When the cameraman had finished, Klein bent over the cone, swung the hinge fitting towards him, and examined the broken end through his magnifying glass. 'Doesn't look like an impact break. More like a fatigue fracture.'

Bradley peered at the broken surface. 'It's been worked back and forth as if the cone flapped about before impact.'

'Impossible,' Klein said, straightening up. He paused,

scratching his cheek. 'By hell!' He whirled around and looked towards the back of Crowthers' farm. 'I bet those kids broke the damned thing off for a souvenir.'

'What kids?'

'Before the cops secured the site, a bunch of kids, probably from that neighbouring farm' – he swept his hand towards a distant farmhouse – 'roamed over this area.' He paused, subduing his anger. 'I want Armstrong to visit every farmhouse that borders on this place, and I want it done immediately.' He pointed to the nose cone lying like an upturned shell in the weeds. 'Arrange to get it to the labs, Howard. Fly it out by helicopter if you have to. I want it in Hugh Turney's lab by tonight.'

'I'll take care of it.'

Klein ran towards the edge of the roped-off area, conscious of cars in the distance bumping down a side road in clouds of dust. Investigators from Regional and the FAA passed him, armed with spades and manual hoisting gear. He found Bob Armstrong by the gear truck.

'Some souvenir hunters have picked off an important piece of evidence, Bob. The nose cone may have come off the aircraft before it impacted, but the hinge fitting's been deliberately broken off. I've got a hunch it was those kids we saw. Get somebody to visit every farm bordering this place and find out.'

Armstrong looked puzzled. 'The nose cone came off before impact?'

'Maybe. Just get somebody on to it.' Klein said. He looked around at the gaping crowd held back by the police: women with babies were clustered in a group, their faces strangely animated as they spoke in hushed voices. A major tragedy always brings either one of two human characteristics to the surface, Klein reflected; unselfish heroism by the few or non-involvement and gloating by the many, like the rubbernecking of drivers on a highway as they slow down to view a rear-end collision. A gang of youths sitting astride motorcycles vroomed their engines and surveyed the scene, pointing out to each other the smashed corpses yet to be covered with plastic sheets or put in body bags.

'I'll get it organised,' Armstrong said.

Klein turned on his heel and strode towards Houston, who was standing by the remains of the rear engine with another man.

As Klein approached, Houston remarked, 'It ain't exactly factory fresh.' He addressed an engine specialist named Corski, a young man from the Regional office, recently graduated from the Dulles school and on his first Major.

Houston stood with his hands on his hips, head on one side, weighing up what he saw. For an engine that had slammed out of the sky from five or six miles up, he was surprised that it was not completely destroyed. It was wrecked, but not devastated. He looked at the sky, now darkening with the approach of night, speculating on the path of the aircraft as it fell. Between active accident investigations Houston headed the group devoted to the study of trajectory analysis, the science of tracing the path of components of aircraft that break up in mid-air, working, as he put it, 'from the ground up'. In recent years trajectory analysis had assumed greater importance owing to several cases of explosive depressurisation of aircraft, the most spectacular being that which had torn apart a Turkish Airlines DC-10 wide-body jet after taking off from Paris, spilling passengers and bits of debris over miles of countryside. The accident had been blamed on the blow-out of an improperly closed rear cargo door, causing explosive depressurisation of the cargo compartment, collapsing the passenger cabin floor, and damaging the elevator control cables. The aircraft took a sharp dive. Several passengers were sucked out of the stricken aircraft at twelve thousand feet, and trajectory analysis had been used to trace the paths and velocities of their bodies as they plunged to the ground. The final toll had been three hundred and forty-six dead in that accident.

'The front of the aircraft cushioned the shock,'

Houston said at last. 'When the tail snapped off, the engine broke loose.'

Corski nodded. Being on his first Major and in the company of an old hand, he wisely thought it best not to pass an opinion.

Houston ran a hand over his pockmarked face and gave his pants an upwards heave under his coveralls. Beneath the coveralls his stomach overhung his belt, the result of his gluttonous appetite, and periodically his belt slipped down. He bent over the battered outer casing of the engine and inserted his hand through the broken steel casing surrounding the combustion chambers. Several of the chambers were split open. With his fingernail he scooped out a fragment of carbon deposit, put it under his nose, and sniffed noisily. Nothing out of the ordinary: the usual odour resulting from burning a mixture of kerosene and air. He walked around to the smashed jet pipe nozzle and sniffed inside. The reverse thrust buckets, he noted, had been torn off, and lay some distance away. He bent to inspect broken fuel lines and oil pipes that stuck out at awkward angles from the gearbox, removed a clod of earth from a filter casing, and cleaned it with a rag.

'Got any sample cans?'

'Right here.' Corski eagerly handed him one.

Houston took a wrench from his tool kit and applied it to the drain plug of the fuel filter. A smear of liquid spread over his fingers and ran down his sleeve. 'Here it comes.' He yanked away the plug and held up the can as a thread of light amber kerosene poured out. Before it all drained away, he reinserted the plug and handed the can to Corski, who screwed the cap on tightly.

'Wipe off the excess,' Houston said. He turned back to the engine. 'Now an oil sample.' He unscrewed another drain plug. 'A fresh can, quick.'

He grabbed the container before the trickle of luminescent oil grew into a thick stream. Then he rubbed his little finger on his backside to clean his fingertip and held it under the oil.

'Still warm?' Klein inquired.

Houston nodded. 'Sure. It was circulating through a hot engine a coupla hours ago.'

'Make sure the cap's on tight,' he said, handing the can to Corski. 'The lab'll analyse it and compare it with the correct specification. And do a spectrometric analysis for metallic bits and pieces. Same with the fuel,' he added, knowing Corski was a new man. There was no harm in reconfirming the lectures Corski had attended at Dulles.

Corski took a china marker from his pocket and scrawled identifying words on top of each container.

'Get them off to the labs right away,' Houston said. 'Got any more of those metal cans? We're going to need samples from whatever's left of the wing fuel tanks.'

Corski looked embarrassed. 'Only these glass and plastic containers.'

'Not worth a boxful of horseshoe nails. Glass lets in light and spoils the sample. Plastic gets absorbed in the fuel and wrecks it chemically. See if they've got any metal cans in the equipment truck.'

When Corski left, Houston went around to the front of the engine. The air intake was obscured by a mess of buckled aluminium, parts of the rear fuselage and fin fairing, and he wondered if debris had been ingested into the engine. He looked around. The photographic team was nearby, focusing on the tail unit. 'Hey, fellas! When you're through there, come over here.'

Corski reappeared. 'Found these,' he announced, putting three metal containers on the ground.

In a few minutes the photographers came over. 'Shoot that crap in front of the intake so's I can move it. I want to look inside.'

It took several minutes for the photographers, now using flashbulbs, to complete their work. When they moved away, Houston put on his work gloves and bent back the bits of metal obscuring the intake. He peered inside.

'Jesus Christ! Take a look, Steve.'

Klein bent to stare at the forward stages of the compressor rotor. All the wing-like blades were rooted in the rotor disc, distorted and twisted out of shape – but still in position.

'If the engine had been turning when it hit, those blades would have sheared off like stripping corn of the cob,' Houston exclaimed.

'Flameout?' Klein suggested.

Houston nodded doubtfully. It was easy to jump to conclusions at the first sign of something out of character with an engine. On the other hand, if the engine *had* been rotating at normal cruising revolutions at the moment of impact, the blades would have been flung outwards by the tremendous centrifugal force of the rotating compressor and turbine. Blades had been found half a mile from the site of an engine rotating on impact. He shone a flashlight into the engine, looking for signs of fire. He must know unequivocally whether the engine was in fact not burning *and* not turning at the moment the aircraft hit the ground. He remembered an accident he'd investigated where a Boeing 727 had crashed and burned after take-off. The compressor and turbine blades had stripped and been flung a hundred yards to each side; on first investigation a clear case of a crash under full power. But when they recovered the flight data recorder, the tape showed that all engines had failed because of fuel starvation. Hitting the ground soon after take-off, the engines had not had time to run down after failure and were windmilling at high speed.

He moved the flashlight around. There were no signs of soot or smoke, but he'd have a look in the mid-section, where the turbine blades were located, to make certain.

'Help me get this turbine casing off,' he said to Corski.

'The bolts are all jammed,' the younger man replied.

'We'll try it anyway,' Houston said, applying a wrench

to the bolts securing the casing around the engine mid-section. Carefully lifting a bundle of electric cables out of the way, he discovered an inspection panel. 'Here, this'll show us.' He unscrewed the bolts, hinged the panel out of the way, and pointed the flashlight into the aperture.

'Not a turbine blade gone. Battered like hell but all in place. And no fire.'

'Then it *was* a flameout, Mr Houston?' Corski said.

'Darn well looks like it. We'll ship it to the labs for a detailed examination.'

'Maybe a main bearing failure,' Corski ventured.

Houston shrugged and hitched up his pants. 'Can't say anything for sure at this stage. But if there're metallic particles in that oil sample and steel shavings in the gear-box when we strip it down, it might mean a ball bearing failed.'

'Oil starvation?' Corski asked in a slightly bolder voice. 'From a conked-out oil pump?'

'Maybe. Sludge or carbon deposits in the oil galleries will tell. Close up this inspection panel to stop any dust getting blown in.'

Corski leaned over the engine, and Houston stood back and rubbed the side of his face, leaving an oily smear across his chin. He'd have to look for the tiny tell-tale signs of bird ingestion too, in the compressor air bleeds, and check the blades individually under a micro-scope for suspicious stains. But bird ingestion at over thirty thousand feet? The Caravan would have been somewhere around that flight level. Bird flocks around airports had caused catastrophic accidents at take-off, being sucked into engine air intakes and causing power to fall off at a critical moment. But at six hundred miles an hour at high altitude? Migrating flocks didn't fly that high, although radar had tracked birds at twenty thousand feet. On the other hand, the aircraft may have descended to a lower flight level for some unknown reason and run into a flock. He'd settle the altitude question with Dave Jacobs when the Air Traffic Control tapes were available.

'Guess that's all we can do on this engine for the time being,' he said to Klein when Corski had finished. 'We'll get over to the wing engines. They're probably cratered.'

Bradley looked at the mess in the hole in the ground, where he had returned after Klein had called his attention to the nose cone. It was now dark, and floodlights had been rigged up to illuminate the site, the heavy cables snaked everywhere, leading back to a mobile power generator. Kruger, one of the structures men from Regional, with a pink complexion and red thatch of hair, shook his head.

'Where the hell *do* we start?'

Bradley hesitated, trying to make up his mind where they should commence digging through the debris, painstakingly looking for the part numbers stamped on the components that made up the main section of the fuselage, tagging the parts as they went. For several seconds he stood still, staring down, trying to shake off his feeling of helplessness.

'Over here,' he said at length, indicating a crumpled length of aluminium skin about eight feet long near the edge of the crater, one of the biggest pieces of wreckage in sight. His first job was to separate in his mind in-flight structural damage from ground impact damage. He grunted, thinking of the phrases they taught at the Dulles school. This hunk looked all ground impact damage, but he must search for clues that might indicate in-flight failure; then he had to look for the initial failure. Finally, he must try to isolate the exact cause of the initial failure. It sounded easy the way they taught it: in actual fact, the work he was starting might not turn up anything. The cause of the crash might have nothing to do with structural failure, and he knew it.

He carefully climbed down and stood near the twisted skin. Taking a magnifying glass from his pocket, he peered at various areas of the surface for telltale signs of paint or oil smears and for the almost invisible scratches that resulted when one part of an aircraft lightly slid over another, signs to the trained eye of the probability of a mid-air breakup resulting from depressurisation. Smears from an in-flight structural breakup came from deposits of paint, primer, or oil film transferred from one part to another as components hit against each other. He looked along a line of rivets pulled through the alloy sheet leaving a line of semicircular perforations like the serrated edge of a postage stamp.

'This is goddamned useless,' he said, slipping the glass into his pocket.

He withdrew a blueprint from his satchel and spread it on the earth. 'Here's the general arrangement drawing of the CA-100. A three-man crew,' he said pointing. 'Major joints are where the rear fuselage is attached to the main fuselage and the nose to the main. Right here.' Kruger and two other Regional investigators who had joined them leaned over. Bradley pointed to the spot a hundred yards away where the bits of the rear fuselage rested on the ground, glinting under the powerful lights. Liss stood near it conferring with a group of other men. 'Looks like we've got most of the main fuselage and the nose fuselage down here,' he remarked, suppressing his doubts that anything could be learned by sifting through the bits. They could dig until they came to the wing centre section, and examine the joints where the wings were bolted to the fuselage.

At the thought of digging deeper, he wondered about the dangers he and the others might be exposed to by the cargo he'd find under the cabin floor. In recent years airlines had become the victims of unscrupulous shippers who evaded federal packaging regulations for airfreighting radioactive materials and industrial acids. Shippers sent radioisotopes by air freight without proper radiation shielding, and deadly bacterial cultures wrapped in flimsy packages. When an aircraft hit turbulence, packages sometimes broke open, exposing passengers to radiation or bacterial infection. Even in calm air, airline passengers, unknown to themselves, were exposed to radiation from industrial radioactive shipments stowed in the cargo compartment below the cabin floor.

Bradley frowned and looked again at the wreck. 'Let's begin by laying out some bits and pieces on the ground, tagging as we go.'

He burrowed into a hollow created by the impacted metal and let his mind drift back to the accident he'd helped investigate at Boston International Airport. A Boeing 707 all-freighter aircraft had crashed when attempting an emergency landing, killing the three-man crew. Crates of nitric acid in the cargo had broken open after the aircraft had taken off from New York, bound for Glasgow, Scotland. One hundred and sixty miles out over the Atlantic the air-conditioning system picked up fumes and smoke, which surged forward into the flight deck. The crew put on smoke goggles, and the captain turned back to attempt a landing at Boston. The aircraft crashed, killing him and the other two crew members. Investigation disclosed that the captain needed to wear corrective glasses when flying, and the smoke goggles would not fit correctly at the temples. Semi-suffocated, and blinded, he'd lost control on the approach.

'The nosewheel's under here,' Bradley exclaimed, spotting a hunk of black rubber curled back under a dented panel he'd removed. 'Impact shoved it up through the wheel well,' he called up, feeling around with his hand.

'Then we're not far from the flight deck,' Kruger said, worming his way into the hole to join Bradley.

'Oh, Jesus,' Bradley said, suddenly withdrawing his hand.

'What's up?'

'Look.'

Bradley pointed to a piece of torn blue cloth about the

size of a man's handkerchief. Four gold braided stripes were sewn to it. A man's shoulder blade poked through the cloth, the raw white bone speckled with red blotches.

Kruger turned away and spewed the contents of his stomach into the wreckage.

Bradley, although feeling sick himself, was able to control his retching. 'You okay?'

Kruger nodded. 'Yeah.' He wiped the sleeve of his coveralls across his mouth. 'Never came across a body suddenly like that before. Usually – ' He broke off.

Bradley made a mental note to tell Downey where the captain's body was located as he saw the glint of steel beneath the shreds of aluminium. 'We may have something here,' he said, his voice muted amid the wreckage. He manoeuvred a solid-looking mechanism towards him. 'It's the nosewheel uplock.'

He pulled it towards him, and turned it over and over in his hands. 'Locked solidly in the Up position.'

'So they weren't expecting a forced landing,' Kruger said, his face the colour of ash.

Bradley handed the mechanism to Kruger and made a note on his clipboard. Kruger swallowed, tied a cardboard tag to the uplock, and wrote on it: *Nosewheel uplock. Lock secured in Up position when found.* He rubbed the earth off the steel surface with his glove until he could read the part number, and wrote the number on the tag.

Bradley paused again before thrusting his hand into the metal rubble, thinking about the luggage passengers had taken aboard Flight 137. Few people read the small print some airlines put on their tickets, prohibiting them from carrying aboard lighter fluid, matches, aerosols, and explosives. Every year thousands of hunters packed live ammunition into their baggage in cheerful ignorance of the potential danger in the event of turbulence, a heavy landing, or even a collision with another aircraft while taxiing. Whatever had been taken aboard this Caravan was now his problem.

'Here goes,' he said, lowering himself deeper into the

tunnel he had dug, focusing his flashlight.

'Look out,' Kruger called. 'There's a tangle of flight control cables where you're putting your foot.'

'I see it. Get the photographers over here to shoot that uplock.'

He ducked his head and picked up the frayed ends of a snapped control cable. It gave no clue: simply a cable snapped by tension as the structure smashed into thousands of pieces on impact. But *this* is something. He knelt and stared at a metal panel with bits of electrical wires hanging from it, housing several warning lights. The stencilled white letters on the front read 'Generator Charging'. He turned the panel over and examined the warning light bulbs. The glass envelopes of all the bulbs were intact, but the filament in each bulb was stretched into a shapeless loop.

'Hey,' he shouted. 'Take a look at this.' He held the panel up high.

One of the other Regional investigators leaned into the hole and took it from him.

'The filaments look like spaghetti, so the generators were charging,' he exclaimed. He recited a phrase every investigator knew from the Dulles school. 'Lit-up filaments are hot and stretch; unlit filaments are cold and snap.'

'A textbook example if I ever saw one,' Bradley shouted up. 'Get it tagged, photographed, and over to the IIC right away.'

Bradley took off his work glove to wipe the sweat off his palm and dug deeper into the fragments. He felt more eager now. He touched something furry and warm, and his hand recoiled. The air was stagnant in the burrow, and he fought back his fear of discovering some other dismembered part of the flight crew. Cautiously he put out his hand and explored again, and felt a sticky soft round blob with a spike in the middle. He gingerly put his hand around the object and brought it into the light. It was bloodied, yellow, and round. The spike turned out to be the beak of a day-old chick. 'Good

God,' he muttered, relieved. He put it aside and felt around, finding several other squashed chicks, and soon dragged up a broken cardboard box. He held it up to the light. Printed in heavy black letters were the words: 'RUSH DELIVERY – PERISHABLE.'

He climbed out of the hole, feeling drained. 'Let's take a look at what's left of the wings,' he said to the men from Regional. 'We can come back here later.'

'Start at this end,' Liss told the three men in his group. 'The FDR and the CVR are mounted between Stations 1210 and 1232.' He rechecked a diagram he'd grabbed from the Bureau library before boarding the Gulfstream. 'Up behind the ceiling near the aft galley.'

He crawled inside the squashed rear fuselage. Strips of ceiling decor hung in tatters, and skeins of electric cables sagged crazily between the sharp edges of the metal floor, thrust upwards by the smashed, crooked floor support members. Upholstery from passenger seats had burst through the seating fabric, covering cadavers with layers of stuffing. At the front of what had been the rear economy cabin bodies were piled in grotesque attitudes against the crushed bulkhead, with legs and arms reaching out, fingers frozen in clawing action. Facing him was the decapitated body of a man wearing a red and green plaid jacket and, by a curious juxtaposition of the parts of the dismembered bodies, a baby's head had rolled down the aisle and come to rest on top of the man's severed neck. Seats had snapped from their anchorages as easily as a child breaks a matchstick, and lunch trays, bits of plastic food containers, strips of ham, snippets of lettuce, tomatoes, unstuck sandwiches, and plastic knives and forks were everywhere.

Liss ducked his lean form to avoid sharp tongues of metal driven inward by the impact, and moved to the side of the floodlighted aircraft, looking for the numbers stamped on the once circular fuselage frames. 'The twelve hundreds should be about here,' he said to one of the men, an FAA investigator named Anderson.

'Here's Station Twelve Ten,' Anderson said. He was a tubby man with a big wart on the side of his face and a bent nose, the latter the result of a flying accident. All air accident investigators were, or had been pilots.

Liss examined the frame Anderson indicated, and peered at the roof, angling his body awkwardly, trying to see if the recorders were still in position. Embedded in shockproof insulation in a steel sphere the size of a beach ball, the flight data recorder was a tape deck that recorded seventy electronic signals as soon as a captain stepped aboard his aircraft and switched on the anti-collision lights before starting engines. It tape-recorded engine start-up, take-off, climb-out, cruise, descent, approach, landing, and taxiing, through accurately measuring and recording the angles of deflection of the elevators, ailerons, landing flaps and rudder, the pilot's movements of the control yokes and rudder pedals, engine throttle settings, positions of undercarriage, the G forces, and the time to a tenth of a second. In the event of a catastrophe, the flight recorder, in its crash-proof, fireproof, waterproof steel shell, was an electro-mechanical witness. Costing more than one and a half million dollars, it was the price airlines paid in the hope of tracking down the causes of otherwise unexplained crashes, to enable them to take action to prevent a recurrence.

The cockpit voice recorder also was in a tough crash-proof sphere located in the rear fuselage. Through three microphones in the flight deck ceiling it recorded all the words spoken by the crew members, from take-off to landing, including the conversations between the crew and the ground air traffic controllers. Only the past thirty minutes of flight deck conversation was stored in the tape, which automatically erased as the flight progressed, and then restarted for the next thirty minutes. The system had an unsuspected flaw, as Liss had discovered after a crash landing by a small privately owned jet. Puzzled on that case, he had called Klein down to the laboratories late one night to listen to a cockpit voice recorder that was utterly silent.

'How many people aboard?' Klein had asked.

'Pilot and co-pilot. On a return flight after flying a group of executives to the Bahamas.'

Klein had listened in amazement to the soundless tape in the special audio lab Liss had designed for playback of cockpit voice recorders. The chamber was absolutely soundproof, and Liss had surrounded it with fine copper wire mesh to shield it from electromagnetic waves emanating from electrical machinery in the labs, and from broadcast waves from television and radio stations in Washington. He'd also designed an electronic gadget that he could use to reduce the noise of the slipstream rushing past the flight deck of an aircraft to enable the crew's voices to sound more distinctly. He'd further improved the device by making it possible to reduce engine noise.

'Something's goddamned screwy, you gotta believe. What happened after he bent the undercarriage?'

'A mechanic saw the plane taxi around the back of the hangar and stay there for about a half hour with the engines idling.'

Klein, with the authority vested in him, had interviewed the pilots. Ultimately he ferreted the truth from the pilot in command, who'd idled the engines behind the hangar as he sat, without speaking with his co-pilot, waiting for the tape to scrub itself clean, erasing incriminating evidence. A charge of violating a federal air regulation had been levied, and the pilot's licence suspended for six months.

Liss was a damned good man to have around, Klein had reflected at the time. He was ambitious and wanted promotion to IIC, and had been sore when he'd been passed over during a reorganisation of the Bureau several months ago. Malik, Klein suspected, thought Liss was too specialised, wrapped up as he was as chairman of the Systems Group. With eight experts reporting to him, he was responsible not only for flight data and cockpit voice recorders but for hydraulics, electronics, electrical, and flight systems.

Liss had come to the Bureau from NASA, where, as a former jet fighter pilot, he'd done work researching the biological changes in human bodies subjected to high acceleration forces at extreme altitudes. Liss had designed and developed a new electronic sensor, since used by astronauts. When NASA's budget for research was slashed, he had come to the Bureau of Aviation Safety. He was a bachelor, still in his thirties, and his gaunt appearance made him appear cold. In reality, he had a warm personality masked by shyness. His gawky walk had once prompted Houston to say that 'Jeff stutters with his feet when he walks.'

'That's Station Twelve Ten all right,' Liss said to Anderson and the other men. 'Start probing around here.' He indicated a spot about twenty feet away, towards the front of the wreck.

They stepped wearily over sprawling bodies and spread out, digging into the debris below the floor. Liss held up a flight bag he had found below the floor and put it aside where Downey would find it. He was uptight, teeth clenched. It was always like this until he found the recorders. He levered a heavy floor beam out of the way, ripping his protective glove, and swore under his breath.

'There's nothing under this section,' a Regional man said. 'How about trying near the bulkhead?'

'Carry on,' Liss replied, taking off his glove. Damned thing's useless, he thought. You lose your sense of feel working with gloves on anyway, they make them too thick and inflexible. He stuck his hand under the beam. To his surprise, he felt crumbly earth. There was a hole through the fuselage skin, and a hollow directly below. He worked his hand around in an exploratory sweep and suddenly froze in numbed terror. Something moved under his hand; something cold and clammy. He felt the sweat gather on his forehead as the thing insistently pushed against his fingers.

'Hey – my God! ' he yelled in a cracked voice. 'There's somebody alive down – '

'Christ almighty, where?' roared the Regional investigator as he stumbled towards him.

'Right here. Somebody's shoving against my hand. Oh, Jesus! Where's George Downey? Get Downey, for God's sake! '

Liss suddenly reacted as his reserve of nervous restraint left him. He yanked his hand out of the hole so quickly he smacked the Regional man across the face and left him with a bloody nose.

'Man, I'm sorry. Get Downey and his men over here fast.'

'What exactly did it feel like, sir?' inquired another man from the regional office. He was about sixty, grey-haired, and had a line of deep wrinkles etching his forehead. His name was Pfeiffer, and he was Armstrong's assistant and had spent some twenty years in air accident investigation.

Liss wiped the sweat from his forehead with a handkerchief. 'Cold – and sort of wet,' he replied.

'Then it's not human,' said Pfeiffer with conviction.

'No?' Liss asked doubtfully.

'If it was human it would still be slightly warm. And so would the wetness you felt.' As an afterthought he asked, 'Was it sticky?'

'No.'

'Not blood. Let me have a feel around.'

Pfeiffer removed his glove and knelt. He felt in the hole while Liss and the others gathered around, silent and expectant. Pfeiffer withdrew his hand.

'This is what you felt,' he said, holding up a green turtle the size of half an orange, which blinked at them with solemn reptilian eyes from the safety of its shell.

'They're probably more of 'em down there,' Pfeiffer said, putting his hand into the hole. 'Probably a shipment from the aft cargo compartment. Their shells protected 'em in the crash.'

'Dammit,' somebody said in an indignant voice. 'Four

hundred and six human beings killed and some goddamned useless pets get saved.'

'Not necessarily useless,' said Pfeiffer, scooping up two more live turtles and the remains of a splintered wooden crate. He pointed at the label still stapled to the wood. 'They're addressed to the California State Biological Research Laboratories, Los Angeles. They were going to be used for scientific testing purposes.' He glanced at Liss as the others returned to where they had been digging. 'You okay?'

Liss forced a smile. 'Sure. It was feeling something move that – '

'Yeah. I know,' Pfeiffer said with understanding, returning to the space he had been searching.

Mustn't show them I'm afraid to feel around in this hole, Liss thought, taking the precaution of pulling on the torn glove. He thrust his hand boldly into the hollow, working in another direction. He touched something solid. Breathlessly he slid his hand around, feeling its shape. It was a sphere about the size of a beach ball.

'Hey! I've got something, men,' he shouted. The others scrambled to help him lift it out. 'It's the cockpit voice recorder,' Liss said. 'One down, one to go.'

At that moment Klein stuck his head through a hole in the fuselage.

'We've got the CVR,' Liss said triumphantly. 'The damned thing went clean through the aircraft's skin.'

Klein examined the steel globe. The flanges joining the halves were still sealed tight, but closer inspection showed that they were bent, distorting the bolts that held the halves together. Several deep gouges on the hardened steel surface showed where it had slammed against the ground. 'Hope it's okay,' he said. 'Get it down to the car, and lock the car. When we find the FDR, we can fly them both to Washington. Get it wrapped up right away,' he added. The sphere had to be protected by a two-inch-thick layer of special plastic wrapping to guard against accidental exposure to electromagnetic radiation. Liss called to a man from Regional to get the wrapping material from the equipment truck.

Klein left them, and looked around the site. It was a scene straight out of hell. The harsh glare of floodlights starkly illuminated eviscerated bodies and horribly disfigured faces. He heard the metallic scrape of steel on aluminium as investigators dug with skilled and controlled haste into piles of rubble. Policemen paced behind the roped-off area, ordering back the crowd where it pressed too close. Workmen had already begun to erect big tents for the arrival of the relatives of the dead passengers, to shelter and succour them before the relatives tried to identify the grisly remains of a husband, a wife, children, a lover, a mother, a father.

A knot of nurses huddled near a police car, talking in hushed tones, looking helpless. They knew they could do nothing for the dead: they could only wait for the relatives, to try to alleviate their distress. Red Cross workers hurried from group to group of investigators, carrying trays of steaming coffee cups, soup, and sandwiches from an industrial catering truck.

Klein walked towards the cratered right wing, searching for Houston. He found him with Corski and another of Regional's powerplant men standing in a pit that had been dug around the right wing engine. The four-ton engine lay horizontally with its support pylon sticking up into the air, like a huge dead bird with stiff feet pointing skyward. Houston looked up with a grimy face. 'Same as the rear engine. Blades in position. Bent like hell, of course,' he called up.

'Liss's found the CVR, so we may get a clue on the throttle settings. What about Number One engine?'

'We're just going over. They should have dug down to it by now.' Houston climbed up to ground level, puffing. 'Looks certain two engines had a flameout,' he said in a confidential tone.

Klein rubbed his chin. Two flameouts seemed an impossibility. And there might be a third. They walked over to the mound of exposed earth where men had dug to expose the left wing engine. Houston lowered his bulky form into the hole. The engine lay on its side, the assembly of intricate outer casing lying in a shattered pile. Klein peered down at the compressor and turbine blades, distorted and twisted as if a giant's hand had tightened around them, crushing and flattening the rotating blades in one direction. Houston looked up with a defeated expression on his face.

'I want those engines dug up and into the lab as soon as possible,' Klein called down. 'And a thorough examination of the relight systems, every fuel valve, and every fuel feed pipe.' Crew mismanagement of the fuel system was a factor in some accidents. Fuel valves had been left open to empty tanks and inadvertently closed to full tanks, despite the fuel warning lights and semi-automatic cross-check systems on modern jets. He'd read of a flameout due simply to running out of fuel, but that had been on a military aircraft. But flameouts on three engines? 'Bird ingestion, Bill? Make sure nobody disturbs any feather or bone deposits in the air bleeds and compressor tappings. And what about the fuel samples?'

'We got about half a gallon,' Houston shouted up. 'Enough for analysis. Not much around except in the regulators and a bit in the filters. The main tanks are completely busted and the fuel's all drained away.' He bent over the engine and swore as his wrench slipped off a nut he was loosening.

Klein made a sudden decision.

'Bill, climb out of that goddamned hole and fly back to Washington with me. We'll pick up Liss. I gotta hear that cockpit voice recorder.'

Part III
Analysis

FIVE

'Queerest damned thing I ever heard,' Klein muttered. He turned to Houston, who sat on the next bench stool in the recorder playback chamber. 'What do you make of it?'

Houston swallowed. He was visibly moved, his ebullient spirit dampened. 'They didn't even have time to call an emergency on the radio or press a seventy-seven hundred,' he said in a subdued voice. 'And no bang at the end that might indicate depressurisation. But the cockpit mikes don't always pick it up.'

'Nothing like a bomb going off, either,' Klein said. He turned to Liss. 'Run it through again.'

'On the copy?'

'Yes, don't risk jamming or breaking the original. I'll lock it in the safe later. Have your guys got printouts ready?'

Liss carefully wound the tape into the feed rollers and adjusted knobs on a panel. 'They should be ready,' he said, swinging back the metal-lined door on silent hinges.

Klein stuck his elbow on the bench, rested his chin on his hand, and stared into space until Liss returned with a stack of computerised printout forms. He collated the forms and handed the others a thin pile of papers. The sheets had square holes punched in the outer edges where they had been driven by gears through a computer line printer. 'Sorry we didn't have time to bind them in a folder,' Liss said. 'At least they're edited. Just ignore that list of names in my group. In the rush they stuck that in from an old report, although I expect I'll be working with the same guys on this case.'

Klein took the papers and studied the top sheet.

TRANSCRIPTION OF COCKPIT VOICE RECORDER, COLLINS MODEL NO. 642C-1. ASTRAL AIRCRAFT CORP. CA-100 CARAVAN, U.S. REGISTRATION NO. N98734NE, AMERICAN CONSTITUTION AIRLINES FLIGHT 137, CHICAGO (O'HARE) – LOS ANGELES INTERNATIONAL, MAY 16, 1978.

Warning

The reader of this report is cautioned that the transcription of a CVR tape is not a precise science but is the best product possible from an NTSB investigative group effort. The transcript, or parts thereof, if taken out of context, could be misleading. The attached CVR transcript should be viewed as an accident investigation tool to be used in conjunction with other evidence gathered during the investigation. Conclusions or interpretations should not be made using the transcript as the sole source of information.

Cockpit Voice Recorder Group

Jeffrey Liss, National Transportation Safety Board, Systems Chairman
Oscar J. Condotta, Federal Aviation Administration
Benjamin M. Rexford, Air Line Pilots Association

Klein turned to the second sheet and ran his eye down the list of explanations for the symbols.

Legend

CAM	Cockpit area microphone
CAM-1	Voice identified as Captain Vernon A. Colley
CAM-2	Voice identified as First Officer Sidney A. Roberts
CAM-3	Voice identified as Second Officer Lawrence P. Tanzella
-?	Voice unidentified (male)
STEW-1	Voice identified as Stewardess Elizabeth D. Lindquist

CC	Chicago Centre (Frequency 125.4)
MKC	Kansas City (Frequency 112.6)
*	Unintelligible word
#	Nonpertinent word
%	Breaks in continuity
( )	Questionable text
(( ))	Editorial insertion
——	Pause

NOTE: Times transposed from Greenwich Mean Time to local time.

He pressed the corners of his lips down when he scanned the symbol #. *Nonpertinent word* was a euphemism Legal insisted they insert to substitute for obscenities uttered on the flight deck. He turned to the next page and noted the time printed on the first line to the nearest half second.

'Where do you estimate they were at the beginning of the last thirty minutes?' he asked.

'I put them just leaving the Kirksville beacon,' Liss replied. 'As you can see, the printout shows the last twelve minutes and twenty-eight seconds of flight, the relevant portion.'

Klein bent over the navigation chart headed 'Chicago–Los Angeles, Hi-Level Route 6', tightly thumbtacked to the wooden bench. He put his finger on it and cross-checked the printout. 'He's just leaving Chicago Air Traffic Control?'

'Yes.'

'Run it.'

Liss moved a switch. For several seconds there was no sound, then the high-pitched whine of jet engines broke from the speakers, overlaid with the softer tone of the airstream rushing past the nose of an aircraft. Liss turned a knob and the airstream sound diminished. He rotated another knob and the engine noise was reduced to a low hum. Looking pleased with himself, he turned to Klein, but Klein was already absorbed in the printout.

	INTRA-COCKPIT COMMUNICATION		AIR-GROUND COMMUNICATION	
TIME	SOURCE	CONTENT	SOURCE	CONTENT
Hr. Min. Sec.				
10 40 09	CAM-2	So I told this guy to park his car and –		
10 40 12			CC	Flight One-Three-Seven. What is your altitude?
10 40 15			CAM-1	Flight level three-one-zero
10 40 18			CC	Roger. Contact Kansas City one-one-two decimal six and report flight level three-one-zero. S'long
10 40 30			CAM-1	Contact Kansas City one-one-two decimal six and report flight level three-one-zero
10 40 35	CAM-2	I'll tell you some other time		
10 40 40			CAM-1	Kansas City Centre. American Constitution Airlines Flight One-Three-Seven. At flight level three-one-zero
10 40 48			MKC	Hi, there, One-Three-Seven. Welcome to Kansas City. Check you at three-one-zero.

INTRA-COCKPIT COMMUNICATION			AIR-GROUND COMMUNICATION	
TIME	SOURCE	CONTENT	SOURCE	CONTENT
Hr. Min. Sec.				
				Squawk ident two-one-zero-zero.
				——Roger. Radar contact. No further position reports required. Have fun in L.A.
10 40 56	CAM-2	Wise guy		
10 40 58	CAM-1	Friendly people		

(EDITORIAL NOTE: No further air-ground communication from this point to end of CVR tape – J. Liss, Systems)

INTRA-COCKPIT COMMUNICATION

TIME	SOURCE	CONTENT
Hr. Min. Sec.		
10 41 05	CAM-1	How's the coffee, Larry?
10 41 07	CAM	Sound of chime
10 41 12	CAM-1	Where's the next report point? We'll report everything's routine to the company
10 41 16	CAM-2	Just a minute. These # maps are all fouled up
10 41 16.5	CAM	Sound of paper rustling
10 41 18	CAM-2	Ah, Vern, uh – Garden City. Frequency one-three-zero decimal four-five. It's three hundred and forty miles west of Kansas City

TIME			SOURCE	CONTENT
Hr.	Min.	Sec.		
10	41	24	CAM-1	We can wait a bit before calling
			CAM	Sound of movement on flight deck
10	41	26	CAM-3	How's coffee?
10	41	28	STEW-1	I'll get it
			CAM	Sound of movement on flight deck
10	41	40	STEW-1	Fresh pot
10	41	41	CAM-1	Okay. I have it. No sugar, thanks. How are things back there?
10	41	44	STEW-1	Busy. Getting ready to serve—— snack.
10	41	50	-?	I heard we've got to congratulate you, Elizabeth
10	41	58	CAM-2	Yeah – congratulations. Sam told me on the ramp
10	42	07	CAM-1	You getting spliced, Elizabeth? Er, what's the fuel burnoff, Larry?
10	42	11	STEW-1	Ah-hum——
10	42	15	CAM-1	Congratulations. Who's –
10	42	20	CAM-3	Five thousand pounds. Inner tanks pumped to outboard. Yes – tell us who's the lucky guy
10	42	31	STEW-1	——you wouldn't know him. Works in * base department in L.A. Gotta go
10	42	37	CAM-3	All the best

TIME	SOURCE	CONTENT
Hr. Min. Sec.		
10 42 44	CAM-1	Nice girl. I knew her on DC-9s. Works hard. Not like some of the girls they're bringing on
10 42 53	CAM-2	Some fella told me a lot of them fail the semi-annual emergency procedures exam
10 42 59	CAM-1	The – er – that burnoff's okay—— Maybe the wide-body aircraft are getting them down. Too many people
10 43 12	CAM-2	That snack smells okay. This fella said girls are turned off stewardessing. Makes 'em feel like a waitress
10 43 31	CAM	Whistling
10 43 39	CAM-2	Last trip——Then layover in Hawaii. I figured I'd take Shirley this time. She's looking forward to it. Talked her mother into baby-sitting the kids
10 43 47	CAM-1	How long for?
10 43 50	CAM-2	Fourteen days. Part of my annual leave % took a long walk around the city——didn't wake up till half after eleven. Wound up in a tavern called the – er – Red Spot Inn – right at the end of the bridge
10 44 10	CAM-1	Don't know Chicago very well. What's the next report point, you say?
10 44 17.5	CAM-2	Garden City. DME shows three hundred and ten miles

INTRA-COCKPIT COMMUNICATION

TIME	SOURCE	CONTENT
Hr. Min. Sec.		
10 44 27	CAM-3	That's Kansas City——apartments, see them there?
10 44 35	CAM-2	Oh, the white ones there
10 44 36	CAM-3	Yes
10 44 44	CAM-2	It's quite a good view out over the countryside there. Housing must be # expensive over there – on the outskirts
10 44 54	CAM-1	Expensive, all right
10 45 01	CAM-2	Yeah. A lot of people must've made a lot of money
10 45 07	CAM-1	Yes – I'll say. Oh – what d'ya know? Hear that?
10 45 10	CAM-2	There're an awful lot of women flying today * pilots

'Stop the tape!' Klein called abruptly. Liss pressed a switch and the sound cut out. 'Can't you get it?'

'I've tried. I'll try again.'

Klein thumped his fist against his forehead. 'The powderpuff league'll be on our backs if *that* comes out in the final report,' he said.

'Dave Jacobs will have it on his ATC tapes. Sounded like a woman pilot asking for landing clearance at Kansas City,' Houston said.

Liss backed up the tape and adjusted the knobs on his control panel. 'Here it is with as near to zero unwanted sound as I can get.'

'Run it.' Klein strained towards one of the speakers. A rushing noise sounded, then:

'*Yeah. A lot of people must've made a lot of money.*'

'*Yes – I'll say. Oh – what d'ya know? Hear that?*'

'There're an awful lot of women flying today' – an indistinct sound like a guttural *'goddamned'* came from the tape – *'pilots'*.

'Can't you get rid of the slipstream noise and separate the voices some more?' Klein asked.

'It's the best I can get,' Liss said.

'All right. Carry on. Try to get what he said later.'

INTRA-COCKPIT COMMUNICATION

TIME Hr. Min. Sec.			SOURCE	CONTENT
10	45	16	CAM-1	((Crackling–mike noise))——*would you be going up into – uh * in L.A.?
10	45	29	CAM-2	Yeah. I think so. * I wonder if that new contract will be okayed by – er – the company. It's a # long time getting approved
10	45	40	CAM-3	Why do they always wait until the contract nearly expires? You'd think ALPA would get on to it
10	45	51	CAM-2	Yeah – er – they have I believe. I heard the company's holding things up. They've ordered seven new CA-100s – the new stretched jobs that I heard have just gone into production. Business must be booming again
10	46	12	CAM-1	I'll put – uh——the red. Until they amortise them. Look what happened to Pan Am
10	46	19	CAM-2	Pity about that. Ed told –
10	46	22	CAM-1	You got that compass heading?
10	46	22.5	CAM	Sound of click
10	46	23	CAM-2	Same as yours. Check. Look at that glorious day. ((Sound of whistling))

INTRA-COCKPIT COMMUNICATION

TIME			SOURCE	CONTENT
Hr.	Min.	Sec.		
10	46	29	CAM-1	Kinda nice——when d'ya say you're going to Hawaii?
10	46	36	CAM-2	Huh – the trip after this one——I mean after we go back to Chicago and return to L.A. Guess you're due for leave, Vern, eh? Soon?
10	46	48	CAM-1	Gotta see the schedule. Silvester's ahead of me. Can't – ah – bid all my own flight scheduling yet. Not enough seniority. What's the DME for Albuquerque?
10	46	56	CAM-2	Albuquerque – oh, where are you, Albuquerque? Ah –
10	46	56.5	CAM	Sound of click
10	46	57	CAM-2	Five-five-five miles
10	47	00	CAM-1	Got anything you want to report to Garden City?
10	47	05	CAM-2	Nope. Just that it's a nice day
10	47	10	CAM-1	I think we can skip it. We'll soon be in their control area. Albuquerque
10	47	17	CAM-2	Albuquerque——This guy told me about how some airline passengers fly under assumed names. Craziest thing
10	47	31	CAM-1	What's that?
10	47	33	CAM-2	This guy back in Chicago. Passing through the dispatch office. Works for the National Transport Accident Board or something. Ah, er - Bureau of Aircraft Safety – er, maybe it was aviation safety or something. Not the FAA –

TIME Hr. Min. Sec.			SOURCE	CONTENT
10	47	45	CAM-1	Yes, I know. They've got nothing to do with it
10	47	51	CAM-2	That's right. Anyways, this guy was telling me about the people they found up on this mountain in California. A taxi plane came down in the mountains——shuttling people from San Francisco to a gambling casino at Lake Tahoe——Yeah. One of the guys was a banker - very respectable ((laughter)) All the others, women an' all, had given false names. An' the - er - bodies all had lots of # cash on them
10	48	21	CAM-3	Ah - I see. Incognito, eh?
10	48	24	CAM-1	Wonder how many passengers on this flight with assumed names ((laughter))
10	48	28	CAM-2	Maybe just heart condition cases ((laughter))
10	48	31	CAM-1	To get wheelchairs for boarding, you mean?
10	48	36	CAM-2	Yeah, that old trick. Wifey tells a ground hostess her old man's got a weak heart. Gets pre-boarding help. Wheelchairs yet
10	48	44	CAM-1	Who can blame them with - er - three hundred and eighty - er - odd people on these things——Then the husband practically runs off the plane at the destination ramp ((laughter))
10	48	56	CAM-3	Or yells whiplash if we bump twice

TIME	SOURCE	CONTENT
Hr. Min. Sec.		
10 48 57	CAM	Sound of paper rustling
10 48 58	CAM-2	Shall I tell 'em our ETA?
10 49 01	CAM-1	Wait until we get the real weather picture in L.A.
10 49 06	CAM-2	Yeah. Met reported smog
10 49 08	CAM-1	There's some traffic this morning. Sounds like Air Canada out of Toronto
10 49 13	CAM-2	Coming up astern. Sounds like he's getting the welcome from Kansas City
10 49 18	CAM-3	Western hospitality. Don't knock it
10 49 23	CAM-2	Route Six is getting like the San Diego Freeway when you're trying to break away from the airport in the five o'clock rush. They'll soon have to put traffic lights here. * two-way route and they just feed them in
10 49 32	CAM-1	Get the L.A. weather soon as we contact Albuquerque
10 49 36	CAM-2	Yeah ((sound of person imitating a bugle))
10 49 37	CAM-1	Burnoff is?
10 49 39	CAM-3	Just working it out. Looks good——
10 49 50	CAM-1	That head wind's down to twenty-five knots
10 49 56	CAM-3	Here's the – er, burnoff figures
10 49 59	CAM-1	Yes, good. You said it was. Looks like the airliner'll make dough this flight ((laughter))

TIME			SOURCE	CONTENT
Hr.	Min.	Sec.		
10	50	05	CAM-2	Manifest shows three hundred and – uh – eighty-eight. No complaint on that load factor
10	50	11	CAM-3	The week-in-L.A. business crowd
10	50	14	CAM-2	How can you tell, Larry?
10	50	16	CAM-3	The black-attaché-case fellas take United's early-morning Flight Four-Zero-One. Come back on our Flight Seven-Three-Four same night
10	50	21	CAM-1	Better tell the veepee sales
10	50	23	CAM-2	Guess it's – er – somethin' with the scheduling. Vice presidents should know
10	50	25	CAM	Sound of movement on flight deck, followed by click, click
10	50	28	CAM-1	Finger trouble, Larry?
10	50	30	CAM-3	Er – nope. Just – er – wondering why it——it got so warm
10	50	36	CAM-2	May sun ((laughter)) I can pull the visor over
10	50	41	CAM-3	It's the – ah – the air temp's up
10	50	44	CAM-1	Outside temp's forty-two below
10	50	46	CAM-3	It's up four degrees
10	50	48	CAM-2	Anything unusual about that?
10	50	51	CAM-3	Mm——checks okay ((sound of clunk, followed by click)) Cabin temp's normal on the remote gauge
10	50	57	CAM-1	* you mention the heat, it's kinda warm

TIME			SOURCE	CONTENT
Hr.	Min.	Sec.		
10	51	01	CAM-2	The spring sunshine tra-la-la
10	51	03	CAM-1	Turn it down——the cabin temp if you think it's too high, Larry
10	51	08	CAM-3	Durned right it's too high——don't understand –
10	51	13	CAM-1	It's warm % my feet – can you feel anything?
10	51	21	CAM-2	Nope – just——now you mention ——queer if you ask me
10	51	26	CAM-1	It's smells sorta warm. Hey – anybody smell anything?
10	51	31	CAM-3	My nose isn't that sensitive——instrument shows temp's still up
10	51	34	CAM-2	Can't smell
10	51	35	CAM	Chime——followed by sound of door latch
10	51	41	CAM-1	Your galley burners okay, Elizabeth?
10	51	43	STEW-1	Sure. We're nearly through with the snack at this end
10	51	46	CAM-1	There's something smells warm—— By – er – the pedestal
10	51	47	CAM	Sound of fire warning bell
10	51	47.5	CAM-1	We've got a fire
10	51	48	CAM-3	Collision avoidance circuit breaker's popped ((sound of click))
10	51	51	CAM-1	Can you locate *
10	51	52	STEW-1	Huh – is it – ?
10	51	53	CAM	Sound of landing gear warning horn begins

INTRA-COCKPIT COMMUNICATION

TIME			SOURCE	CONTENT
Hr.	Min.	Sec.		
10	51	53.5	CAM-1	Power – we've lost power ((three above statements occur almost simultaneously, some overlapping))
10	51	55	CAM-2	Looks like – ((engine sound diminished))
10	51	56	CAM-1	Get on it, Larry
10	51	58	CAM-3	Lost power on Engines One, Two, and Three
10	52	01	CAM-2	Oh my God
10	52	05	CAM-1	——gone like – ((engine sound ends. Slipstream sound continues, louder)) Give me power – she's rolling right over – the ailerons won't correct –
10	52	07	CAM-2	She's rolling * other way we've lost four thousand feet
10	52	09	CAM-1	I just gotta get this back. It's % swinging like mad –
10	52	11	CAM-3	I'm sorry ((sound of slipstream increases))
10	52	14	STEW-1	((Yell, followed by words)) Holy Mother –
10	52	16	CAM-2	* out. Pull fire bottles?
10	52	17	CAM-?	((Shout))
10	52	18	CAM-1	Re-ignition. Try (all) three –
			CAM	Increasing noise of slipstream ((noise rises in frequency; voices indistinguishable))
10	52	22	CAM-?	She's flipping –

INTRA-COCKPIT COMMUNICATION

TIME	SOURCE	CONTENT
Hr. Min. Sec.		
	CAM	((Slipstream noise rises in frequency and merges with sound of landing gear warning horn))
10 52 25	STEW-1	((Scream))
10 52 29	CAM-2	Shirley – ee – eee – eeee ((barely distinguishable above noise))
10 52 37	CAM	Sound of impact ((end of recording))

The soft whir of the tape spinning out was the only sound in the little chamber. Klein continued to stare at the last sheet of paper. After a long silence he said, 'In the final printout delete the stewardess's last words, her scream, and the first officer's last shout. Mark it "nonpertinent words" in all cases.'

'Yes,' Liss said, stopping the tape.

'Let's go back to the line where the first officer offers to adjust the sun visor,' Klein said.

'On the paper?'

'Yes. There's no need to run the tape through again.'

Reading the conversation was bad enough: he couldn't take it three times on the tape in succession. 'Check Zulu 10.50.28,' he said, using airmen's and Air Traffic Control jargon for time.

'I've got it,' Houston said.

Klein moved his fingers on the paper. 'Go up to the previous line, where there's the sound of movement on the flight deck followed by two clicks.'

'Got it.'

'The clicks sound like he was checking switches. Possibly the cabin air conditioning. The first indication that something's wrong comes in the next line when the captain asks the second officer if he's got finger trouble,' Liss said.

'Okay. The line after Zulu 10.50.30.' Klein turned to

Liss. 'What do *you* think happened there?'

'Obviously the second officer was alert. He was on to something.'

'Elevated flight deck temps aren't normal,' Klein said. 'We can take that as our starting premise.'

The talking-out process for the reconstruction of what had happened on the flight deck was a method experience had taught Steve. He'd developed the idea from a detective inspector he had met in New York, who since had become a good friend. He had explained, 'On homicide, when we're up against a blank wall, I call the guys together and we sit in the room where the crime was committed and nobody speaks. We just absorb the atmosphere in the room. Then one of the guys'll say something pertinent, and pretty soon we've got a train of thought that sets us off on a new angle. We've solved several difficult cases that way.'

Investigating a major air accident was like solving a murder case, Klein had philosophised, except that his investigators didn't talk it out on wreckage sites. Carrying the analogy further, he'd likened the pathetic piles of twisted metal to the murdered person, and it was his job to find the killer. He'd do it by discovering the modus operandi rather than the motive. No wonder the Go-Team had been called air crash detectives in a recent magazine article.

'So the second officer was alert – I think we all agree on that,' said Houston, fidgeting with his belt. 'And the captain was right on the ball. He spotted the second officer's concern.'

'Check,' Liss said.

'The second officer denied he was having finger trouble,' Houston said, putting a pencil mark on his copy of the printout. 'He said, "Er – nope," at Zulu 10.50.30.'

'Check.'

'The first officer didn't take it seriously – the remark about it being so warm,' Klein said.

'Check. He says "May sun," and he's the one we

might suspect did the laughing,' Houston said. 'He seems a light-hearted type all through.' He flipped the paper sheets. 'Back here at Zulu 10.40.56 he makes this remark about the Kansas City en-route controller being a "wise guy". And at Zulu 10.43.50 there's a hint of his character where he says he wound up in a tavern called the Red Spot Inn –'

'I don't think it's pertinent, Bill,' Klein interrupted.

'Okay. Challenge.'

'Lots of airline pilots drink. We all know that. But I challenge you to name one who's reported for duty with the smell of liquor on his breath. Ninety-nine point nine per cent of professional pilots stick to the eight hours from bottle to throttle rule, or phones Operations and asks them to get the pilot who's on the alternate list to take his flight.'

'I wasn't implying that. All I'm saying is that his reference to finding the tavern indicates part of his character. All the way through he's the guy who laughs easily. And he likes spinning yarns. The story about the incognito passengers and the bit about passengers' pre-boarding tricks. And at Zulu 10.49.36 he imitates a bugle sound.'

Klein nodded. 'I accept. What about you, Jeff?'

'I agree with Bill.'

'At Zulu 10.50.44 the captain checks the outside air temp,' Klein went on. 'The second officer says "It's up four degrees." We don't know for certain whether *he* was referring to the outside or inside temp.'

Houston tilted his stool closer to the bench and peered at a diagram in a handbook. 'On the CA-100 the outside air temp gauge is on the captain's instrument panel. The inside air temp gauge is on the second officer's panel.'

'Check.' He turned to Liss. 'Okay with you?'

'I accept.'

'We're agreed that the captain was checking the outside air temp and simultaneously – well, almost – the second officer was checking the inside air temp. But at

Zulu 10.50.48 the first officer asks, "Anything unusual about that?" '

'What about the clunk in the next line?' Houston asked. 'Followed by the click.'

Klein turned to Liss. 'The flight data recorder won't show that?'

'No,' Liss said, then added, 'Unless it affected the cabin air-conditioning system in some extreme way.'

Houston said, 'Before the clunk and click he says – the second officer – he says "Checks okay." What d'you suppose he meant?'

Klein wiped the sweat from his forehead and said, 'Can't we open the door? It's goddamned hot in here.'

'One day they'll invent a *quiet* air-conditioning system so's it won't interfere with the playback sound,' Houston said. 'Then we can install one.' He lumbered down from the stool and opened the door.

'Thanks, that's better,' Klein said. With his thumb he twirled the signet ring on his little finger. 'The clunk may have resulted from his retesting the air-conditioning lever.' He took a blueprint from a shelf and spread it out on the bench. It showed the layout of the CA-100 Caravan flight deck, with the levers, switches, circuit breakers, control yokes, and rudder pedals. 'It's a hell of a hefty lever.'

'The click that followed could have been him testing the gauge for the cabin temperature,' Liss suggested.

'Sounds logical. He says "Cabin temps normal on the remote gauge." I think we can safely adopt that. Anybody challenge?'

Houston pushed out his lips for several seconds before saying, 'I accept.'

'Same here.'

'Let's go on. The next line is the captain speaking. That unintelligible bit, Jeff –'

'I tried every which way. It simply won't come through.' Liss made a helpless gesture.

'We'll have to accept it,' Klein said. 'He might have

said "now". "*Now* you mention the heat, it's kinda warm." '

'Reasonable assumption,' Houston said.

'Then at Zulu 10.51.01 we get our first officer tra-la-la-ing and full of the joys of spring. Where's his history? It should be in Ackerman's draft file.'

Houston reached up to a shelf and took down a manila folder, placing it in front of Klein.

'First Officer Sidney A. Roberts, 33,' Klein read aloud. 'Held Commercial Aeroplane Certificate Number so-and-so. Hired by American Constitution Airlines on May sixteenth, nineteen hundred – say, do you see the coincidence?'

'I never realised that,' Houston said. 'Poor bastard. Wiped out on the anniversary of the day he joined the company.'

'Maybe that's why he was full of the joys of spring,' Liss suggested. He suddenly realised the irony of his remark and his face reddened. 'I mean –'

Klein quickly read on. 'Qualified on single-engine types, land, sea, and instrument ratings and upgraded to first officer on June twenty-ninth, nineteen hundred and seventy-five.'

'Was he ever a second officer, Steve?'

'No. Went straight into the right-hand seat after being upgraded on Boeing 737s. Completed initial training on the DC-9 and was assigned as a first officer on American Constitution's approved routes on this type of aircraft. Three months later he took initial training on the CA-100 Caravan. Hey – listen to this. On October eighth he flew an unsatisfactory proficiency check, but passed a subsequent recheck on October tenth. His last proficiency check was January fifteenth and his latest line check on March thirty-first.'

'How many hours did he have, Steve?'

'Six thousand two hundred and forty-seven.'

'Wasn't short on hours.'

'Last checked out in the CA-100 simulator on April fifth. His most recent first-class medical certificate was issued, without limitation, on December second.' Klein paused as he scanned the page. 'The first officer had a rest period of twenty-three hours during the twenty-four hours before reporting for duty at Dispatch at Chicago O'Hare.'

He threw the folder on the bench. 'He's okay. Just the happy sort,' he remarked. 'D'you agree now, Bill?'

'Sure. He was just happy. I change my mind.'

'No challenge,' Liss said.

'Now look at Zulu 10.51.08. The second officer is puzzled – doesn't understand why the cabin temperature's up, and then the captain says it's warm – something – his feet and asks the first officer if he feels anything.'

'The first *real* indication that something's abnormal,' said Liss.

'The first officer says he doesn't feel anything, then changes his mind. "Queer if you ask me," he says,' Klein continued. 'Any comments?'

'Isn't he a bit undecided?'

'His attitude in some places is – uh – flippant,' Liss said.

'It's the way it comes off the tape,' Klein said. 'You should know that: you've listened to enough of these things. Let's separate the apparent flippancies from the remarks about the real job of flying the aeroplane.' He turned to Houston. 'I imagine the first officer is the type who takes a positive view of everything.' He paused, realising that he was using the present tense to describe a dead man. God, the co-pilot was only thirty-three, and with over six thousand hours flying time, might soon have been upgraded to the left-hand seat, depending on his seniority rating. He shook his head. 'Definitely not the flippant type. Let's go on.' He studied the printout. 'At Zulu 10.51.26 the captain is worried about the possibility of a fire without showing the others his alarm, and in the next line the second officer is convinced that something is wrong. Like a good pilot he rejects his sense organ, namely his nose, and relies totally on the instrument reading. Then the captain, as a long shot, calls the stewardess to ask her if her galley burners are overheating. What do we think about that?'

'His action?' Liss inquired.

'The *philosophy* of his action. What was going through his mind? What was his logic? He may have wasted precious seconds calling the stewardess to the flight deck, waiting for her to appear – although she came instantly – inquiring about a totally irrelevant cause of the smell they were all conscious of by now. Depending on our interpretation, we may have to return a verdict, as it were, that the captain failed to ascertain the location of the source of the burning smell in as expedient a manner as possible.'

'Goddamned weasel words, Steve,' Houston said sternly.

Klein frowned. 'It's the only way to get anything past Legal these days. Did you hear what they did to my draft report on the Avianjet case?'

'No.'

'Chopped it to hell. "Too redeeming of what was" – er, "apparently" was the word I think they used – "too redeeming of what apparently was a gross flying error." '

'Jesus. That's a new one.'

'I was trying to be fair to the pilot,' Klein growled. '*Too redeeming!* Where were we?'

'The captain's just asked the stewardess if the galley burners are okay, meaning they're not overheating,' Liss said. 'Zulu 10.51.41. He couches his language in such a way as not to alarm her.'

'He also says, or implies, something's warm by the pedestal,' Houston said. 'Zulu 10.51.46.'

'Followed by the fire warning bell,' Liss added.

'Let's stop right there,' Klein said authoritatively. 'We're going too fast.' He turned to Liss. 'See if Don Ackerman's back from Chicago. If he is, get him down here with the Ops handbooks. I want to know what systems trigger the fire sensors.'

When Liss had gone, Klein picked up the manila

folder and leafed through it. 'The captain's medical certificate had a limitation for near vision, Bill. Wore glasses.'

'We'll keep that in mind as we go on,' Houston said.

'Had more than twenty-two thousand hours, of which three hundred and sixty were on the CA-100. You'd expect that low hours with a new type of aircraft, of course. Been with the airline for twenty years.'

'Must've racked up some seniority.'

'Here's an interesting note. The check pilot on the captain's initial line check in the CA-100 remarked, "Good knowledge of the aircraft and procedures." '

'*Most* interesting. Never heard of a check pilot being free with compliments.'

Klein read on. At the bottom of Captain Vernon Arthur Colley's flying record and statement of most recent requalifying tests were some personal biographical notes. Age: 56. Married, five children. Eldest son, Richard, is a 2nd officer with Eastern Airlines, Boeing 727s. Capt. Colley was cited for bravery as bomber pilot in action, World War II, European theatre of war, Holland and Germany.

He turned the page. Second Officer Lawrence Paul Tanzella. Age: 46. Married, three children. Graduated, honours, powerplant engineering course, Midwest Aviation Engineering College. Cited for devotion to duty as volunteer transport service officer, Vietnam, 1965–1967. Wounded in action.

Impelled by inquisitiveness, Klein's eye followed down the list of dead crew members and stopped at the name Elizabeth Diane Lindquist. Age: 27. Unmarried. Senior flight attendant. Part-time instructor, American Constitution Airlines stewardess training school, O'Hare HQ base.

Liss entered with a slim man in his mid-thirties, dark hair slicked back with brilliantine. He carried several handbooks under his arm.

'Hi there, Mr Klein.' He nodded at Houston. 'How's it going?'

'So-so. What sets off the fire warning bell on this aircraft?'

'An engine fire, naturally, and there're sensors for the auxiliary power unit, and the generators of course.'

'Anything else?' Klein asked.

'Let's take a look.' Ackerman put his books on the bench and opened a volume. 'There's fire protection for the anti-icing system. It's a carbon dioxide system, same as the other fire protection systems. There're detector sensors in the engine nacelles, the cabin, underfloor cargo holds, and one on the flight deck –'

'Hold it right there,' Klein said sharply. 'Where on the flight deck?'

Ackerman turned the page and consulted a diagram. 'Here.' He slid the book along the bench for Klein to see. 'Down in front of the control pedestal.'

'Captain Colley said something smelled warm near the pedestal, at Zulu 10.51.46,' Klein said. 'We may be on to something.' He looked at Ackerman. 'What system does it protect?'

Ackerman riffled the pages and shook his head. 'As far as I can tell it's simply a general fire detector. Doesn't protect any particular system.'

'Are you certain?'

'No.'

'Check with Astral Aircraft.'

'Right away.' Ackerman moved to pick up his books.

'Leave them here,' Klein said. 'We may need them.'

Houston bent over the CVR printout sheets. 'As soon as the fire warning bell starts to ring the captain says, "We've got a fire." He doesn't say where.'

'The collision avoidance circuit breaker tripped,' Klein reminded him. 'Second Officer Tanzella says so. That was a click. Isn't the Caravan the first aircraft to be installed with a fully automatic collision avoidance system?'

'Yes,' Liss said. 'It's an optically scanning system designed by Aero Opta Devices Corporation in California.'

FAA regulations called for an effective collision avoidance system to be incorporated in all designs of new commercial aircraft and gradually retrofitted into the older generation of jet aircraft. It was wired into the aircraft's automatic pilot. When the scanner sensed another aircraft – or a mountaintop or other obstruction – electronic signals automatically manoeuvred the aircraft away from the danger.

'Why in hell's name would the collision avoidance CB trip?' Klein continued, smoothing the lock of hair at his forehead. He turned to Liss. 'Supposing it scanned a target, say another aircraft on a collision course. Surely to God the CB wouldn't trip at a critical time like that.'

He consulted one of the handbooks. 'The power supply for the collision avoidance system comes off the main line here.' He jabbed a finger at symbols on an electrical diagram. 'The cables come back through the forward pressurisation bulkhead to the main circuit-breaker panel at the rear of the flight deck.' He drummed his fingers on the page. 'Anything significant about that, eh?'

'Are you suggesting the fire inside the nose cone got through the pressure bulkhead?' Houston asked.

'Why not?'

Houston said, 'That leads us to the possibility of depressurisation –'

'Bradley says we can't rule it out,' Klein interrupted. 'Let's look at it this way. There was a fire inside the nose cone. How it started is a question to be answered – ' Klein broke off and stared at a spot on the ceiling. 'Perhaps,' he continued in a quiet voice, 'perhaps the critical question –'

'Maybe the fire worked the other way,' Liss interjected. 'From someplace aft of the nose cone, then spread forward *into* the nose cone.'

'But Tanzella said the collision avoidance circuit breaker had popped. That throws suspicion on the fire starting in the nose cone,' Klein said. 'That's where the equipment is located.'

'I'll go along with that, Steve,' Houston remarked. ' 'Cause right after that Captain Colley says, "Can you locate," followed by some unintelligible words.'

'That's my point,' Liss said. 'It was *after* Tanzella said the collision avoidance CB had popped that Colley asked if he could locate the fire. At Zulu 10.51.51. If he knew for certain it was the collision avoidance system he wouldn't have asked.'

'It's a valid point,' Klein admitted. He counted lines on his copy of the printout and stabbed the paper with his finger. 'These five lines from Zulu 10.51.46 through to Zulu 10.51.51 are the most critical in the entire printout. Somewhere in those five seconds, you gotta believe, is the answer to the question: why did this aircraft crash?'

It went suddenly very quiet in the listening chamber. The only sound was the distant whine of an electric drill from the Air Accident Investigation Laboratories along the corridor, the noise oddly muted in the echoless chamber. At last Klein spoke. 'Stewardess Lindquist begins to ask a question. It could be "Huh – is it – ?" meaning "Is the fire at such and such a place?" or she might have been asking "Is it going to crash?" You flip a coin for the answer. Let's go on.'

'At Zulu 10.51.53 where the landing gear warning horn goes off, we know he's lost power,' Houston said. 'That's definite. It's preset to go off at thirty knots above stalling speed. I checked the flight handbook.'

Klein turned to Liss. 'Can you separate these three statements that occur almost simultaneously and overlap?'

Liss shook his head. 'We've tried. I even re-recorded the tape on three separate tapes to see if that would work.' He moved his hands, palms up. 'Hopeless.'

Klein took a clean sheet of paper from the shelf, and picked up a pencil. Holding flat the paper on the bench with the elbow of his floppy right arm, he drew one horizontal line. Then he added vertical lines to divide the horizontal line.

'Here's the beginning of Flight One-Three-Seven,' he said. 'Our first passenger boards here.' He printed a statement to this effect alongside the first vertical line, and shuffled the papers of the CVR printout. 'The Lead Event's here. At Zulu 10.50.25, where the cockpit mike picks up the sound of Tanzella clicking a switch. It goes through to Zulu 10.51.47, when the fire warning bell sounds. Agree?'

Houston and Liss turned the pages of their copies of the printout. 'Okay with me,' Houston said.

'And me.'

'Okay. Lead Event.' Again Klein printed on the paper. Below it he extended a large arrow and scribbled 'WHY?' and the words 'CAUSE UNKNOWN'. He then divided the horizontal line several times as he mentally analysed the reactions of the individual members of the flight crew and the action of the aircraft.

'This is the Point of Inevitability,' he said, drawing a thick line at the right side of the paper. He consulted the printout. 'At Zulu 10.51.53.5, where Colley yells "Power – we've lost power." And here's the Terminal Event.' He printed in other critical remarks between the vertical lines, straightened up, and checked the diagram. 'I think that's it,' he said conclusively.

The others nodded. 'Now let's press on,' Klein continued. 'Colley is aware that he's lost power, and the first officer also knows it. He asks Tanzella to get on it, and Tanzella announces a power loss on all three engines.' He screwed up his mouth. 'Y'know, that guy was really cool. Sticks to the book throughout. I heard a second officer on a 707 tape when all engines cut out momentarily. He yelled, "Lost all power." It means the same thing, of course, but to stick to the rules and call out the engine numbers at a moment like that – ' He paused, visualising the desperate moves on the flight deck of Flight 137, the three men going through the engine flameout drill they had learned in the simulator. But the practice emergency procedures had been for two engines out: a total engine failure on a three- or four-engine jet was a rarity. Then Elizabeth Lindquist, recently engaged to be married, crying, 'Is it – ?'

Klein looked at Liss. 'Take it back to Zulu 10.52.05, where the captain says "Gone like – " and the engine sounds die, and he says "Give me power – she's rolling right over – the ailerons won't correct – " '

Liss moved a switch, and the reel whirled. He stopped it, checked the numerals in a little aperture, and said, 'Ready? I've taken it back a few seconds earlier.'

'Close the door, Bill,' Klein said. He waited until Houston shut the door and locked it. 'Okay.'

The whine of the turbines came from the speakers, then *Oh my God*. The three men strained forward, eyes shut. *Gone like –* . The whine suddenly ended and was followed by a shrill, hollow sound, steadily rising in pitch. The plea *Give me power!* followed by *She's rolling right over – the ailerons won't correct –* burst from the speakers . . . *we've lost four thousand –*

Four thousand feet in four seconds. My God!

I just gotta get this back. It's – swinging like mad – He could visualise Colley struggling with the yoke and rudder pedals, trying to get the wildly rolling, diving aircraft on an even keel.

'Cut! ' Klein shouted.

Liss pressed a button. The tape stopped.

'Cross-check this Zulu with the airspeed when you get the flight data recorder charts printed. He nodded at Liss. 'Roll it.'

The almost apologetic *I'm sorry* from Tanzella, the man responsible for power output, and then came Elizabeth Lindquist's terrible scream *Holy Mother* above the rising crescendo of air rushing past the nose as the aircraft began its near vertical plunge. *– out. Pull fire bottles?* Roberts, the first officer, thought the engines were on fire. A shout followed by Captain Colley's hopeless request for re-ignition on all engines. The sound of rushing air rose to a resonating scream, a live thing that filled the chamber with an insistent, piercing cry. God, do aeroplanes die like this? Somebody yelled *She's* *flipping* – Was it Colley? And the racket of the landing gear warning horn was swallowed by the rising pitch of the airstream until Klein thought his eardrums would burst. He gripped the edge of the bench. Roberts screamed *Shirley –ee – eee – eeee* – from a great distance – shrieking the final syllable; an explosive crack, then silence.

Klein looked down at his white knuckles and wondered how he'd kept his feelings under control when the tape had played through the first time. Huh – *queerest damned thing I ever heard.* But that was a stupid thing to say. Listening to the tape a second time was always worse than the first. A psychologist acquaintance had told him that when they first listened to it their senses were attuned to technically interpreting the voices on the tape; when they listened to it a second time, reconstructing and analysing the events taking place on the flight deck, they were aware that the voices they heard were the voices of human beings who *knew* they were only seconds away from obliteration. Whatever the reason, it cut an ineradicable bloodless wound deep into the psyche. It was so much more powerful than any war movie with planes being shot down. Maybe that was because it was just voices – and the imagination leapt to supply the images of terror. At that moment he was too upset to analyse the aircraft's action resulting from the sudden loss of power. It had lost height rapidly, rocking violently from side to side. If the others were thinking the same analytical thoughts, which he doubted, they certainly didn't feel like expressing an opinion, as he could see by Liss's strained face and Houston's sagging jaw.

Houston broke the silence. 'Jesus Christ,' he said in a husky voice, bending his head. He was thinking of the screaming women, children, and men shot headlong to the front of the cabin behind the flight deck as the aircraft spiralled almost vertically into the ground. He glanced at his watch. When he was through down here, he'd go back to his office and dream up some excuse to phone Bette. And he wanted to talk to the kids. It would be reassuring to hear their voices; all five of them.

Klein reached into his desk drawer and pulled out a blank NTSB Form 1765.2. At the top was printed: 'Security Classification of This Document.' Holding the form under his right wrist, he printed in bold letters with his left hand: 'RESTRICTED – NOT FOR PUBLICATION.' In the next line, 'Title of Document,' he wrote 'Air Accident Report No.' and leaned over to examine the Investigations-in-Progress board, where Lena Shaw had stuck a plastic tape on which she'd punched out the accident number Derrigan had phoned in. He wrote down 'DCA 78-A-22' and added 'Preliminary' in parentheses.

Completing the other details, he came to the heading *Abstract:* and nibbled the end of the ballpoint, mentally arranging the sequence of events. For several minutes he bit the pen, deep in thought, before writing without interruption: 'American Constitution Airlines Flight 137, a CA-100 Caravan, crashed on a farm 30 miles southwest of Topeka, Kansas, at 10.53 local time, May 16.

'The aircraft was completely destroyed. The 406 passengers and crew were killed.

'Last contact with Flight 137 was by the high-level controller at Kansas City Air Traffic Control Center. The aircraft reported an altitude of 31,000 feet twelve minutes' – Klein turned the pages of his cockpit voice recorder printout and subtracted Zulu 10.40.15 from Zulu 10.52.37 – 'and twenty-two seconds before the blip disappeared from the radarscope. No emergency radar code 7700 was transmitted by the aircraft. No radio Mayday was called.

'Preliminary investigation at the crash site indicated that all three engines were at zero power on impact.

'The cockpit voice recorder (CVR) confirms that simultaneous flameouts occurred on all engines. The CVR indicates that the aircraft went into a dutch roll, rapidly lost altitude, and dived into the ground.

'Further investigation at the crash site and subsequent analysis indicate that the fibreglass nose cone of the aircraft separated from the main structure immediately before impact.

'THE NOSE CONE INTERIOR SHOWS EVIDENCE OF BEING SUBJECTED TO EXTREME HIGH TEMPERATURE OF CAUSE UNKNOWN.

'The fire was contained within the nose cone and did not spread to the aircraft main structure.

'*Action:*

'This Investigator-in-Charge recommends that the Federal Aviation Administration immediately ground all CA-100 Caravans in worldwide airline, freighter, and/or charter service until the probable or actual cause of the accident is determined.

'*Key Words:*

'Flameout, nose cone, fire – cause unknown.'

Klein read it over carefully. Under 'Key Words' he scratched out his script 'cause unknown' and rewrote the words in capital letters: 'CAUSE UNKNOWN.' Then he pressed a button. Nothing like being prepared, he thought, wondering how Malik would react when he received his copy. Shaw appeared in the doorway.

'Shaw, here's a preliminary report on the Caravan crash. I've marked it Restricted. Please get it duplicated and send a copy to all board members, and a copy to Malik. I want him to get a chance to digest it before I see him.'

She saw the worry on his face. 'Is it that bad, Steve?'

'Read it.'

She sat in the opposite chair, her black, loose hair falling forward as she read.

'D'you think Grewson will agree to a grounding directive?' she asked.

'He'd better, for God's sake. Before we have more people killed.'

'This isn't like any of the other crashes we've worked

on, is it, Steve?' She looked at him with concern in her eyes.

'I've never seen anything like this in sixteen years of aircraft crash investigation. There's something goddamned fishy.' He got up and walked about agitatedly, shaking his head. 'I haven't got *one* solid clue,' he added.

'You'll solve it, Steve. You always do.'

'Thanks for your confidence, Shaw.' He stopped walking about. 'I'm going down to the site tomorrow. Probably be back the next day. I've got to see Malik after he's read that.' He pointed to the report in Shaw's hand.

'I'll make sure he gets it,' she said, rising.

SIX

Early the following morning Klein, with Liss and Houston, flew back to the crash site; Klein to continue his coordination work and attend the press conference Reynolds was to hold, and Liss to supervise the search for the still missing flight data recorder. Houston had to oversee the packing and shipment of the remains of the three engines to the Washington labs. Driving from Kansas City Airport, Klein said, 'Some press guy's sure to ask about the recorders. The official line is that we've found the CVR but haven't had a chance to listen to it. I'll tell Reynolds.' The others nodded in agreement.

They stopped at the cordoned-off area. At that moment a car with Reynolds, Harrilyn, and two Regional investigators drew up. Klein hailed them.

'Where did you stay last night?'

'We found a motel in Little Cedars,' Reynolds replied. 'Booked it for a week with an option on another.'

Klein drew Reynolds and Harrilyn aside. He told them the relevant points they'd heard on the CVR tape and his decision not to publicise its contents until the investigation had developed further.

'A wise decision, Mr Klein,' Harrilyn said without condescension.

'Let's go,' Reynolds said. He winked. 'Mustn't keep the press boys waiting. I've arranged to hold it in the farmhouse.'

Klein allowed the others to go ahead while he looked over the site. Mobile cranes and other lifting equipment were now in operation, hauling up chunks of the heavier debris from the craters, and Downey and Armstrong had enlisted the help of state troopers and policemen from Kansas City to search for bodies and carry the pathetic bundles on stretchers towards the temporary morgue in the barn. But the barn, although big, was not large enough to lay out four hundred and six corpses, and several large canvas tents had been set up as extra morgue space. A Red Cross flag fluttered from a smaller tent near the others, and Red Cross volunteers were still carrying coffee and Coke to the recovery teams. He looked for Armstrong but couldn't see him, then hurried after Reynolds to the farmhouse. The farmer, George Crowthers, was a sad-looking man, who ushered him into the front room. Reynolds and Mrs Harrilyn were already seated there at a table pushed to the end of the room, facing a crowd of newsmen armed with notebooks, television cameras, and floodlights.

'I'll answer all your questions if I can answer them with facts,' Charlie Reynolds said. 'If you expect me to make speculations, guesses, or pass an opinion on the cause of the accident, you may leave right now and save your time.'

Reynolds always started his on-site press conferences with the same statement, leaving no doubt in reporters' minds where he and they stood. Reynolds was a former newsman, who had worked in the public relations department of a major airline and later become chief of public affairs for the NTSB Bureau of Aviation Safety. He was tough, but fair, with the press. But despite his efforts to get news stories of aeroplane crashes off the front pages of papers as quickly as possible, he had no control over the facts he stated once they were in the hands of reporters who had no technical background of aeronautics. One editor of a local newspaper had sent his society page reporter to a particularly harrowing crash site. She'd interviewed eyewitnesses, spoken to injured passengers, and written a story filled with emotionally charged accounts of human tragedies, and concluded that the aeroplane had exploded in the air.

The actual cause of the crash had been mismanagement of the fuel system and a stuck undercarriage, and the explosion had occurred *after* the aircraft had belly-landed and skidded off the runway. The front page headline screamed: 'PLANE EXPLODES IN MID-AIR. PASSENGERS HURLED INTO SPACE.'

At one time it was NTSB policy to keep newsmen as far away as possible from a crash scene. Photographers were even forcibly ejected from accident sites. Now, in an effort to prevent exaggerated and inaccurate reporting, the working press and photographers were allowed to inspect the debris after the initial stages of an investigation had been completed.

'What I have to say is the result of a meeting Mr Steven Klein, the Investigator-in-Charge, had with the group leaders of the investigation. As a result we can state the following.' Reynolds paused while the newsmen readied their ballpoints.

'The aircraft was a CA-100 Caravan, belonging to and operated by American Constitution Airlines. It was Flight 137, from Chicago to Los Angeles. All the passengers and crew, totalling four hundred and six persons, are dead – '

'Does that make it the biggest death toll in aviation history?' interrupted a young reporter in the front row.

Here we go again, Klein reflected bitterly. The front pages of the next editions will be splashed with photographs of corpses in grotesque positions, and there'll be highly conjectural accounts of what caused the crash. Newspapers were sold with stories of horror, human suffering, sex, and sports, and his Bureau was high on the list as an innocent supplier of information about the two top best-selling items.

Reynolds' lips clamped into two thin lines as he tried to control his temper. A crimson glow spread upwards from his neck and suffused his deeply lined face. 'I've just finished telling you I answer questions with facts,' he said. 'I don't know about other crashes. If you want to compare death statistics, check the records of the

International Civil Aviation Organisation. Their headquarters are in Montreal.' He paused. 'In case you didn't know,' he added sarcastically. The reporter unfazed, jotted down the name and city.

'Here's what we *know*,' Reynolds continued. 'The aircraft hit the ground at a high impact angle. It appears – ' He raised his eyes from his notes and repeated, 'It *appears* that there was no power from the three engines at the moment of impact. The CA-100 Caravan as you know, is a three-engine wide-body jet – '

'Sir, does that mean – ' interjected the young reporter.

'I don't know what that means,' Reynolds snapped. 'Let's get this straight and clear. I'll answer questions when I'm through making my statement. Correction. I'll *try* to answer questions when I'm through with this statement.'

He glared at the reporter, who stared right back at him with challenging eyes.

Reynolds glanced at his notes and went on. 'The nose cone of the aircraft became separated from the main structure before the moment of impact. The nose cone is made of laminated fibreglass and the inside shows signs of burning.'

Several newspapermen looked up expectantly when they'd finished scribbling. A television cameraman zoomed in for a closeup of Reynolds' face.

'Part of the hinge fitting that attached the nose cone to the structure of the front fuselage is missing. Examination of the remains of the fitting leads us to believe that the missing part was removed by souvenir hunters.'

'For Chrissakes,' muttered a grey-haired man.

Reynolds' voice softened. 'In the past we have not entirely seen eye to eye with the press on the way some air accidents have been reported, but this is a free country and we respect the First Amendment. On the other hand, we appreciate the cooperation we've had from some of the media when some past cases were under investigation. You acted with the public interest in mind. It's obvious from what I've told you that the hinge fitting is a vital bit of missing evidence. If, in writing your stories, you could point out the importance of this fitting and that it should be returned to any official concerned with this investigation, or to the police, we would appreciate your doing so.' He looked around the room and said, 'Now I'll try to answer your questions.'

Two reporters near the front started speaking at the same time. One sat down, and the other continued. 'Will the person who stole the hinge fitting face charges, sir?'

'No. We're only interested in getting it back. No charges will be made.'

'I'm Smithers of the Little Cedars *Sentinel*.' Klein looked towards the centre of the room where a diminutive, wiry man stood with an air of importance. Despite his size, he spoke with a demeanour that left no doubt that he considered all the other newsmen in the room to be outsiders trespassing on his territory. 'Is it not true that airliners flying from Chicago to Los Angeles use the township of Little Cedars as a turning point to correct navigational errors? The Subcommittee for Noise Reduction of our local Committee for Protection of the Environment has studied the paths of all air traffic from Chicago.' He pulled the lapels of his tweed jacket together and sat down with a smug expression.

Reynolds sighed and adjusted his bifocals. 'I can say unequivocally, Mr Smithers, that modern air navigational methods have long ago eliminated the need for pilots to check their en-route positions by ground reference.' He bowed slightly. 'With due deference to your subcommittee's work.'

Smithers shot to his feet, but a wide-mouthed, big-featured man at the back of the room shouted, 'What's the significance of the burning inside the nose cone, sir?' Smithers slowly sat down.

'We don't know,' Reynolds replied. 'I told you I only report facts.'

'Was there an explosion before the plane crashed?' the man persisted.

Reynolds said, 'We have a statement from a witness who was on the farm. He says there was a flash like an explosion from the aircraft as it dived.'

'A violent depressurisation, sir?' The reporter had his pen ready.

'We don't know,' Reynolds replied firmly. 'I might point out,' he added dryly, 'that not all depressurisations of pressurised aircraft are violent.'

Unchastened, the reporter went on, 'But your witness said there was a flash. Doesn't that mean it was a case of depressurisation? Like the accidents to the DC-10s a few years back?'

Reynolds tapped his fingers on the table. A man like this, using a specious argument, could easily trap an inexperienced investigator into making a statement resulting in distorted headlines. That was why the standing instructions forbade individual investigators to speak to the press. He fielded the ball expertly.

'What newspaper or news service do you represent?' he asked.

The man looked surprised. 'Kansas City *Star*. What has –'

'You didn't mention your name. Mr Smithers, of the Little Cedars *Sentinel*, introduced himself at the beginning.' From the corner of his eye he saw the smirk on Smithers' face.

'Morganston. John Morganston.'

Taking advantage of the reversal of roles, Reynolds zeroed in. 'Your question, Mr Morganston, is illogical. It is in the form of a syllogism, and in your case a fallacious form of argument. Because of this, therefore that. The *this* you refer to, the DC-10 accidents, has absolutely nothing to do with the accident we are investigating. Depressurisation does not necessarily follow a flash. A flash may be caused by sunlight reflecting on the wings or other surfaces of an aircraft.' He fixed his piercing eyes on Morganston. 'A flash may even be in the imagination of the beholder.'

A snigger arose from the back of the room. Morganston looking contrite, lowered his head and pretended to scribble furiously.

'Sir,' said a photographer doubling as a reporter, addressing Reynolds, 'have you found the black box yet?' Remembering the previous questioner, he added, 'The name's Allen Duluth with the Wichita *Eagle and Beacon*.'

Here it comes. Klein looked down at his fist clenched on the table, nails grooving his palm.

'No. But we found the cockpit voice recorder.' Seeing the puzzled expression on Duluth's face, he went on, 'The flight data recorder, the so-called black box, gives information about the aircraft's operation. The cockpit voice recorder tapes the voices of the flight crew and their conversations with the ground controllers.'

'What was the last message sent from the plane, sir?'

'That is presently being investigated. The Operations Group is impounding the ground tapes at all Air Traffic Control Centers that the aircraft passed through from its moment of take-off from Chicago's O'Hare International Airport to the moment of impact.'

'But was there a cry for help? A Mayday?'

'We don't know. If there was such a message, the cockpit voice recorder will record it. And if the transmit button in either the captain's or the first officer's position was open, the ground tapes will corrobate the last words spoken on the flight deck.'

A hand shot up. 'What about the seventy-seven hundred code, sir? Did the radar operator on the ground report he saw it?'

Klein sighed with relief, and slowly released his fist. They weren't going to press Reynolds on the cockpit voice recorder.

Reynolds turned towards his questioner, a middle-aged man with a bald head, round face, and black-rimmed glasses. Obviously he'd covered air accidents before.

'The Systems Group chairman has yet to make his report on whether the emergency transponder code was used,' Reynolds lied. Seeing questions shaping themselves on several faces, he went on. 'The numerals seventy-seven hundred are the international code indicating an emergency aboard an aircraft. It is a radar code, not a radio code. By turning the transponder code numbers to seventy-seven hundred and pressing a button, the pilot can send a radar signal to Air Traffic Control, which results in the radar blip on the ground radarscope blossoming into a large shape, signifying an emergency. 'It's equivalent to a Mayday spoken over the radio.'

'When do you expect to know?'

Klein clenched his fist again.

'Just as soon as the Systems Group chairman finds out.' Reynolds kept his features tensed.

'When will that be?' Klein recognised the persistence of an old hand.

'In several hours' time, we hope,' Reynolds said. He threw out his hands. 'I can't be more specific than that, because I don't know.' Lying in the public's interest was justifiable under the circumstances, he told himself.

A tall dark-haired woman of about thirty rose at Klein's left. 'Doreen Brailey, Chicago *Sun-Times*,' she announced in a robust voice. She looked at her notebook. 'Mr Reynolds, you said in your written statement that it *appears* that there was no power on all three engines at the moment of impact. I have a two-part question: one, how certain are you at this stage of your investigation that the aircraft did in fact lose power on all three engines, and, two, what has been confirmed in past accident investigations as the cause, or causes, of simultaneous power failure on all engines of a multi-engine jet airliner?'

She's put Reynolds on the spot with a perfectly valid question, Klein thought. On the most important factor in the case, something the others had neglected to pursue. It was a pity that the best question was a throwaway to the other reporters: they didn't deserve it.

'Let me answer part two of your question first,' Reynolds replied. 'In past investigations, simultaneous or individual engine failures, or flameouts, have been caused by various factors, including such elementary things as running out of fuel, mismanagement of the fuel system, failure of booster pumps in the fuel tanks, problems with valves in the fuel system, especially cross-over valves, and failure of the fuel regulators that meter fuel to engines. I, uh – ' He paused, scratched his head, and looked past Madge Harrilyn at Klein. 'Have I left any out?'

'Bird ingestion,' Klein replied promptly.

'Ah, yes. Bird ingestion.' The reporters wrote in their notebooks.

'On the first part of your question,' continued Reynolds, 'I can only elaborate on our preliminary findings. When a jet engine rotating at cruising speed or at full power hits the ground, the compressor and turbine blades usually fly off tangentially due to the shock of being stopped by a hard object, the ground. If the blades are still rooted in position, but of course bent out of shape, or broken, this usually indicates that the engine was not rotating at the moment of impact.'

'Are the blades still in position on all three engines out there,' Brailey asked, waving towards the window.

'Yes. This was brought to the attention of a number of reporters during the press tour.'

'I arrived late,' Doreen Brailey responded. Reynolds looked at his watch. 'I have another question bearing on the same subject,' she added quickly. 'Obviously bird ingestion at the cruising altitude of the aircraft could not take place – '

'We can't rule it out,' Reynolds interrupted, beginning to lose patience.

'Why, sir? Have you found feathers or bits of birds in the engines?'

'Only microscopic examination will reveal that. But flocks of birds, especially at migration time, have been found on rare occasions up to altitudes of twenty thousand feet.'

‘But the Caravan was probably flying at over thirty thousand feet. Birds can’t breathe at that altitude,’ Brailey said.

‘Only if they wear oxygen masks,’ someone called. The other reporters laughed.

‘That is an assumption,’ Reynolds replied sternly. ‘The thirty thousand feet, I mean. We won’t know the altitude at which the aircraft was flying when it suffered an apparent loss of power until we do a printout on the flight data recorder and cross-check with Air Traffic Control.’

‘I accept that, sir,’ Doreen Brailey replied. ‘You’ve shot me down.’ She smiled and sat down.

Reynolds, glad of a moment of relief in the proceedings, checked his watch. ‘This meeting is now closed,’ he said determinedly. ‘There’ll be a press release published on what we’ve discussed, and further releases made as the investigation proceeds.’

‘When do you expect to hold another press conference?’ asked the aggressive young reporter in the front row. ‘By the way, for the record, I’m Ivar Reesey of the New York *Post*,’ he added.

Reynolds looked at Klein, who said, ‘Just as soon as we have something more to say.’

‘When will that be?’ Reesey demanded.

‘I don’t know.’

‘What do you expect to say at that time?’ the reporter persisted.

Klein glared at him. ‘The reason or reasons for the apparent power failure,’ he snapped.

The man in the dark grey suit who looked like a banker extended his hand. ‘Lampton, FBI, Mr Klein.’

‘Pleased to meet you.’ Klein gestured towards Madge Harrilyn. ‘This is Mrs Harrilyn, one of the board members.’ The fact that the FBI was on the scene did not surprise him: it attended investigations of major air accidents as a matter of course.

‘We’ve met before, I think, madam,’ Lampton said

courteously, taking Madge Harrilyn's hand, and then, to Klein, 'May I see you alone for a moment, sir?'

As Klein turned away, Harrilyn said to him, 'I'm heading back to Washington for a day or two, unless you think I should stay.' Klein saw the numbness that lay behind her eyes, distress kept under control by a strong will. Unwittingly, Harrilyn had put him in an embarrassing position. She was one of his bosses, and she was asking his opinion on whether she should stay on site. She'd done everything expected of her. She hadn't spared herself. He evaded a direct reply.

'I'll get Charlie Reynolds to arrange transportation.'

'Thank you.'

Klein followed Lampton out of the farmhouse into the sunshine. The two men slowly walked along the path that led to the back field. Lampton withdrew an envelope from the inside pocket of his jacket.

'A copy of the passenger manifest, sir. Have you seen it?'

'I have it back in Washington. Haven't had a chance to study it,' Klein replied.

Lampton handed him the photostated pages. 'Does the name Lionel Arthur Weinberger mean anything to you, Mr Klein? It's at the bottom of page seven.'

Weinberger? The name was vaguely familiar. There had been an article in the *National Observer* recently. Weinberger – Weinberger – the guy had been quoted on something. He looked at the tops of the sycamores in the distance. What the hell was the story about? Environmental protection? Airline security? Security – sabotage. God –

'The name's familiar,' he blurted, feeling a numbness in his belly.

'Mr Lionel Arthur Weinberger is president of the American Zionist Organisation,' Lampton said portentously. 'He was on American Constitution Airlines Flight One-Three-Seven to attend a World Zionist Conference due to open in Los Angeles at nine o'clock tomorrow morning.'

SEVEN

'The FAA's got a couple of tracker dogs sniffing around, Mr Lampton.'

'I know. But I've sent for our own bomb squad all the same.'

'Any other famous or suspicious names on the manifest?'

'Washington's going through the computer checks now.' Lampton frowned and put the list back in his pocket. 'Don't expect anything'll turn up. Easy enough to buy a domestic airline ticket under an assumed name. Not like an internationl flight, where we can cross-check with the Passport Office.'

'There's at least one passenger with a passport,' Klein said. 'Belongs to a girl named Olive Patricia Williams. United States citizen. Domiciled in Chicago.'

'Do you remember where it is?'

'See that tree?' Klein pointed. 'It's lying by a bush right alongside. There're several black passengers lying around there.'

'I'll take a look. It's something else my men can start on.'

'Mr Downey, my Human Factors Group chairman, will be listing all the passports he finds, foreign and domestic. I'll ask him to give you a copy.'

'Thanks.' Lampton turned to go.

'Please put anything you lift up back in exactly the same position.'

Lampton smiled. 'Sure, sure, Mr Klein. I understand very well.' He walked off.

'Steve!'

It was Armstrong, waving his clipboard and running towards him. Perhaps he'd tracked down the missing hinge fitting.

'A couple more witnesses,' Armstrong said, rushing up breathlessly. 'A guy named Don Chudak and his daughter Janet, age seven. They live in an old converted farmhouse a half mile from here and saw it happen from beginning to end, and drove over today. Says he couldn't come the day of the crash because he had to rush his wife to hospital in Kansas City. That's why he was off work.' He paused to catch his breath. Klein felt encouraged. 'Chudak's an ex-Air Force pilot,' Armstrong went on. 'Has an aircraft maintenance engineer's licence, too. Works as an assistant foreman at Kansas City Airport.'

Klein frowned. The most unreliable witness was one with aviation experience. Such a witness mentally analysed what he *thought* he'd seen and fitted those observations to the analysis. But a child of seven made the best witness, not preconditioned by life's experience and knowing nothing technical about aviation.

'Have you taken statements yet,' he asked.

'No, I'm just going over.'

'Where are they?'

'I put them in a police car. I'm going to take Chudak's statement separately. If I allow him to prompt the kid, she'll get all mixed up.'

'Anything on that hinge fitting?'

'My guys haven't reported back yet. They're still going over the farms in the neighbourhood and interrogating all the kids they can find.'

Klein stared across the countryside, bright under the Kansas sun. Miles away a barn roof glinted. 'Keep on to them, Bob. We're broadcasting an appeal. About these new witnesses. Get somebody else from the Witness Group to interview the father. Do the interview with the girl yourself. You're good at it.'

'Okay, Steve.'

Klein glanced towards the barn where Downey had set up his temporary morgue, and saw a stretcher party enter. He hoped George had got the flight crew before the county coroner arrived. County coroners could be damned awkward, and when suddenly thrust into the glare of publicity, they often exerted new-found authority and tried to direct operations. It had happened before.

It was important to confirm that the captain had been flying the aircraft at the time of the accident, as the CVR had indicated. Unsophisticated county coroners knew nothing about lactate profiles, a newly developed technique that identified muscles under strain because of their low lactate levels. It was a more reliable way to confirm which crew was holding the control yoke than the older method of examining smashed thumb bones.

Downey would test the remains of the flight crew for alcohol in the blood, signs of drugs, carbon monoxide, and hypoxia. It would then be up to the pathologists to examine muscle tissues, heart, liver, and kidneys to determine their lactate levels.

He saw Downey some distance away, with an assistant, bent over a shape in the weeds. He went across and waited for him to withdraw a syringe from the body of what was apparently a young boy; his face was smashed beyond recognition. One of the helpers tied a tag to the body's wrist.

'How's it going, George?'

Downey looked up and wiped sweat off his forehead with the back of a rubber-gloved hand. 'Everything's just about under control, Steve.' He nodded at the body at his feet. 'This is one of the last. We've managed to get most of them laid out in the barn and the tents, where the pathologists are working on them.'

'There's a guy named Lampton from the FBI snooping around, George. Suspects sabotage. I said you'd give him a list of all passports you find.'

'It'll take a coupla days, Steve.'

'Don't rush.' Klein glanced in the direction of the

barn. 'You've got enough to deal with.'

Downey looked up with distressed eyes, and Klein felt the aura of sadness that radiated from him. Downey slowly stood up, and Klein noticed the nervous jerk of the rounded shoulders.

'You okay, George?' he asked quietly, so that the others couldn't hear.

'Sure, sure, Steve,' Downey replied quickly, and walked with a limp to another corpse twenty paces away, his assistants following.

I'll check Downey's file, Klein thought. He might have had more Majors than were good for him; a man could only take so much in this line of work. Fate and the roster system played unfair tricks on investigators: you could go for a year without being called out on a Major, and then, by coincidence, find yourself involved in two investigations in three months.

Klein found himself again wondering about the legendary Downey. The man must be over sixty now. He'd been lecturing at the Dulles school even before Klein had enrolled, and insisted on staying with the Human Factors Group while people about him were promoted. Everything about Downey was gentle, Klein reflected: his name, the voice, the great hunched shoulders and pear-shaped body, even the furry eyebrows and kind grey eyes. Nobody seemed to know when Downey had started in air accident investigation, or why. There was a story around the Bureau that he had designed and built his own light plane and had taken off with his nine-year-old daughter to fly to the family cottage upstate. The aircraft had run into a sudden thunderstorm, and Downey had crash-landed in a wheatfield. The little girl had been hurled through the windshield. 'I had my seat belt fastened, Daddy!' she cried, and fell back dead. The seat belt anchorages had pulled right through the floor. Nobody at the Bureau knew where he had first heard the story, and nobody ever asked how Downey had got his limp.

Klein recalled his first Downey lecture. It had been

such a traumatic experience he could still remember almost the exact words.

'Get blood and tissue samples right away, before rigor mortis sets in,' Downey had explained. 'The main purpose of examining the bodies of flight crew, cabin attendants, and passengers is to get evidence on the cause, sequence, and effect of the accident,' he'd continued. 'The identity of the victims will automatically emerge through the efforts of the Human Factors Group, pathologists, police, fingerprint experts, odontologists who check dental charts, and radiologists.'

A hand had been raised at the back of the class.

'Yes?'

'I see why we have to examine flight crew bodies for drugs and alcohol, sir, plus all the other factors you mentioned,' said a curly-headed man. 'But why examine the remains of cabin attendants and passengers as thoroughly as the flight crew's bodies?'

'Because it might tell you if the aircraft was sabotaged, either by a bomb hidden in a baggage hold or by a maniac with a bomb in the cabin. Look for wounds or punctures on the skin, and try to get the airline's seating plan or the passengers' boarding passes so that you can trace where each passenger sat. From this you may trace where the bomb was located or where the bomber sat. Shrapnel penetrates deeper into the flesh the nearer passengers sit to the centre of an explosion.'

The curly-headed man had nodded his thanks, and Downey had gone on.

'Position of bodies on the ground may give clues on the sequence of breakup of an aircraft. There was the case of a Convair 440 that crashed on final approach short of the runway. We had no problem establishing the sequence of breakup; it was an unusual case. The left side of the aircraft ripped open on impact. The first body along the wreckage path, farthest from the runway threshold, was the captain's, followed by several passengers who'd been sitting on the left side of the aircraft. The body farthest down the runway – in other words, the last one out – was the co-pilot's . . .

'So you see, sometimes the order in which bodies fall out can give you a clue on the order of the aircraft's structural breakup. Don't disturb bodies until their exact position has been plotted.

'Back to flight attendants. Were the attendants braced for an emergency – strapped in – or were they found unsecured, as though they'd been going about their normal duties? The position of food trays, liquor cart, and remains of the galley will give useful evidence. If the galley heating compartments are empty, and trays littered about the cabin, it may have been mealtime, with nobody suspecting trouble.

'You'll get vital clues from possessions found on cadavers. Look for drugs, or a doctor's prescription in the pocket or billfold of a flight crew member, or a letter in a passenger's pocket indicating a disturbed or suicidal state of mind.

'Speaking of identification, you'll have to deal with the deceased's relatives. You may have to ask them to try to identify the remains. Keep in mind that people looking at a mangled or burned body, or even a fragment of garment or other personal possession, are terribly distressed and may make wrong identification.'

There had been more to Downey's lecture, and it flashed through Klein's mind like a film unrolling as he watched the object of his sympathy help lift some human remains on a stretcher and cover them with a black plastic sheet.

'Consider the dead person's religion and funeral rites. Take the Jewish religion for example. A Jew must be buried within twenty-four hours after death. You'll have legal authority to keep a body until you're through with the pathological work and have positively identified it. It can be released after these two conditions are met and a death certificate issued. So you may find yourselves in the distressing position of having to break religious laws, and under duress from grieving relatives.

'It's important to determine the cause of death of

each person. In a major accident, where there's fire on impact, some bodies will be both burned and injured by excessive G forces, and it's easy to be tempted to say that death was due either to burning or to multiple injuries, based on a superficial external post-mortem examination. This can lead to medico-legal wrangles.'

Downey had paused and looked around at the group of a dozen investigators-in-training. 'You must distinguish between ante-mortem and post-mortem injuries. Let me give you an example from an actual case.'

There had been absolute silence in the classroom. 'A DC-6 crashed in dense forest on a mountain in Oregon. By the time the police arrived, most of the plane had been destroyed by fire. The Go-Team arrived about six hours later, a difficult climb scrambling on our hands and knees over rocks and through the woods, and we found sixty-five passengers and crew dead. The aeroplane had gone in at a shallow angle, chopping off trees like matchsticks, and flipped on its back. I'd had some experience on human factors then – it was in the early days of accident investigation and we sort of overlapped our duties – and we came to the conclusion that because the plane had turned over before landing, everybody died of mulitiple injuries and was then incinerated. The pathologist-in-charge came to the same conclusion. But that was before we examined the passenger manifest in more detail. On board had been a millionaire pulp and paper magnate and his wife. We discovered their remains in what was left of the first-class section. We were sure we had identified them correctly because the forward part of the aircraft had not been completely burned out.

'Then the lawsuits started. The biggest claim was from the millionaire's eldest son. The father had left most of his estate to his eldest son because he was the only one of the children – there were four sons – who had gone into the business, and he wanted the business to stay in the family. A minor but substantial fortune was provided for the widow. But the will stipulated that in the event of common death, husband and wife dying simultaneously, the whole of the estate, including the mother's, was to be divided equally among the four sons.

'The eldest son privately hired pathologists to prove that the father survived the mother. The case dragged on for months, and some of the brainiest medical experts were called in – I remember we were grilled for hours – to prove that the father had survived the impact and had died of asphyxia from smoke, and that the mother had been killed on impact. Eventually, medical experts from Switzerland proved conclusively that the father survived the mother, and the eldest son inherited the full estate.'

Someone had asked a question: 'How *do* you tell the difference between death caused by asphyxia and multiple injuries, Mr Downey?'

'That's the topic for next week,' Downey had replied. 'An expert from the Armed Forces Institute of Pathology will be here.'

Now, as he stood watching Downey and his little group move off, Klein again became aware of the scene of devastation around him. God, wrecked aeroplanes never looked like this in those days, he ruminated. And never all these bodies. He slowly turned away and walked towards the barn.

A line of covered trucks was unloading a seemingly endless flow of loosely nailed pine coffins when he got there. Men carried the empty boxes into the barn and the tents, past the telephone linesmen rigging temporary lines into the morgues. Klein entered the barn and recoiled from the odour of putrefying flesh. The weather had turned warm in the past two days, and the pathologists, whose number had been bolstered by forensic specialists from the Chicago and New York police departments, had not been able to process the hundreds of cadavers that had to be minutely examined. Most major air accidents occurred within four miles of an airport, and many airport authorities set aside unused basement space as emergency mortuaries, with corpse refrigeration facilities, running water, and separate rooms where autopsies could be done. Some airlines retained firms of funeral directors to provide embalming services and arrange for the ultimate disposal of crash victims.

He held a handkerchief to his nose and looked around. The brilliant glare of the bare electric bulbs strung to the roof cast a cold light on triple lines of open coffins, each containing a shapeless form of pulverised flesh, splintered bone stumps, and a few personal possessions – smashed dental plates, a cracked artificial eye, a gold ring, a crushed powder case. One coffin was shared by a small mound of mangled flesh with blood-clotted golden hair and a plastic doll with blue eyes that smiled at the barn roof from unblemished rosy cheeks.

A group of workers, wearing face masks, moved from coffin to coffin: the pathologist-in-charge, his stenographer, morgue attendants from Downey's Human Factors Group, missing persons police detectives, and a property officer, co-ordinating their findings. If they positively identified a victim and the chief pathologist was sure of the cause of death, he gave a discreet nod to waiting helpers, who put the lid on the coffin and drove home the nails, their hammering echoing in the cavernous building. Occasionally the pathologist shook his head.

'Another John Doe,' he said to the stenographer, a woman of about forty, and moved on to the next box without nodding to the men with the hammers.

Klein caught his eye. 'I'm Steve Klein, Investigator-in-Charge.'

'John Shelley, Mr Klein,' the doctor said, rising.

'How many positively identified, and cause of death definitely known, Doctor?'

Dr Shelley motioned to the stenographer. 'One hundred and seventy-one positives, ninety-four negatives, and – er – fifty-three John Does,' she said in a slow, flat voice. A negative referred to human remains impossible to identify. John Does were remains where there was still a chance of positive identification.

Klein pulled out the microphone and spoke the figures and date into his tape recorder.

'What times are you finding on their watches, Doctor?'

Dr Shelley gestured to the stenographer. She flipped the pages of her notebook. 'Those that smashed and stopped point to between ten-fifty and ten-fifty five. Many stopped at various times as they ran down, of course,' she said. 'Some battery-powered watches are still running.'

Klein noted the average times of the stopped watches on his recorder. 'Thank you.'

He moved towards the wide barn doors. Near the entrance he stared at two negatives, the barely distinguishable remains of two child-sized bodies deposited together on a blood-stained stretcher. It was impossible to tell what sex they were, and they lay in a heap with bloody arms outstretched as though clutching each other for comfort. One of Downey's men gently lifted the bodies one at a time into a pine coffin. Then he numbered the box with a black crayon, crossed a number off his copy of the passenger manifest, and tossed his head in the direction of the hammerers. When they had driven in the nails, he motioned to other men who lifted the coffin and slid it into a van waiting outside the barn.

Klein entered the nearest tent, where the same activity was going on. A middle-aged woman supported by two Red Cross nurses was led to a stretcher, and a man and wife, tightly gripping hands, were directed to a coffin containing the remains of a girl. In the Red Cross tent, he saw coffee urns and piles of untouched sandwiches on trestle tables. Ashen-faced relatives sat in a daze on benches, and from time to time morgue attendants hurried by, wearing rubber gloves and stark white aprons flecked with blood. They paused and spoke to people in quiet voices, holding up a torn billfold, a fragment of a sweater, a ripped shoe, a squashed plastic baby's bottle with milk still in it, or a battered cigarette case for identification.

Klein lingered a moment before going out into the fresh air. The husband and wife had identified their little girl and came out of the tent, where television cameramen and news photographers pounced on them. The woman was sobbing, and tears streamed down the man's face. He held a protective arm around his wife's shoulders.

'Look up, sir!' a cameraman shouted.

The dazed man looked up, saw the camera, and threw his hand in front of his face.

'Who did you lose?' demanded a familiar voice. It was the young reporter from the New York *Post*.

Klein swung into action. 'Get the hell out of here before I break your neck!' he yelled at the reporter as he signalled to a policeman. 'Officer, remove these newsmen from this site as fast as you can or I'll charge them with public mischief, you gotta believe.'

The policeman hustled the protesting newsmen away to the other side of the cordoned area. Klein watched to make sure they had been thrown off the site. Beyond the barrier a young couple strolled hand in hand along the side road, away from the crash site. They were some of the many idly curious or morbidly interested who thronged to the disaster site every day.

Satisfied that the newsmen were safely off site, Klein moved among the crowd of police. Some sat on the ground, resting after their exertions.

'I found this skinny little guy with half his clothes torn off under one of the electric cookers in the galley,' he overheard a policeman tell another. 'I tell yer, I never want to go through that again.'

'What happened?' his colleague asked.

The policeman seemed anxious to supply the answer, as though by doing so he was relieving himself of a great burden that he had been forced to bear alone. 'His flesh was burned like hell, third degree by the looks of it. I grabbed him under the armpits to get him on a stretcher, and his body fell apart like meat on an overcooked Thanksgiving turkey.'

'For Chrissakes, Al. Stop me next time I ask.'

Klein felt sickened. He turned back towards the wreckage. There he'd be among the professionals, men who over the years had become inured, at least on the surface, to grisly scenes, and hardly spoke about them any more. But as he threaded his way through the crowd of workers, he heard a young Red Cross girl say to a policeman, 'God, it's been the rottenest day of my whole life.'

'Don't look at it that way, kid,' the policeman said consolingly. 'You're alive. And so am I.'

'Have you found the recorders?'

The man with the brusque voice who addressed Klein was Christopher H. Grewson, head of the Federal Aviation Administration. Klein disliked him: he was a bureaucrat and Klein detested bureaucrats. If Klein had had the capacity to hate he would have hated Grewson. The man represented officialdom, red tape, and specious legal arguments that he arranged with conniving lawyers at public hearings on aircraft accidents. He was a political appointee and he resisted change. He had been accused by the press of being in the pockets of several aircraft manufacturers when the NTSB recommended design changes for safety reasons following a series of crashes of a particular type of aeroplane. He was heartily disliked by everyone in the Bureau. Of stocky build, he was turning flabby from sitting at a desk too many years, and he had a moonlike polished face crowned by short white hair. His small, suspicious eyes were close-set, and crinkles splayed from the outside corners to his ears.

'We've got the CVR, but no luck with the FDR yet,' Klein replied.

'When did you find the CVR?' Grewson demanded.

'Day before yesterday. We've listened to it, and I sent a copy of the printout to your office yesterday. Classified it restricted, *not* for publication.'

'Hmm. I was out of the country the last two days.'

A typical Grewson evasion, Klein reflected. No explanation of where he had been, or why he hadn't flown back immediately when his office contacted him. He stepped aside as two men lugged bent undercarriage struts to the centre of the site.

'Have you intensified the search for the missing recorder?'

'My Systems man, Liss, has all the men and facilities he needs,' Klein replied.

Grewson looked around at the piles of metallic rubble with dark, troubled eyes. He looked dejected and out of place in his impeccably tailored charcoal grey business suit. He twisted his overweight body this way and that, sniffing the air, as if trying to determine where enemies lay in wait. Klein felt a sudden pang of pity for him. He wouldn't be in Grewson's shoes for a half million bucks a year. It was part of the FAA's job to help Klein find the cause of an accident to an aircraft that had been designed and constructed according to FAA specifications, given a Certificate of Airworthiness by the FAA, flown along air routes designated by the FAA, by pilots examined and licenced by the FAA, directed by ground air controllers licenced by the FAA, using electronic equipment designed to FAA specifications. Currently Grewson and his investigators were partnered with Klein's own Go-Team. In a few weeks Grewson and his men might be playing the role of defendants instead of detectives, defending their designs and procedures at a public inquiry.

The NTSB had been set up, Klein reflected, as an independent body that was not responsible to the FAA but to its own board members appointed by the United States President. Whatever final conclusions the NTSB came to about the cause of an air accident, it was free, indeed obligated, to publish, revealing all the facts it had discovered, and make recommendations to the FAA to change its aircraft design requirements, equipment standards, or operational methods. Unfortunately, the NTSB could only recommend: it had no mandatory powers, an inherent weakness in the system.

Grewson let out a long sigh. 'What showed up on the CVR?' he demanded, fixing Klein with distrusting eyes.

'Simultaneous flameouts on three engines, and it sounds like they went into a dutch roll.'

Grewson's eyes opened wide. 'Three flameouts?' he echoed. 'Dutch roll?'

'The nose cone dropped off the aircraft before impact. We found it over there, about two hundred yards away from the main wreckage,' Klein said, pointing.

Grewson looked in the direction Klein indicated. 'What sort of interpretation do you put on that? The nose cone falling off before impact?'

Klein shook his head. 'I don't put any interpretation on it. Not until we find the flight data recorder.'

'For Christ's sake. Nose cones don't fall off aeroplanes just like that.' He snapped a pudgy thumb against his forefinger.

Klein took a step backwards and studied Grewson's face. He wanted to savour the full effect of what he was about to say.

'The inside of the cone was burned to a frazzle.'

Grewson's chubby jaw dropped. For several seconds he was unable to speak. 'Burned? Burned?' he repeated, a look of bafflement flushing his features.

'It's made of reinforced fibreglass, as you know. The laminae are peeled back with heat.'

'Where is it? I want to see it.'

'I sent it to the labs. We're doing some experiments, and comparing it with a new cone taken off the production line.'

'You've got *our* structures men working on it?'

Klein nodded. Despite differences of opinion that arose between the two organisations, mainly political, the FAA and NTSB cooperation at the working level was excellent. 'Your guys have been on site since we first got word,' he said, unable to resist turning the knife.

Grewson's attitude suddenly softened. 'Let me know immediately you find the FDR, Steve.'

'Sure.' Poor bastard. He's worried about what the flight data recorder might show up: perhaps incipient faults in the design of an aircraft carrying the FAA's Certificate of Airworthiness. And if it turns out that the aircraft *has* a clean bill of health, there's always the possibility that the FAA's Air Traffic Control system might have some blame attributed to it. Nope. He wouldn't have Grewson's job for a *million* a year.

'Any witnesses?'

'Only two so far. The farmer and his teenage son.'

'What're their stories?'

'The farmer didn't know an aeroplane was diving out of the sky towards his farm until it impacted about two hundred yards away from where he was driving a tractor. The kid says there was a flash as the plane dived.'

'An expert opinion,' Grewson said sarcastically.

'I forgot to mention part of the nose cone hinge fitting was stolen by a souvenir hunter.'

'Where the hell was your security?' Grewson demanded, his manner suddenly hardening. He looked accusingly at Klein. 'Was Regional here first?'

'Yes. And Armstrong made a damned fine job of security.'

It hadn't been Armstrong's fault that the police had been slow in putting a barrier across the far end of the site. And even if Armstrong had been to blame, he wasn't going to admit it to the head of the FAA, or anybody else.

An official from Grewson's group, some distance away, called Grewson's name. He turned to go. 'Inform me as soon as you find the recorder,' he instructed Klein in a schoolmaster's tone.

Klein stalked towards the rear fuselage hulk, men stepping aside as they recognised him. He peered at the bits of structure above ground, and Jeff Liss's head poked up from beneath a pile of broken floor truss members.

'It's here,' Liss shouted. 'Jammed under the galley cooker.'

'Is it okay?'

'Can't say. Only part of it's showing.'

Klein thought of the galley heat's effect on the delicate tape of the FDR. Although designed to stand high temperatures, there was a limit to how much heat the steel case and its internal insulation could absorb.

'I'll get help. Looks like you need a block and tackle.'

'A small tripod type will do it,' Liss said. Fifteen minutes later Liss hefted up the recorder to one of the FAA experts, who laid it carefully on the ground. Klein knelt beside the beach-ball-sized sphere, discoloured by heat, and ran his hand over it. He examined the steel lip where the halves were bolted together. Except for three boltheads that had been sheared off, the container appeared undamaged. He looked under the lip.

'My God!' he exclaimed. Cemented by intense heat to the undersurface of the lip was a charred pencil-thin shape. He fought to control his stomach as he stared at the crisped cinder of human fingernail at the tip of the incinerated form. 'Get Downey over here right away.' He paused. 'And somebody tell Mr Grewson we've got the FDR.'

EIGHT

Martha Crowthers' parlour was an oasis of peace after the turmoil in the field at the back of the farm.

'A coffee, sir?'

'I could use a coffee. Thanks,' Armstrong said politely.

Mrs Crowthers turned to stare through the curtainless windows, eyes filling with tears. 'Terrible, terrible. Who'd have thought . . . on our farm. I was shopping in Topeka when they told me. At first I wouldn't believe it.' Then, recovering control, she patted the top of Janet Chudak's head and said, 'I've got something special for you.' She went into the kitchen, returned with a brown jar, and placed four cookies on a plate. Janet Chudak sat stiffly on a chair, feet crossed, hands tightly clasped in her lap.

'Don't be shy, dear. Andy's friends come from miles around to eat my home-made cookies.'

Armstrong looked at the child. This wasn't going to be easy. He helped himself to a cookie and put the plate in front of Janet. 'Now I know why Andy likes them, Mrs Crowthers.' From the corner of his eye he saw a slim, freckled arm slide towards the plate.

'What about a glass of milk, dear?' Mrs Crowthers said. She was rewarded with a dimpled grin. Armstrong waited for the child to take the glass with both hands before withdrawing a small tape recorder from his pocket.

The girl's eyes lit up. 'Have you got music?'

Armstrong smiled. 'No, Janet. This is a blank cassette.' He left it running.

Janet took another long gulp, put down the glass, and looked at the cookie jar. 'Help yourself, dear,' Martha Crowthers repeated.

'Janet, your Dad told me you saw the plane. The plane that crashed and killed many people.'

Armstrong lifted his chin towards the window. Don't be too direct, but get the conversation going. Interviewing witnesses was a delicate art. Encourage the witness to tell the story herself, avoid asking leading questions, don't make suggestions, and don't interrupt. And try not to put questions that elicit simply a yes or no reply. Remember that witnesses had legal rights and could refrain from answering if they wanted their lawyer present. On the other hand, reluctant witnesses could be subpoenaed to give evidence at a public inquiry.

'It fell straight down.' Janet paused while she swallowed. 'It wasn't like the crash I saw on television. There was a bang, like a big bomb. And then it fell with sorta clouds of smoke – black smoke – out the back. And then these people started falling out of the plane.'

'You mean the one you saw on television, Janet?'

She nodded earnestly, her fair curls bobbing up and down.

'Tell me about the plane you and Dad saw in the sky,' Armstrong said offhandedly.

'It didn't go bang. It just sorta fell.'

A bluebottle buzzed angrily against the window, and Armstrong heard crockery being washed in the kitchen. Ten seconds passed. Then Janet said, 'There was a kinda flash and it came down.' She drained the glass with a gurgling sound and squirmed uncomfortably in the chair.

Armstrong stood and went to the door. 'Mrs Crowthers, may Janet use your bathroom, please?'

'Sure. Come with me, Janet.'

Armstrong switched off the recorder. This was going to take a long time. He crossed to the window and stared at the low rolling hills on the horizon. An early butterfly flitted across the vegetable garden. He heard Janet chattering to Martha Crowthers, and went to the table and switched on the recorder.

'Mrs Crows – Crowsthers' got pretty toilet paper. Green and pink flowers,' Janet said, reappearing.

'It sounds beautiful, Janet.' Armstrong suppressed a smile. The girl sat in the chair and he waited for her to get settled. 'You were telling me about this aeroplane.'

'It came down like this.' She put her hand up and brought it down in a near vertical slope until it touched the lace tablecloth. 'But there was this flash before it came down.'

Armstrong nodded encouragingly.

'Like a bunch of Reynolds Wrap flashing up in the sky,' the child continued, licking her lips and looking at the cookie jar. Armstrong pushed it towards her.

'And after the flash, Janet. What happened after the flash?'

'I already told you. It fell down.'

'You saw the aeroplane up in the sky. There was a flash. The aeroplane fell out of the sky.'

Janet nodded, big brown eyes wandering over the room. She was losing interest: he must work fast.

'Where were you when your Dad and you first saw the aeroplane, Janet?'

'Oh, *I* saw it first. I was on the back porch. Dad was up on the ladder fixing the roof and was hammering like crazy.' She stopped to swallow. 'I had to stick my fingers in my ears.'

Then she wouldn't have heard the aircraft's approach. A jet approaching at more than six hundred miles an hour at a flight level of over thirty thousand feet was rarely heard until it was level with an observer. Was the flash the kid saw caused by sunlight reflection, indicating that the aircraft had changed its *attitude*, or had it flashed because of an explosion? To the child it was simple. She had seen an aeroplane in the sky. There was a flash. The aeroplane fell out of the sky.

'Janet, you said you saw the aeroplane first –'

'I *did.* I told you. Daddy was up on the ladder fixing the roof. Mommy has been telling him about it for ages and ages,' she said with a touch of womanly indignation.

'And then?'

'I saw this flash, and I pointed to the aeroplane and told him it was flashing.' She paused and turned earnest big eyes on him. 'Were you ever in an aeroplane that crashed?' she asked.

'A long time ago.'

'You were a pilot like my Dad?'

'Yes, Janet.'

She stared at him critically. 'You must have flown the old-fashioned planes. You look ever so much older than my Dad. He flies jets.'

Armstrong smiled. 'You know a lot about planes, Janet. Your Dad must be a very good pilot to have taught you all about them.'

'I'm going to be a pilot when I grow up. And jump out with a para – para –'

'Parachute.'

'Yes, that's it. A parachute. And float down like on the end of an umbrella.' She giggled. 'That'll be fun.'

'Janet, all good pilots remember exactly what happens up in the sky. I want you to think back very carefully about the aeroplane that flashed and fell out of the sky like that.' He duplicated the child's hand movement.

Janet squeezed her eyes tightly shut. 'I can remember better when I close my eyes. Just like when Daddy and Mommy kiss me goodnight in my bed. I always close my eyes after they kiss me and then I can remember everything that happened in school and what Normie Johnson and Beryl Black said during playtime and things like that.'

'Keep your eyes closed, Janet, and listen to what I'm saying.' The child jerked her head up and down.

'What did your Dad do?' he asked encouragingly.

'He didn't do anything 'cause he was still banging this nail into the roof.' She suddenly opened her eyes and pointed to the window. 'Oh – look at the butterfly!'

'Now, Janet. Close your eyes and try to remember what *you* did.'

'I pulled his foot and he stopped hammering and said, "*Now* what is it?" '

'Yes?'

'So I pointed up at the aeroplane that was falling from the sky, and he said a bad word like swearing and dropped the hammer on his foot and that made him swear some more, and then he put his hands up to his face like this.' She covered her face with both hands, peeking between her fingers.

'Yes.'

'Nothing.' She paused. 'Oh yes. I remember now. He said it must've fallen about a quarter mile away. It made a big bang and I could feel it shake my feet.'

There was another vital point, but how to approach it was difficult. 'After you saw the flash, were you still looking at the aeroplane?'

'I kept looking at it 'cause I never saw a plane fall like that before.'

'Now think very hard, Janet.' Armstrong paused. 'Did you see anything else after the flash? Before the aeroplane fell to the ground?'

'Oh yes. I did see something else. Something fell off the front.'

Armstrong leaned forward, carefully framing his next question. What he heard in the next few seconds might be critically important months from now. 'When did this something fall off the front of the aeroplane, Janet?'

The little girl put her head on one side and sucked the tip of her forefinger. 'Sorta just before the aeroplane went down behind the hill.'

Good girl. So the cone came off just before impact. Now he was getting somewhere. Could there have been an explosion in the nose cone that blew it off? What in hell's name would explode in a nose cone? It was usually an empty space housing the weather radar scanner. Unless some bastard planted a bomb . . . At that moment Martha Crowthers came from the kitchen.

'Oh, excuse me, sir. Another coffee?'

'No, thanks,' Armstrong said. 'But maybe Janet would like some more milk.'

He waited until Janet was settled again with a brimming glass and another cookie before he asked, 'Did you watch the aeroplane until it hit the ground, Janet?' He had to confirm that point.

'I told you before. I saw it fall behind the little hill. It crashed down like this.' Again she moved her arm in a near vertical movement, and began to swing her legs under the table: it was clear her attention span was up. She suddenly jumped from the chair. 'Can I go to my Daddy now, please?'

'Yes, Janet. I'll take you to him.' He scooped the child up in his arms and hugged her. 'One day you're going to be a very good pilot – just like Dad.'

'Where's Chudak's story?' Klein asked. Armstrong handed him a clipboard on which a Statement of Witness form was uppermost. They were sitting in a police cruiser. Chudak and his little girl had been given permission to leave, and now, as he studied the form, Klein's mouth sagged.

'Donald Chudak, former USAF pilot,' he read. 'Flew Phantoms in action, Vietnam. 1st officer, Aero Express Charter Services, twin turbo-props; total flying hours 3,400. Present occ. asst. foreman, maintenance and overhaul base, Kansas City Airport. (Witness belongs to Kansas City Flying Club and flies light aircraft 2–3 hrs weekly.)

'*Where were you when the accident happened?*

'At home, approx. a quarter mile from crash site.

'*Tell in your own words what you saw or heard before and at the time the accident occurred.*

'I was standing on a ladder repairing the eavestroughing on the back porch when I saw the aircraft directly ahead. Janet, my daughter, age seven, was standing near the ladder, and she drew my attention to it. It was a jet at cruising flight level and nothing out of the ordinary as we're on the main southwest airway from O'Hare to the West Coast.

'Then the pilot made a course correction. At that precise moment there was a flash and the aircraft depressurised. Then the machine lost flying speed and came down at an estimated angle of about seventy degrees and ploughed in behind a rise in the ground. I could not come over to the scene of the accident the day it happened because my wife was expecting our second child and I had to take her to the hospital.'

'So much for expert opinions,' Klein said, flipping the page. 'What did the kid say?'

Armstrong pulled out his tape recorder and switched on. Klein listened. When it clicked off, he said, 'A flash followed by a dive and something fell off the nose.' The flash would be the sun reflecting off the wings as the aircraft began to roll and lose height. But the child's statement confirmed that the cone detached only seconds before impact. Children usually had keen eyesight, Klein reflected, and the child's statement sounded reliable.

'The question is,' he said to Armstrong, 'at what point during the descent did the cone part company with the airframe? Plastic material has a low density, and there was about a ten-knot wind on the ground. The Met report will show the upper winds.'

Armstrong stared out of the car window at the crowd still gaping at the scene beyond the roped-off area. 'One thing both witnesses agree on is the high angle of the fall. Chudak says seventy degrees and his daughter indicated a steep angle with her hand. At such an angle aerodynamic forces wouldn't force the nose cone off the fuselage. I haven't seen the cone yet, Steve. Is it badly burned?'

'Interior's like a cinder. The laminae are unstuck. Peeled back like onion skins at the edges.'

'Trajectory analysis may help pinpoint the exact point of separation,' Armstrong suggested.

'Maybe,' Klein said doubtfully.

Armstrong looked puzzled. 'Your guy Houston's the expert. What's the problem?' he asked cautiously.

They got out of the car and Klein picked up a twig and pointed. 'There's what's left of the main part of the fuselage, Bob.' He pivoted towards the spot where he had found the nose cone two hundred yards away, the spot now marked with a pole driven into the ground. 'And there's the nose cone. The aircraft was at thirty-one thousand feet.' He turned to Armstrong.

'Go on.'

'The pilot makes a course correction, according to our witness Chudak, and the aircraft depressurised. Let's assume the nose cone blew off and started its trajectory towards the ground. The rest of the airframe, assuming it was in one piece, weighing many times the weight of the nose cone, began its own trajectory. Even if the wind strength at the higher levels was zero, the chances of the main part of the airframe and the nose cone hitting the ground only two hundred yards apart are so remote as to be impossible. They'd be miles apart.' He stuck out his jaw. 'No depressurisation, Bob. The pathologists' reports on the lungs in the bodies will confirm it, you gotta believe.'

A low-loader carrying a mobile crane trundled towards them. Klein watched it come up the dirt road, preceded by a state trooper on a motorcycle.

'I had to send to Kansas City for it,' Armstrong said.

'It's only a five tonner. Too light to handle the rear fuselage, the biggest chunk of the wreck in one piece.'

'There're two more on the way. They're turning off the side road now.'

'Supervise them, Bob. And for God's sake don't let them mess up the wreckage.'

Armstrong set out, and Klein looked at his watch, side-stepping the rumbling low-loader. He spoke the time of its arrival into his microphone. 'Hey Bob!' he called above the roar of the low-loader.

'Yes?' Armstrong shouted.

'I'm flying back to Washington. Take over again and supervise the digout. I'm arranging for the reassembly to take place at Kansas City Airport.'

Armstrong nodded vigorously. 'I'll look after it.'

NINE

Klein spun the telephone dial. 'Dick Demsar, Maintenance Records,' a quiet voice answered.

'It's Steve. Have you got the maintenance records for the CA-100 Major yet?'

'Everything, including the snag sheets.'

'The aircraft's log book?' Hardly possible, but he'd better check.

'No. Waiting for them to pull the wreckage out. I've got the airline's copy of the snag sheets right up to the flight that took place before the crash.'

'How do the maintenance records look?'

'A-okay right through. All the snags reported by the crew had been corrected before Flight One-Three Seven took off.'

'How many flight hours on the airframe and the engines?'

'Half a moment, Steve.' The line was silent for a few seconds. 'The airframe structure and wing engines had only one hundred and seventy flight hours – it was a brand-new aircraft. Only been in service two weeks. But the rear engine had even fewer hours of operation. Only seven.'

'Oh, how come?'

'The airline changed it because there was consistently below-normal oil pressure. The pressure was down by half a pound.'

'Does Bill Houston know about this?'

'Yes. We've been over the records together.'

'Was the flight deck gauge checked?'

'Yes. American Constitution removed the flight deck pressure gauge and had its calibration checked. You know they've got a hell of a fine reputation for good maintenance. I've just checked the instrument manufacturer's test report. The instrument read A-okay.'

'They replaced the *complete* engine for only half a pound pressure loss?'

'Yep. If it had been me I'd have just replaced the oil pump.'

It was an extraordinarily cautious step, Klein reflected. But it was true that American Constitution had an excellent reputation for maintenance.

'When was the oil pressure loss last reported?' Klein asked.

'On May fourteenth, two days before the accident. By a Captain John W. Hoffman, who was flying the aircraft on the Los Angeles to Honolulu leg of the Chicago to Hawaii flight. The records show airline maintenance picked it up in Honolulu and recorded it on the snag sheet. Since it was only a half pound pressure loss, they cleared the engine for the return flight to O'Hare.'

'What then?'

'O'Hare maintenance decided to swap engines.'

'Dick, were there any FAA fixes involved? Any mandatory modifications to the rear engine mountings, for instance?'

'No FAA fixes on either the airframe or engines. But there's a major mod in the Modification List that added stiffening plates to the mounting anchorages on the rear engine. How did you know?'

'A hunch, you gotta believe. What reason do they give for the mod?'

'Vibration in the fin at cruising speed. The stiffening plates cleared up the problem. The test flight programme records show FAA test pilots cleared it after Astral's pilots were through.'

Klein sucked his lip thoughtfully. It appeared that all three engines had clean bills of health from take-off to the moment of the unexplained flameouts, but he'd have to check the ATC tapes to make sure the pilot hadn't reported anything in flight. A slightly below-normal oil pressure would not cause a flameout. And there had been flameouts on all three engines simultaneously.

'All right, Dick. Send me your reports as soon as possible.' He rang off and stared into space before dialing another number.

'Don Ackerman, Ops,' a deep, well-modulated voice announced.

'It's Steve. Have you secured all the flight operations records?'

'Nearly everything. I've already given you copies of the flight crew histories. The only thing to come is the Weight and Balance Record, and I've got a man on that.'

'You'll cross-check the crew histories with Downey's group?'

'I've made a note. When will the flight data recorder printout be ready so that we can correlate flight planning?'

'Jeff is working on it now. I don't know when it'll be ready. Anything out of the ordinary in the flight plan?'

'No.'

'Have you checked the forecast weather with Davies?'

'Yes. CAVU in theory and for real.'

'That's a change. Any SigMets?'

'No significant meteorological reports. But there were three Notams.'

Nothing unusual about that. A pilot might pick up four or five Notices to Airmen in his mailbox in the operations office before take-off. Klein recalled a time when he'd found a half dozen waiting for him before a transatlantic flight, and none of them was important.

'What were they about?'

'Prohibition on using Lake McMillan in New Mexico for seaplane operations, except for emergency landing. Seaplane floats might contaminate the water.'

'Environmentalists lobbying,' Klein commented.

'Probably. Another Notam on restricted air space.'

'Where?'

'A big oblong between latitude 38 degrees north and latitude 40 degrees north. And longitude 97 degrees west and longitude 101 degrees west. Issued by order of the Department of Defense.'

'Limitation on altitude?'

'Below ten thousand feet's okay. No flights above ten thou allowed.'

'What's the third Notam?'

'Errata for one previously issued. Entitled "Hazards to Air Navigation." Scientific balloon flights from an unnamed Air Force base in Nevada between the period March fifteenth to May thirty-first. Er – it says the balloons will rise to an altitude between one hundred and fifteen thousand feet to one hundred and fifty thousand feet, and will ascend at a rate of approximately one thousand feet per minute. Total flight duration of each flight will be approximately eighteen hours. They will drift eastwards and possibly northeast, and be tracked by telemetry ranging systems.'

'What was the original Notam?'

'Class One. It gives the altitude for the balloons between eighty-five thousand feet and one hundred and twenty thou.'

Typical government bureaucracy. It didn't matter what ultimate height the balloons reached: it was flight levels between the ground and forty-five thousand feet that mattered, the flight levels of commercial and general aviation flights.

'What about that restricted air space Notam? Does it give any reason – balloons or Air Force exercises? Anything like that?'

'No reason given. Simply a restricted air space.'

Restricted air spaces over the United States were a fact of life these days, and had increased in number and extent as more Defense Department military installations had been established. Flights over them were prohibited, even by commercial aircraft of U.S. registry.

'I see.' Klein thought of the other factors in the Operations investigation. 'Have you got the cargo manifests, Don?'

'Yeah. Including the weights of each package.'

'You're a fast worker.'

'American Constitution are pretty thorough,' Ackerman replied modestly. 'I've also got the list of cargo and baggage taken over from connecting flights, mail, and the forwarding agents' paperwork. And the passenger manifest, of course.'

'I've already seen a copy,' Klein said. 'The FBI beat you to it.'

'It's not the first time. They work fast.'

For the present it would be well to keep the FBI's suspicions to himself. Klein changed the subject. 'Was the cargo as clean as the airline claimed, Don?'

'According to the freight listed – yes. But you know how shippers cheat on labelling.'

'Assemble your material as fast as you can. We'll be calling a review board meeting early next week.'

'An internal meeting, or with all interested parties?'

'Internal.' He rang off and leaned back in the chair. His gaze rested on the cork bulletin board directly opposite. The photo of a pocket calculator printed on a pamphlet caught his eye. It was something Shaw had pinned up during his absence at the wreckage site. Inquisitive, he got up and read the printed matter: *'Safety Note: Tests confirm that electronic pocket calculators carried on board light aircraft and used to work out navigational problems can interfere with radio compasses. Three cases have been reported where the compass was deflected to an extent that the pilots were off course. In two cases the aircraft ran out of fuel and forced-landed on highways.*

'Of five pocket calculators tested, two paralysed the radio compass when held within three feet of the loop antenna. The other three caused varying degrees of deflection of the radio compass needle. Tests on these calculators are continuing and we will keep you

informed. If you receive reports of problems linked to a calculator, please keep me informed.' It was signed 'J. Liss, Systems.'

Klein raised his eyebrows. Something new and unexpected was always turning up in air accident investigation. He returned to the desk and studied his Investigation Check List, then picked up the telephone and dialled.

'Is the Wreckage Distribution Chart for the CA-100 Major ready? It's Steve.'

'I was just going to call you, Steve,' replied a female voice. 'I've just completed it. Would you like me to bring it to your office?'

'Please.'

A few moments later a dark-haired woman of about thirty-five appeared at his door.

'Quick work, Helen,' Klein said, pointing to the drawing rolled under her arm.

Helen Dimitry smiled warmly and walked to the desk. She had what fashion magazines euphemistically referred to as a 'full figure', and walked with a sensual grace that reminded Klein of Houston's wife. She unrolled the drawing on the desk. As she leaned over, Klein noticed with amusement the strip of cellophane tape she always struck across her neckline when she wore a V neck, to stop the cloth from sagging when she leaned over her drawing board. He knew she was a centre of attraction for the men in the drafting department.

'Use this for a paperweight,' he said, moving into position the half section of an aluminum piston now used as an ashtray by visitors to his office. It had a crack down one side, the cause of a crash that had killed five people. 'And put this handbook on the other end.' To put her at ease by not having to bend over, he added, 'Draw up a chair.'

He was rewarded by a friendly flash of black eyes. 'I was completing the list of bits and pieces when you called,' she said, pointing to a list she had printed in a neat hand on the right side of the chart, with numbers keyed to big dots on the chart. 'Here're the continuation sheets.' She held up several pages of a typed list.

Klein put his finger on one of the squares Helen had drawn, each square representing a five-foot gridded area of the actual site. There was a big dot with the numeral '1' against it near the edge of the square. He checked the list. 'Main fuselage,' he said.

Helen nodded. 'The low numbers refer to the fuselage bits. Outer wings and appendages like landing flaps, leading edge flaps, and ailerons start at number fifty.' She placed an impeccably manicured fingernail on a thick cluster of crosses between the bigger pieces of wreckage. 'These are bodies. I had to group them together. Each cross represents ten cadavers.'

'And here's your base line – in red. Between the farmhouse and the barn.'

'Yes. It was a good datum.'

Klein studied the chart. The main scatter area was no bigger than a shape about three hundred yards by two hundred yards, although the smaller dots in the outlying areas indicated bits of wreckage hurled farther away. Everything confirmed a high impact angle, perhaps seventy degrees. The list of dots in the oblong cross-referenced an inflatable life raft, several oxygen bottles, a Bible – airliners carried one as standard equipment in case a dying passenger requested last rites – one right undercarriage door, hundreds of pieces of luggage, cargo crates, one of which Helen had listed as *automotive parts,* and the rudder. She had drawn in the outlines of three major craters; those for the main fuselage and the two wing engines. A notation *Slash through treetops* identified the sycamores, and arrows pointed to *Freshly cut branches* nearby. He read other items on the list: generator indicator panel lights, nosewheel uplock, right and left hand landing gear uplocks, parts of left elevator, aft gallcy, trim tab, port engine pylon, aft cargo door – with their part numbers taken from the aircraft manufacturer's Parts List and corresponding with the numbers the investigators had crayoned on the tagged parts in the field. The same numbers, Klein knew, were at the moment being entered in an index in the photography department across the corridor, where a woman was cross-referencing the numbers on the backs of the pictures taken at the site.

'From your experience in drawing these charts, what do you think was the aircraft's heading, Helen?'

'Two-two-two degrees,' she replied with conviction, sweeping a pink-tipped finger across the chart. 'The scatter pattern shows that clearly. Southwest.'

Klein picked up the letter opener and pointed. 'Here's the rear fuselage, and the main fuselage's cratered here.' He threw down the opener, took a pencil, and drew a line through the dots. At the end of the line he drew an arrow. 'Dead on two hundred and twenty-two degrees.'

'On course and probably not suspecting anything,' Helen added.

Klein nodded, thinking of the cockpit voice recorder tape. The telephone rang.

'Klein.'

'It's Hugh Turney in the labs. The samples are ready, Mr Klein.'

'I'll be right down.' He turned to Helen. 'Make the usual number of copies for the Go-Team members and copies for Mr Malik and the board members.' He paused, looking over the drawing neatly done on transparent drafting paper. 'The Dimitry high standard.'

'Thank you.'

'I have to go.' He left Helen Dimitry to reroll the drawing and stepped through the door. Shaw sat outside, typing furiously. She grabbed his arm.

'You'll be pleased to know, Mr Hurry, that all five board members have signed the report on the Miami mid-air. I'm typing the final draft right now.'

'Thank God for that. It's been hanging around for I don't know how many weeks. *There* was a case of pilot error, you gotta believe. It came through conclusively on the CVR and FDR tapes.' He prepared to rush away.

'Just a moment, Steve.' Shaw sifted th pages of the material she had already typed a up the title page of the Miami collision report

'I added three more Key Words here, Steve *emergency action.* You mentioned them, but r forgotten to write them in.'

'Shaw' – Klein leaned over and squeezed her – 'what the hell would I do without you?'

'You couldn't do without me.' She grin inserted a cigarette in the holder before lighting

'The indispensable Shaw. Sounds like the ti novel.'

'Yeah, but not an aircraft whatdunit.'

He laughed and hurried away, his right arm sv wildly as he swerved to avoid a girl carrying a photographic negatives into the photo departme loped down a staircase and entered a door m 'Engineering Laboratories, No Admittance to thorised Persons'. Facing him was another, wider dor with offices and several small laboratories on side. Lining the walls were glass cases containing ney's museum, a collection of wreckage samples t from crashed aircraft. Without reading the labels l knew they were samples of steel bolts that had f because of fatigue, fittings that had broken in f because of corrosion by sea, air, and several cabine Turney's favourite examples of engine turbine bl that had failed because of creep fatigue. Creep fati was the characteristic of hot metal to elongate ur tremendous centrifugal force in a jet engine. He pas the last case, the bottom of an engine oil pump filled w a heap of steel filings. The tiny pieces of metal l plugged a valve in the lubricating system of an engi caused the engine to seize, and set off a chain of eve that resulted in forty-eight people being killed. Turne tousled head appeared through a door along the co ridor. Over the door hung a sign: 'Wreckage Analy Laboratory'.

'We're all set,' Turney called.

Bradley was sitting on a bench stool in the small boratory, staring at a blank television monitor, unching a sandwich. He acknowledged Klein's arrival ith a wave of his arm. 'Help yourself,' he said, indicatg a pile of sandwiches Turney had had sent in. 'Coffee's ver there.'

'The samples,' Turney announced, holding up a tray f black plastic discs, each the size of a checker piece. mbedded in the top of each disc was a gold-plated iver of metal as wide as a matchstick.

'From the nose cone hinge fitting?' Klein asked, elping himself to a cheese sandwich.

Turney nodded, crossed to a desk, and dug under an ntidy heap of paper, tossing sheets aside until he found vhat he was looking for, a sheaf of photographs held ogether by a big paper clip. The usual Turney mess, Klein commented to himself, studying the jungle of engineering reports scattered on the desk, a dozen stubby pencils, and a broken ruler. Above the desk was a massive chart headed 'Laboratory Workload and Projects Completed', with green and red lines climbing ever upwards. It was, Klein knew, Turney's way of hinting that he was overloaded with work and wanted a bigger budget. Alongside the desk was a small bench with lapping wheels and jars of etching chemicals used to prepare samples for photographing under a powerful microscope. Turney thrust the pile of photographs at Klein. The top picture was like a moonscape, with sharp-sided hills, sudden valleys, and craters that looked big enough to swallow a truck.

Klein leafed through the other photos and handed them back to Turney. 'It wasn't fatigue. No beach marks,' Klein said, using the jargon he'd picked up in the laboratories. Beach marks, so called because they looked like the lines on a sandy beach left by the receding tide, characterised metal fractures that had failed because of fatigue.

'That's what I thought – at first,' Turney said, leaning over so close that Klein averted his eyes to avoid seeing

the pimples on Turney's face. 'But watch this,' He vanished behind the electron scanning microscope in the middle of the room. 'I've got a gold-plated sample in the machine now.'

He pressed a button and the room was filled with the hum of the television monitor warming up. An oscilloscope adjoining the monitor lit up with a green luminescent glow, and a blip crossed it in a regular wavelike motion. The monitor screen flooded with white light, and Turney adjusted some knobs on a control panel. 'One thousand magnification,' he announced.

He tuned in the picture, and instantly the screen was filled with dozens of huge stationary amoeba-like blobs, with dark spaces between.

Klein flashed a glance at Bradley, who sat rock-still in front of the monitor, chin cupped in his hand.

'Three thousand magnification,' Turney said, clicking a switch. The picture expanded into a landscape of jagged peaks and black valleys. 'Much the same, eh?'

'Go on. You can get it up to six thousand, can't you?'

'And if the tightwads holding the purse strings relent, I may one day be able to go to twelve thousand,' Turney said petulantly.

He flipped another switch, the roughhewn peaks jerked and rounded, and the hollows liquefied into pools of black. 'Like a chunk of Swiss cheese full of holes,' Turney said. 'Indicates fatigue. Now, if I had twelve thou magnification – '

'How d'you explain no beach marks on the microphotos?' Klein interrupted.

'Not enough magnification for this type of fatigue.'

'Hugh thinks it's a kind of – uh – ' Bradley said, between bites on his sandwiches. 'What did you call it?'

'*I* call it quickie heat fatigue. They don't call it that in the textbooks.' He jerked his head towards the window. 'Too simple for the types over in the National Academy of Science.' He switched off the electron microscope and sat on a stool facing Klein near the workbench, a squat figure dressed in a green sweater with worn elbows and a brown shirt, shoulders hunched from hours bent over the microscopes. He turned his attention to unwrapping a sandwich.

'What the hell are you talking about?' Klein snapped. Turney's offhanded manner annoyed him.

'It means the hinge fitting, at least the bit we got from the wreckage, was quickly softened.' The fingertips of one hand unconsciously searched out tiny bits of debris on the bench and swept them on to the floor.

Klein turned to Bradley. 'But it's a solid forging, Howard.'

Bradley stuck out his lip. 'Sudden heating followed by *rapid* cooling from the slipstream – ' He broke off and shook his head doubtfully.

'The quick heating and rapid cooling would produce internal stresses in the microstructure and cause it to snap off?' Klein suggested.

'I think so,' Turney said. 'But Mr Bradley isn't sold on the idea.'

'Have you analysed the chemical composition of the metal used in the fitting in the X-ray unit?' Klein asked.

'The percentages of aluminium, copper, silicon, and magnesium match the metallurgical specification exactly,' Turney said.

Klein took a sip of coffee before asking, 'What physical tests did you do on the hinge fitting, to compare it with a batch of forging material made to the same specification?'

Turney's triangular-shaped face glowed with self-satisfaction. 'Tension and hardness tests. Tension was forty per cent less than the batch material, and the hardness was way down. By seventy per cent.'

'Soft as putty,' Klein said.

'And as strong,' Turney added sarcastically. He perched himself on the bench, legs swinging.

'Whatever flared into flames in the nose cone heated the hinge fitting very quickly,' Bradley said. 'When will they have the bits dug up, Steve?'

'I'm waiting to hear from Bob Armstrong. He's supervising the digout.'

'As soon as we get our hands on the corresponding hinge fittings attached to the fuselage, we can check some more,' Turney said. 'With luck, the locking catch will be intact.'

'More'n likely that failed too,' Klein reminded him. 'We found the nose cone two hundred yards from the main fuselage wreckage.' Can't blame Turney for not realising that: he hadn't visited the site.

'Any news about the rest of the fitting? The part you suspect souvenir hunters stole?' Bradley asked.

Klein made a helpless gesture. 'We've broadcast radio appeals and put ads in the local newspapers. Nothing.' He addressed Turney. 'We have to decide if the initial fracture was caused by the fire or by the souvenir hunters working the thing back and forth to break it off.'

'If I could get my hands on the missing bit I'd be in a better position to answer that,' Turney replied, a trifle self-righteously.

'We won't ever see it,' Klein growled. He felt defeated. The hinge fitting, he had hoped, would have given some clue to why the nose cone flew off before the aircraft impacted. Heat obviously had played a vital part in the detachment. What about an explosion other than depressurisation? The name Lionel Arthur Weinberger flashed into his mind. Bomb in the nose cone?

'Where's the nose cone now?' he asked.

'In here,' Turney said, slipping off the bench and leading the way into the next laboratory. They entered a small room with workbenches on three sides, and testing machines bolted to the concrete floor. In the centre of the room were two nose cones, the burned one and a factory-fresh cone, each resting on a wooden trestle specially built to support it.

They gathered about the burned cone, like three physicians holding a conference around a patient's bed.

'Bonded, no rivets,' Klein remarked, pointing to the

circular aluminium frame to which the fibreglass part of the cone was attached.

'Stronger,' Bradley said. He eyed the circular frame, took a slide rule from his breast pocket, made a rapid calculation, and said, 'With that surface area, approximately two and a half times stronger than riveting.'

Klein leaned over and put his face inside the cone, examining every square inch. After several minutes he straightened up. 'No bomb fragments.'

'I've been over it with a powerful magnifying glass,' Turney said. 'No explosion. When do you expect re-assembly to start?' he added after a moment.

'They'll have the fuselage bits in the hangar at Kansas City Airport today,' Klein peered into the bright new nose cone and ran his hand around the polished surface. 'They finish the inside smooth as a baby's ass.'

'Sure do,' Turney agreed.

Klein looked at the hinge fittings on the new nose cone and compared them with the remains of the fitting on the burned-out cone. 'Are we *right* to assume the forgings are easy to break off after they're heated?'

'As you said yourself, soft as putty,' Turney replied. 'Remember tension and hardness strengths were down.'

'Weak enough for a kid to break off?'

Turney nodded at the undamaged cone. 'I'll heat one up and try it.'

'Let me know how you get on,' Klein said. He turned to leave, then addressed Bradley. 'You all set for Kansas City tomorrow?'

'Yes.'

'Check with the hangar for the time.' Klein jammed his good hand in his pocket and left the laboratory, head down, a deep vertical furrow dividing his forehead, concentrated at the root of his nose. He was as puzzled as Bradley. What *had* flared into flames in the nose cone with enough heat to weaken two strong fittings and cause the cone to fall off before the aircraft hit the ground? Maybe tomorrow would produce an answer. Instead of walking straight, he turned left, swung open a door, and was enveloped by the pungent smell of kerosene and oil. In a large room, mounted on steel frames bolted to the floor, were three huge, battered shapes, the wrecked engines. The smashed casings that had once enclosed the engines had been pried off, exposing the flattened compressor and turbine blades. He saw the silvery gleam of the main shaft of the rear engine where the aft bearing had been stripped down, and a cord fluttered from it on a piece of string. Houston, in coveralls, bent over the engine with a group of men.

Houston looked up, carefully holding a metal object in a rag. 'Hi, Steve.' He motioned to the others. 'You remember these fellas from General Powerdyne?'

'Howdo,' Klein said, recognising Roy Felden, the chief engineer from General Powerdyne Corporation, the Caravan's engine manufacturer, and Alex Wald, chief metallurgist.

Felden introduced the other members of his team, all power-plant specialists. Several NTSB and FAA engine experts nodded at Klein.

'We're taking apart the internal lubricating system,' Houston said, indicating a circular shape in his hand before holding it against a bright work lamp. Several similar shapes were on a nearby bench, displayed on a sheet of clean brown paper. Klein recognised the coarse oil filter screens. At a far side of the room several NTSB engine experts were arranging twisted copper pipes on a blueprint they had spread on a bench. On the floor was a tangle of broken pipes and connections. They were attempting to do the opposite of what Houston was doing – reassemble the *external* piping of the lubrication system.

'How's it going?'

Houston shrugged. 'So-so.' He squinted through the filter screen and laid it on the brown paper.

'Got reports on the oil and fuel analysis?' Klein asked.

Houston tugged his coveralls at the waist. 'The Chemical Lab sent them over a half hour ago. A-okay. Exactly as per specification.'

Klein pointed to the engine. 'And the fine oil filter.'

Houston indicated another bench. 'We stripped it. The element's clean. This rear engine only had seven flight hours on it.'

Klein turned to Felden. 'American Constitution replaced the rear engine because the oil pressure in the main bearing was down a half pound.

'Mr Houston told us,' Felden replied. 'That's playing it safe. There was really no need to replace the *complete* engine.'

It was an old story, so old that Klein paid no attention to it. An engine manufacturer, like his airframe partner, always stood up for his product. 'What do you think caused low pressure in the rear main bearing?' he asked.

'Our technical representative at O'Hare had a call from American Constitution and went right over. It was a malfunctioning valve in the oil pump. We offered to change the pump, but the airline insisted on changing the whole engine.' He paused and continued, 'It only takes two hours for an engine change, and the aircraft was out of service anyway on a five-hundred-hour inspection.'

'A steel filing on the seat of the valve was the problem,' interjected Wald. 'It put the valve out of kilter. Reduced the oil flow.'

'Have you told the pump manufacturer?' Klein asked sharply. Last year he'd listened to exactly the same story from another engine maker, and the chief engineer had not followed through with a complaint to the pump manufacturer.

Feldon nodded. 'Shipped the complete pump back.'

Klein looked straight into Felden's blue eyes and asked, 'Why did you add stiffening plates to the rear engine mounting anchorages, Mr Felden?'

Felden shuffled his feet and glanced at the chief metallurgist before replying.

'During the initial test flights, before the aircraft went into airline service, Astral Aircraft complained about a vibration in the fin.' He paused and went on in an even voice, 'The vibration occurred at cruising revs only, and the chief test pilot said he couldn't tune it out with the rudder trim tab.'

'What would cause the vibration in the first place?' Klein asked.

Felden shrugged. 'One of those things. A sympathetic vibration at cruising revs – '

'Despite computers and wind tunnel tests, aircraft design is still a rather – shall we say – inexact science,' Wald interrupted patronisingly.

Klein sucked his lip. There was probably no connection between the flameout and the stiffened anchorages. But his job, he reminded himself, was to investigate: investigate every bit of evidence that came to hand, however apparently insignificant. He sensed tension between himself and the other two, and made a mental note to cross-check Felden's statement about the stiffening plates with the chief engineer of Astral Aircraft Corporation.

'Has Bill shown you our Lab Supervisor's museum exhibits, Mr Felden?' he said in an effort to ease the atmosphere.

'Museum exhibits?'

Klein laughed and turned to Houston. 'Don't let 'em get away without seeing Hugh's museum, Bill.'

'Sure won't.'

Felden and Wald looked mystified. Klein quickly changed the subject. 'Any theories on why flameouts on three engines simultaneously?'

'Fuel starvation. Cross-feed valves improperly operated. Fuel shortage,' Felden said, his eyebrow jerking.

A typical engine man, Klein again reflected. Keep steering the blame away from his engines.

'The fuel valves we've already recovered show they were in correct positions,' Houston said, pointing across the room, where valves and bits of fuel pipes had been mounted on a big wooden board. Coloured chalk traced a diagram of the complex fuel system.

'When will you have the flight recorder printout?' Felden said, in an obvious attempt to change the subject.

'Possibly tomorrow,' Klein replied.

'There're at least a dozen engine signals monitored,' Wald said.

Klein shook his head. 'Flight data recorders are not foolproof Mr Wald. The impact shock may have damaged it. Sometimes we get an ambiguous printout.' He stepped closer to the engine and examined a cylindrical device attached by a lever to the fuel regulator. 'I didn't know the CA-100 had an auto-throttle system for all speeds, Bill.' Klein never claimed to know everything, unlike some IICs, who pretended to know everything about all systems, an impossibility with a modern aircraft. 'That puts a different light on it.'

'Don't exactly follow you,' Felden said guardedly.

'No mechanical pushrods between the throttle levers on the flight deck and the three engines, right?'

'Correct. The auto-throttle works entirely by electricity.' Felden pointed to the cylindrical device. 'This electric actuator operates the fuel regulator lever on the engine when the pilot switches on auto-throttle.'

Klein chewed his tongue thoughtfully. 'Do you think there's any connection between a fire inside the nose cone and the auto-throttle system?' He was thinking about the CVR tape and the captain's remark about feeling heat near the front of the control pedestal. The throttle levers were mounted on the pedestal.

'Fire in the nose cone?' Felden asked.

'Haven't you heard?'

'Nobody's *told* us.'

'It was in most of the press reports.'

Felden drew himself up and spoke in an authoritative voice, like a headmaster lecturing a student for misbehaviour. 'I'd have expected to hear through official channels first, Mr Klein. Why didn't we receive a full report?'

'Simply because we've not put anything on paper

yet,' Klein lied. 'There was a fire in the nose cone – of cause unknown. Could that damage the auto-throttle wiring?'

'It's impossible to say without looking at the wreck, if there's anything left to go on. We could theorise, of course, but –'

'I'm sorry you weren't told officially. Will you be at Kansas City tomorrow? The wreckage is being carted back there and reassembled.'

'Of course we'll be there,' Felden said stiffly.

Houston turned to Wald. 'Got a minute to check the metal used on the levers for the engine relight system?'

'Sure.'

Houston, followed by Wald, crossed to a thick pile of blueprints slung over a trestle. Klein called after him, 'See you at Kansas City tomorrow, Bill.'

'I'll be there.'

Part IV
Deduction

TEN

Klein pushed open the door of Liss's electronics laboratory and looked inside.

'Morning, sir. Looking for Mr Liss?' asked a tall blonde girl who looked at him through outsize white-framed glasses. Norma Parker was dressed in a white pantsuit. The jacket was cut low, revealing the tops of her breasts as she leaned with deliberate provocation over a high-speed line printer. I'll never understand women, Klein mused, thinking of Helen Dimitry, who was embarrassed when her cleavage accidentally showed: Norma Parker deliberately wore low necklines to reveal hers.

A swath of letter-width paper shot out of the printer and automatically folded itself into pages ready-punched for a ring binder.

'Is that the CA-100 flight data recorder printout you're collating?' he inquired.

'Yes, sir. I gave Mr Liss the first copy a moment ago.'

An inner door opened and Liss appeared, a ring binder under his arm. His usually immobile face was quivering with excitement.

'I was just on my way up to see you, Steve,' he said. 'Let's go into my office where we can talk.'

He led the way through the inner door, into a room where several technicians stood before electronic test equipment. Against one wall was a vertical tape deck that transposed digital data from the delicate tape and stylus Liss had skilfully extracted from the inside of the battered flight data recorder casing. He had deciphered the data into what he called square wave form and other terms that Klein did not pretend to understand. All he was interested in was the final results Liss extracted from the recorder.

Liss opened his office door and sat in one of the chairs in front of his desk, which was bare except for a bowl of fresh flowers put there by Norma Parker, and some neatly stacked files. Against the far wall Klein noticed the halves of the earth-caked outer steel shell of the flight data recorder, and the protective electromagnetic plastic covering, in which it had been wrapped, folded in a neat bundle below. On a nearby workbench were the disassembled pieces of a complex electronic steering gear from one of Liss's model aeroplanes, the tiny transistors and delicately soldered components laid out in order on a sheet of clean white paper. Christ, Turney could learn something here, Klein reflected.

Liss opened the binder and quickly turned the pages. Klein caught a glimpse of graphs and tables titled vertical acceleration, pitch attitude, elevator angle, fuel flow, control column position. Liss stopped at a foldout chart headed 'Roll Data'.

'Look at this, Steve.' Liss pointed with a finely sharpened pencil point.

Klein studied the wriggly lines on the chart for several seconds before commenting. 'A dutch roll? That checks with what we heard on the CVR.'

Liss nodded. 'A *divergent* dutch roll, Steve. The aircraft rolled from left to right and back with increasing acceleration until it was uncontrollable. It finally flipped on to its back and spiralled into the ground.' Liss shook his head. 'I've never seen a divergent dutch roll before. Look at the sudden altitude loss and the rapid buildup of airspeed.' He flipped the pages until he came to a graph at the front.

'I had this chart drawn up to simplify things for the public inquiry. A layman will have no problem understanding it.'

Klein looked at the two curved lines that crossed on

the chart. 'They hit the ground at a hell of a speed, three hundred and forty-five knots. That's about four hundred miles an hour,' he said quietly. 'It was over very quickly.' But he couldn't shake from his mind the terror on board the aeroplane as it rocked from side to side with ever-increasing violence, the cries of alarm as it went into a near vertical dive and flipped on its back, hurling passengers, including the babies he'd seen listed on the manifest, in a screaming heap of kicking, struggling bodies towards the front end of the aircraft, breaking legs and arms. He studied the line indicating loss of altitude, where it swept sharply towards the point of impact, and leafed through the other pullout charts. 'Can't remember the last time we investigated a dutch roll case,' he said, leaning his elbow on the desk and rubbing his forehead.

'There've been some near misses, if I can mix my metaphors.'

'How d'you mean?'

'Well, we know fast aircraft with swept-back wings are susceptible to dutch rolls. I've heard of recent cases with British aircraft. But the crew were able to pull out in time, after losing height in a hurry.'

'Checked the library?'

'I was on my way up after dropping this on your desk.'

'Let's go and see.'

Norma Parker dispensed a coquettish smile in Liss's direction when the two men passed her rattling line printer. Upstairs, they were greeted with a warm smile by Miyoko Tezuka, the librarian, a diminutive girl nicknamed The Nippon Memory Drum because of her prodigious memory. Klein asked for all reports concerning American civil aircraft that had crashed owing to dutch rolls.

'There's nothing for civil aircraft of United States registry,' she said in a soft, precise voice, smoothing her black hair. 'But there're two dealing with *recovery* from dutch rolls. I'll check the cards.'

She crossed to a bank of narrow drawers and thumbed through the catalogue cards; extracting two, she brought them over to Klein.

'Dutch roll in clear air turbulence. TWA 707 mid-trans-atlantic. Recovery at twenty-four thousand feet. Flight data recorder stylus at roll limits. No casualties,' he read aloud to Liss.

'What does the other say?'

'Dutch roll from low cloud base at twelve thousand feet on descent into Kennedy. Pan Am 727. Probable cause: turbulent air from thunderstorms and wind shear. Flight data recorder stylus within roll limits.' Klein tapped the cards on the desk thoughtfully. 'What about non-domestic airlines? Foreign airlines?'

'I'll check,' said Tezuka. She went back to her card catalogue and opened another drawer. She pulled out three cards and studied them, put one back in the file, and gave the other two to Klein. 'British Airways Diplomat aircraft and an Aero Frank Alouette,' she said. 'There's one on a Varig 707, but it's catalogued under pitch-roll manoeuvre, not dutch roll.'

Klein read the cards and showed them to Liss. 'Let's see the reports, please,' he said to Tezuka.

She returned with two thin leaflets. One was bound in British Air Ministry dun-coloured covers. It was headed 'Aeronautical Information Circular, United Kingdom, Aeronautical Information Services (AIS 1)', followed by the date. Klein read the title: *Operating All Engines of Multi-Engine Aircraft from One Tank for Fuel Balancing Purposes.* It took him only a few moments to scan the text, written with typical British understatement.

'There have been two recent occurrences where a three-engine Diplomat jetliner went into a serious divergent dutch roll at 37,000 feet at night at 520 knots after all three engines flamed out without prior indication. Although the crew was able to establish the aircraft in glide descent they were unable to return the machine to level flight until it reached an altitude of 26,000 feet, at

which level the crew re-lit all engines and returned all systems to normal operation. This was a near disaster, prevented only by the skill of the crew.'

'I'll say,' said Liss a trifle breathlessly. 'Imagine a flameout at night: generators gone and all lights out.'

'See this,' Klein said.

Liss read: *'The crew reported that they were operating all three engines from one tank to effect fuel balancing. The centre tanks, in the fuselage, had been allowed to run dry.'*

'Goddamned crazy way to operate a fuel system, you gotta believe,' Klein remarked.

'A pal of mine used to do it that way on DC-7s,' Liss said.

'But those things weren't as complicated as modern jets. Nor did they drink fuel as fast. You had more time to make adjustments.' He looked again at the report. *'Roll rate exceeded design limits, as shown by flight data recorder.'*

'What does Aero Frank have to say?' Liss asked, bending over Klein. 'There's an English translation on the other side.'

Klein read it aloud. *'An AL-301 Alouette flying at 41,000 feet on the Paris to Rio de Janeiro route suffered partial rundown of two engines which were operating from the centre tank only. The fuel low pressure warning lights alerted the crew regarding the exact cause of the rundowns. The crew quickly restored fuel flow to the engines by switching on the booster pumps in the wing tanks, but the aircraft entered a divergent dutch roll and recovered at 32,000 feet. The limits of roll rate were exceeded, as shown by examination of the flight data recorder.*

'NOTE: *In this occurrence the captain was not informed that fuel balancing operations were taking place. Also, after interrogation, the crew members responsible for fuel balancing admitted that flight deck distractions had caused them to lose their concentration.'*

'Fuel balancing doesn't apply in our case. What d'you think they mean by distractions on the flight deck?'

Klein shrugged. 'A stewardess bringing the crew their lunch trays; the flight service manager taking his cabin log book to the flight deck for the first officer to sign.' He stared thoughtfully at the reports and books neatly lining the walls of the room. 'Notice anything about the Diplomat and Alouette incidents, Jeff?'

'They were both three-engine aircraft,' Liss replied without hesitation. 'And they were the only aircraft where the dutch roll exceeded the design rate of roll.'

'The sweepback on the Caravan's wings is more than in conventional designs,' Klein said. 'If I remember Bradley's figures correctly, five degrees more than the Lockheed TriStar and the DC-10.'

'Increasing the tendency of the aircraft to dutch roll with power off?'

Klein opened the copy of the flight data printout and restudied the charts. He turned the pages slowly, and stopped at a sheet headed 'Power Settings'. The line on the graph showing the power delivered by each engine ran horizontally across the page before suddenly dropping vertically to zero at the base line. 'Auto-throttle failure. And I have a hunch that damned fire in the nose cone has something to do with it.' He got up. 'Distribute the usual number of copies to all interested parties, Jeff. I'll keep this.' He hugged the binder under his arm and glanced at his watch. 'I've got an appointment with Ray Malik in five minutes. I want to give him a surprise.'

'Are you crazy, Steve? Grewson wouldn't ground CA-100s on this flimsy evidence.' Raymond Malik tossed the copy of the Preliminary Accident Report on his desk and regarded Klein with sharp, shrewd eyes over the tops of his half-frame glasses. 'Huh, you want me to look an ass?' He put his shirt-sleeved elbows on the desk and steepled his huge hands under his chin in a defiant self-confident attitude. Like his hands, the rest of

Malik's body was of gigantic proportions, like a logger's. His big head was topped with a fuzz of white hair, and his face was creased like medieval parchment. After a quarter of a century in air accident investigation he had earned the nickname The Judge, for his proficiency in the art of compromise, in particular for his ability to smooth over differences when the heads of the NTSB and FAA disagreed on draft accident reports and probable causes. Klein, sitting opposite and staring back at Malik now, wondered if the two cards he held in reserve would make The Judge alter his decision.

'Have you read the CVR printout, Ray?'

'Of course.'

'Well?'

'Damned odd.' Malik unsteepled his hands and picked up the printout, casually turning the pages. 'A dutch roll is so unusual.' He studied the printout silently for several seconds. 'And the nose cone dropping off before impact.' He shook his head and suddenly swivelled his chair to stare out of the window, stroking a tuft of white hair that protruded from his ear. He propped a polished shoe on the windowsill, revealing a white expanse of calf between socks and trouser leg.

Klein found himself studying the veined backs of Malik's hands. They often referred to The Judge as the rough diamond of the management team because of his fierce independence and absolute self-confidence. Over the years he had stubbornly refused to enroll in any of 'those bullshit management courses. Managers are born – not made'. Malik's inherent ability to manage had proven itself as over the years he had steadily risen until he was now in charge of the one hundred and twenty air accident investigators at the Washington headquarters and the eleven regional offices.

Klein looked again at the rows of photographs on the walls of the office. Pictures of aircraft on the ground, aeroplanes in flight. Some photographs cracked and faded with age; others, like the coloured pictures of the Boeing 747 and a CA-100 Caravan in flight, were new.

The older photographs, Malik in an aeroplane's open cockpit or casually leaning against the wings of planes on the ground, hung closer to his desk than the others, as if memories physically crowded in.

Malik suddenly yanked his foot off the windowsill and picked up the Preliminary Accident Report. 'Why did you include "cause unknown" in the key words, and why the hell capitalise it?'

'Because I have a hunch they're the most important key words. We're dealing with something that's never happened before. A modern high-speed airliner, at cruising altitude in straight and level flight, suddenly has three flameouts and dives into the ground. Something new.'

Malik glared at him. 'You expect *me* to recommend to Grewson that he ground all CA-100s because you've got a *hunch*?'

'You gotta believe.'

He snorted, and tossed the CVR printout aside. 'Huh – on this flimsy evidence?'

'I think you'll find this is more concrete evidence,' Klein said quietly, pushing the black binder across the desk. 'The flight data recorder printout. Hot off Liss's press.'

Malik seized the binder and quickly found the relevant charts. His eyes widened, and his fingers twirled the ear hair furiously. He looked up, a puzzled expression in his eye. 'Fuel flow normal, throttles chopped, immediate *divergent* dutch roll,' he said shaking his head. 'Doesn't add up.' After a minute of silence, broken only by the metallic tick-tock of an antique grandfather clock against the wall, he looked up and stared at Klein over the tops cf his glasses. 'And you've got a hunch it's going to happen again?' he remarked, with the slightest emphasis on the word 'hunch'.

'Yes,' Klein replied unequivocally.

'You realise what this means, Steve,' Malik said, emphasising each word with stabs of a gnarled forefinger on the leather chair arm.

'Grewson will think you're crazy and the Bureau's judgement will be in question,' Klein said, and added, 'But, hell, we can't take chances with people's lives.'

'Haven't you got any *logical* theory why there was a fire in the nose cone, Steve?' Malik asked, his posture suddenly softening.

'No,' Klein admitted, feeling defeated.

'How far advanced is your investigation?'

'Regional's getting the wreckage reassembled at Kansas City. We've secured the ATC tapes, and I just heard that Downey's identified the flight crew's bodies. The pathologists are doing lactate profiles on them now. He also found the Aircraft Journey Log Book, but it doesn't show anything abnormal. Only minor snags.'

'Why don't we wait until the reassembly's done before running off to Grewson like scared chickens?'

'Because I think there's something mysterious about this particular crash.'

'Mysterious? Malik paused, and by an intuition born of long friendship and mutual respect Klein guessed what the other was thinking. *Steve's been in this game long enough to know when something's fishy.*

The Judge waited patiently for Klein to continue.

'I think some external agency may be responsible for the occurrence.'

Malik said nothing, silently swivelling his seat from side to side. At last he spoke. 'Steve, we've known each other for a hell of a long time, and all that. I've always respected your views. But – for Christ's sake – do you expect me to phone Grewson and recommend grounding about fifty aircraft representing millions of dollars' worth of capital investment and millions of revenue dollars to several airlines because you've only got a *hunch* one of them crashed for some mysterious reason? Like being, uh, shot down by a UFO or something equally crazy. The disruption to the airlines and the financial losses don't influence my judgement, and I'd go along with your recommendation right now if you could produce some concrete evidence.' He made a gesture with his enormous hands. 'But ground planes on a hunch?'

Klein leaned on the edge of the desk. 'That's what I'm asking you to do.' As an afterthought he added, 'It's the first CA-100 to crash.'

Malik turned to stare out of the window. The ticking of the grandfather clock sounded loud in the quiet room. The ludicrous thought passed through Klein's mind that Malik looked like the old clock: solidly built, reliable.

'For Christ's sake, can't you be more specific, Steve?' Malik appealed. 'Can't you figure it might be something that at least *sounds* scientific?'

'I *have* a scientific hunch,' Klein said, drawing his chair closer to the desk. 'I told you I believe this crash was caused by something we've never thought of, like electromagnetic propagation, nothing to do with the wave bands from commercial television and radio broadcast, perhaps not even from the military short-wave bands. I thinks it's something maybe to do with' – he stopped, weighing his words – 'an external cause such as very, very high frequency waves from a passing satellite. Perhaps a Russian Molynia spy satellite searching the radio spectrum with high-intensity microwave sensors as it passes over the United States. Or an infra-red sensing device from a spy satellite. God knows there're enough satellite spy overflights continually probing and taping our military signals which the Russians hope will reveal our military secrets. They even listen in to private long-distance telephone conversations carried on the trans-American microwave system.'

'What the hell has all that got to do with the crash?'

Klein pointed to Malik's copy of the CVR printout. 'The aircraft was at thirty-one thousand feet at cruising speed. The second officer says the flight deck temperature was above normal. The captain confirms it. Seconds later three simultaneous flameouts, an uncontrollable dutch roll, and dive at terminal velocity. At the crash site we found the nose cone, burned to a cinder inside, the hinge fittings weakened by heat. The cone was two hundred yards from the main wreckage. In it was housed the automatic collision avoidance equipment and the weather radar. The collision equipment was recovered at the site, smashed to smithereens of course, but it looks like it was subjected to heat, and I mean intense heat.'

'I'm still listening.'

'The FDR shows the aircraft was on auto-throttle *and* auto-pilot before the flameouts. The auto-throttle works on the new entirely electric system. No mechanical connection between the throttle levers and the engines.' Klein was encouraged by a gleam that appeared in Malik's eyes.

'I think the burnout in the nose cone, the elevated temperature on the flight deck, and the three flameouts are all connected.' To his satisfaction, Malik nodded. 'My hunch is that the damned electrics failed because of something exterior to the aircraft. Something entirely new, something we know nothing about yet.'

The gleam in Malik's eyes vanished. 'Christ, Steve. Not again?'

Klein leaned forward. 'I'm suggesting high-intensity propagation of energy from sources presently unknown. From some top-secret military installation experimenting with countermeasures, for example, or – yes, I'll stick to my goddamned guns – even energy from Russian satellite spy overflights.'

The light came back into Malik's tawny eyes. 'Spurious energy that causes heating? Is that it?'

'Yes.' Klein leaned back in the chair.

Malik's mandible clamped upwards, lips pressed tightly together. He shook his head. 'They'd have to be hellishly powerful energy waves to burn the inside of a fibreglass nose cone. Any burning on the outside?'

'Nothing. Ultrashort waves penetrate neutral material like fibreglass, as you know.'

'You've got me half convinced there *are* mysterious

energy waves out there,' Malik said, waving his hand towards the window.

Klein smiled. If Malik was half convinced, then he *was* on to something. The Judge was the most sceptical man in the Bureau.

'Let's assume you're right, Steve. Just assume, mind you,' he added hastily. 'If these experiments are still going on, possibly in a random manner, other aircraft may be jeopardised. Why do you want to ground only CA-100s?'

'Two reasons. One, the CA-100 is the first civil aircraft to be fitted with the new automatic collision avoidance gear, and, two, it's the first CA-100 to crash.'

'And you think the collision avoidance equipment and the fire are linked?'

'Yes.'

'What have you done about investigating the equipment?'

'This afternoon. At the reassembly at Kansas City.'

'Aren't you rushing it? Asking for a grounding before you've examined the equipment?' Malik asked cautiously, waiting for Klein's reaction.

'We've looked at the bits, and they're burned. This afternoon I'm gonna talk with the equipment manufacturers and the auto-throttle experts.'

Malik still isn't fully convinced, Klein thought. He fished in his pocket and brought out a collection of newspaper clippings and unfolded them with skilful movements of his left fingers. 'Have you seen these, Ray?'

Malik glanced at the clippings, then settled back to read more carefully.

CAUSE OF WORLD'S WORST AIR DISASTER REMAINS UNSOLVED

SAFETY BUREAU HUSHES UP FINDINGS

BY DOREEN BRAILEY

The cause of the world's biggest air crash, in which 406 persons lost their lives, still remains a mystery.

While investigators from the Bureau of Aviation Safety sift through the grisly remains looking for clues, the official word from Washington, after the initial press conference, is still 'nothing further to report'.

The crash of the CA-100 Caravan belonging to American Constitution Airlines raises doubts in many minds about the safety of the latest wide-body airliner to enter airline service, although it is the first accident to this aircraft type.

A random poll taken by *Sun-Times* interviewers at major airports across the United States, including Chicago's O'Hare, Los Angeles International, and New York's Kennedy International, indicates that many passengers are avoiding flying in the Caravan.

It is now a week since the disaster, and the only facts made known to the press are that *perhaps* all three engines of the doomed aircraft flamed out (suddenly stopped), that the aircraft dived from approximately 30,000 feet, and that before the moment of impact the nose cone fell off the aircraft. At the press conference it was also revealed that the inside of the nose cone was burned.

Investigating experts are still appealing to the souvenir hunter who stole a part of the hinge fitting to bring or send the missing part to the Bureau of Aviation Safety, Washington, D.C., or send it to the nearest police station. No questions will be asked. The missing part may have an important bearing in answering the question: why did this aircraft crash from a perfectly clear sky?

He ignored the big news photos showing closeups of the wreckage and bodies strewn over the ground, and picked up another clipping.

LITTLE CEDARS, KANSAS – The environmental safety aspect of the new generation of wide-body jets carrying more than 400 passengers is questioned after the crash of the American Constitution Airlines Caravan near this township.

Noise, smoke, and other environmental dangers are not the only factors to be questioned. One shudders to think what would have happened if the aircraft had crashed into this township (population 2,451).

Malik tossed the paper aside. 'Self-centred alarmist,' he commented. His hand pounced on a clipping from the editorial page of the Washington *Post.* He sat up straight.

WHAT ARE THE AIR ACCIDENT
INVESTIGATORS HIDING?

A week has passed since the worst accident in aviation history, and still the National Transportation Safety Board's Bureau of Aviation Safety, when questioned about a probable cause of the accident, considers that 'no comment' is sufficient to ease public concern.

This is no way for a public body to respond to the public's right to know. If certain facts about the safety aspects of the aircraft concerned, the recently introduced CA-100 Caravan, designed and manufactured by Astral Aircraft Corporation, are being held back by the Bureau, then the Senate Subcommittee recently established to investigate the current state of safety of all modes of transportation in the United States should place this affair at the top of its agenda for their next meeting.

Malik put down the paper and shoved it across the desk with the small pile of unread clippings. He turned and stared out of the window again, whistling an off-key tune through pursed lips, a signal The Judge used when he was in the process of making up his mind. He suddenly turned back to Klein.

'I'll recommend the grounding, Steve. But on one condition.'

'What's that?'

'For a limited time only. Four weeks. By then I expect you to come up with a probable cause.' He jerked his forefinger at Klein. 'And it had better be related to your hunch,' he added grimly.

A measly month. Hardly enough time to arrive at more than a preliminary deduction, and *perhaps* a probable cause. But it was better than nothing, Klein consoled himself, and if anything, God forbid, happened to another CA-100 he'd definitely get an extension.

'I'll phone Grewson and then confirm it in writing.' Malik reached for a file, tacitly indicating that the meeting was over. But Klein remained sitting. Malik looked up. 'Something else, Steve?'

'Two things.' Klein put the draft report of the Avianjet case on the desk. 'Have you read your draft of the Avianjet case with Legal's notes?'

The Judge nodded but said nothing.

'Hell, Ray. You know my beef. Legal's doing an about-turn on pilot error.' Klein tapped his fingers on the report. 'The pilot followed every rule in the book. At his low altitude there was simply no way he could correct the thrust reverser before he hit the deck. And he *hadn't* been drinking.'

Malik took the report and studied it for several minutes, rubbing his lips with a fingertip. He leafed through the pages, reading intently. When he finished, he rested his chin on his hand and cleared his throat.

'You sure you aren't going soft on him?'

'He didn't have a chance. The blame rests squarely on the mechanic. I had a simulated test flight done by the company's pilots with the co-pilot pulling the reverse thrust bucket when the pilot wasn't expecting it. At altitude, of course.'

'I've read it. It's in the report,' Malik said, a trifle impatiently.

'Doesn't Legal read everything we guys write? Would you see them and argue the case? With their top man?'

Malik pushed the report back across the desk. 'I'll take it up with Legal's general counsel.' He looked at a pile of correspondence.

'There's one other thing, Ray. Something that might be none of my business.'

'I'm listening.'

'It's the question of Jeff Liss.' Klein hesitated, forming words in his mind. 'He's the best Systems Group chairman in the Bureau, and you know the improvements he made to the Audio Lab. He's disappointed about being passed over as an IIC when the reshuffle took place.'

'I know.' The Judge's eyes hardened.

'He's very ambitious.'

'I know that too.'

Klein suddenly felt deflated. He had come prepared to argue Liss's case, put in a good word for him. The careful argument he had mentally prepared collapsed.

'Well, er – I was hoping, Ray, that when the next review comes around for the appointment of new IICs you might reconsider Liss.'

'He's a detail man. Doesn't see the whole picture,' Malik snapped.

Klein paused, trying to salvage the bits of his argument. He'd anticipated Malik's belief that Liss was a detail man.

'His beat covers a hell of a lot of territory – electronics, hydraulics, pneumatics, electrics, besides the FDR and CVR. He gets one hell of an overview with that lot.'

'Has he ever taken a structures course?'

'You've got a point,' Klein admitted. 'On the other hand, he's young enough and eager enough to go back to Dulles for a few seminars.'

Malik turned towards one of the faded photographs on the wall, whistling his off-tune notes. Beside an ancient Stearman biplane was the figure of a young Malik in flying gear, leaning against the wing, ankles carelessly crossed, smiling into the camera. In the next photo the same young man stood against the wing of a monoplane, and the next showed him climbing into the cockpit of a Shooting Star jet fighter, with two ground crew standing at the ready.

'I can't promise anything, but leave it with me,' Malik said, standing up, indicating that it was time for Klein to leave.

'Thanks, Ray,' Klein said, gathering up his papers.

ELEVEN

Klein and Houston surveyed the scene in the lofty hangar, a section of the general aviation building near the main terminal at Kansas City Airport. Bits of the fuselage debris Armstrong had sent back from the wreckage site, held together with wire and wooden props, formed as exactly as possible the original shape of the crashed aircraft. Battered parts of the rear fuselage rested on trestles, and the contorted tail plane and fin were supported on scaffolding, with pieces of elevators and rudder positioned in correct relationship. The centre section of the wing and outer wing panels lay on the concrete floor within a chalked outline, corresponding to the wing's shape. Part numbers were red-crayoned on the bigger skin panels, and cardboard tags dangled from the crumpled engine mounting pylons.

The reassembly reminded Klein of the reconstructed dinosaurs he'd seen in the Smithsonian Institution, where ancient chunks of fossilised bones were wired together.

'Let's face it,' Houston said, 'they're doing a hell of a good job.'

Klein nodded, and ran his eye along the sleek lines of a new Caravan CA-100 parked alongside. Astral Aircraft had taken it off their flight production line and flown it up to Kansas City that same morning. Men were comparing skin panels and holding long steel tapes against the fuselage of the new aircraft, to find where corresponding pieces of debris should be placed on the reassembly.

'First time I've seen a CA-100 in one piece,' Houston remarked.

'A first for me too. They only went into airline service last fall.' Klein's eye took in the clean aerodynamic form of the airliner: the cleverly shaped cowlings, for the rear engine mounted on the fin, the raked-back wings, slender silver shapes supporting finely streamlined engine pods, in sharp contrast to the pulverised scene of devastation at the site, and the adjoining miserable reassembly. Above the flight deck he read the blue stylised script: *Caravan – the Shape of Tomorrow's Flight.* Some shape, Klein thought.

'I'll take a gander at the engine pylons,' said Houston.

Liss strode up. 'Forget about the front fuselage,' he said in a disappointed tone. 'There isn't a piece left bigger than my hand.'

'Armstrong's found pieces of the collision avoidance gear, so don't be discouraged,' Klein said. 'Who's in charge of reassembly?'

'Guy named Alvarez. Astral's production superintendent. Here he comes.'

Mario Alvarez was a porcine man, with jet black hair and an olive complexion. Despite the grim work going on about him, he wore a perpetual smile.

Liss introduced him. 'I didn't expect such quick progress,' Klein said, shaking hands.

'Everything's well tagged, sir.' Alvarez gestured towards a flipstand on which layers of blueprints several inches thick had been mounted. 'And the drawings help.'

'Not much coming back on the nose fuselage,' Klein commented glumly, staring at the empty space at the front of the reassembly.

Alvarez shrugged, and pointed to a pile of metal debris embedded in brown earth on a bench. Klein examined the mess, then asked, 'What's over here?' as he moved to another bench.

'Bits of the flight deck floor and –'

'You're going to have a hell of a job making sense out

of this lot,' Klein said to Liss. He carefully extracted the battered casing of an instrument from the tangle of metal.

'Airspeed indicator,' Liss said.

Klein turned the instrument over and looked at the face, indented with glass splinters. The white pointer indicating hundreds of knots was crushed into the dial face at 345 knots

'Corresponds with the terminal velocity readout on the flight data recorder,' Liss said.

'What's this?' Klein burrowed into the metal heap and held up a smaller instrument. He knew he was trespassing on Liss's territory but couldn't overcome his fascination with instruments. They represented the interface where machine and man met, the eyes, ears, and nose of the aircraft. 'A rev indicator. Dead on zero.'

'Confirms the flameouts with the FDR,' Liss said, moving closer to Klein. It was clear he was anxious to investigate the instruments himself.

'Er – before you get into this muck,' Klein said, 'let's look at the collision avoidance gear inside the *new* aircraft. Are the manufacturer's reps here?'

'Yes. And the auto-throttle guy.'

'Get Houston. He's examining the engine pylons. We'll go over it together.'

'You think there's a connection between the collision avoidance gear and the throttles, don't you?' Liss said.

'Yes. And, more important, between the fire and the collision avoidance gear.'

'If we could pin down the cause of the fire, we'd have something to work on.' Liss ran a hand over his pale, hollow cheeks, a distant look in his green eyes.

'How do you react to my theory that an outside cause is responsible?'

Liss snapped out of his dreamlike pose. 'What's that?'

'Supposing it's something we've never heard of before, like a misguided high-frequency microwave homing in on the scanner and burning it up.'

Liss snorted. 'Never heard of such a thing.'

'They never heard of aeroplanes in the seventeenth century, either,' Klein retorted. 'You and your goddamned electronics. Invisible electrons doing exactly what they're told, buzzing along printed wiring boards like white rats scrambling through a maze to get to the cheese.'

'The rats have to be educated.'

'I thought they figured it out themselves.' Klein pointed to the high hangar ceiling. 'There're some uneducated electromagnetic waves up there, you gotta believe.' He looked at Liss's face. Liss was absolutely unimpressed, so he changed the subject. 'Where're those guys?'

'Here's one.' Liss waved to a dark-haired man of about thirty under the nose of the new Caravan, a black attaché case in his hand. He wore a soft grey suit, blue shirt, and red and white polka-dot tie, and looked like any of the hundreds of other aircraft manufacturers' technical sales representatives Klein had met: smartly dressed, efficient-looking, and with the confident air of a man who was sure of the product he sold.

'This is Mr Pelrine,' Liss said.

Klein shook Pelrine's hand. 'Can we get together with the auto-throttle guys and run over your systems operations?' Klein asked.

'Sure, sure,' Pelrine said in a businesslike manner.

Alvarez arranged for a platform to be wheeled into position near the new Caravan's nose, and led the way up the steps. He lifted the recessed locking latch and swung open the fibreglass nose cone. Klein stared inside the cavernous opening exposing the inside of the nose fuselage. The expert from the auto-throttle makers, a man named Qand, peered over his shoulder. Facing them, on the centre line of the aircraft, was a mirror-like, silvery steel dish.

'This is the collision avoidance scanner,' Pelrine announced, touching the dish. 'It's driven by this electric motor to scan around all sides of the aircraft.'

'And that's the weather radar scanner behind?' Klein

asked, pointing to a smaller dish mounted above the other.

'Yes, sir.'

'Where does this electric cable go?' Klein demanded, bending to touch a cable clipped to the back of the collision avoidance scanner.

'To the power supply under the flight deck floor,' Pelrine explained. 'And there's a connection to the control pedestal on the flight deck.'

'To the pilot's master switch for the avoidance gear?'

'Yes, sir.'

'So there's an electric cable that goes from this scanner to the pedestal, passing through the airtight connection in the pressurisation bulkhead?'

'Correct,' Pelrine agreed.

Could the cable have burned right up to the pedestal? Klein wondered. That might be why the temperature rose on the flight deck. But none of the crew had mentioned a burning smell – just heat. And sure as hell a burning wire would be smelled immediately on the flight deck – or would it? An airline check pilot had once told him of an instance where he'd been checking out a first officer in the flight simulator of a Lockheed TriStar. The check pilot, standing at his control panel at the back of the simulator, a panel with switches for simulating emergencies, had flipped the Fire switch. Under the simulator an electric element heated up a pan of oil in the air-conditioning system, circulating an acrid smell in the simulator flight deck. It had taken the pilot being tested five minutes before he'd noticed the smell and taken emergency action.

'Our wires connect at the same junction box,' Qand volunteered. He was a blond man crowding forty, with permanent laughter lines radiating from the corners of his mouth.

'For the auto-throttle?' asked Houston, in the middle of the group on the platform.

'That's right,' Qand said.

Klein and Houston exchanged glances. 'How come?' Klein asked.

'Our wires also take power from the main power supply,' Qand explained.

'Answer me this,' Klein said. Qand's cherubic face grated on him: it was out of place at this type of discussion. 'If a fire occurred in the nose cone, could it spread to the auto-throttle controls on the pedestal?'

Qand looked puzzled. 'There *was* a fire in the nose cone,' Klein said. 'You heard about that, I'm sure.'

'Mr Liss told me. Well, now – ' Qand rubbed his chin thoughtfully. 'I guess a fire could spread to the pedestal by that route.' He nodded, rippling his wavy hair. 'Yes. It could,' he said with conviction.

'Take it a step further, Mr Qand. If the aircraft was on auto-throttle, could a fire in this particular circuit cause the throttles to close, causing a flameout?'

Qand was silent for half a minute. 'Jeez,' he said at length, 'that's a toughie to answer straight yes or no. It depends on many things.'

'Like what?'

'As you know, when the pilot switches to auto-throttle, the throttle levers move by themselves, adjusting the engine speed and fuel consumption automatically to give the best fuel efficiency. It's done through the computer tied into the system.'

'Like the systems on 747s and the other wide-body birds,' Houston suggested.

'*They're* not fully automatic for all flight manoeuvres,' Qand said a little indignantly.

'Don't the throttles automatically open up the engines on those aircraft if the pilot is landing by the automatic landing system and gets waved off by the control tower and has to go around?' Klein asked.

'That's right.'

'Let's face it. The auto-throttle is almost human.'

Qand smiled benevolently. 'We like to think it's better than human, Mr Houston.'

'Meaning?' Houston demanded gruffly.

'Automatic landing by auto-throttle is ten times less liable to error than when the aircraft is landed by the pilot.'

Houston grunted. 'I'll take your word for it.'

'Has Armstrong found the pedestal?' Klein asked, turning to Houston.

Wordlessly Houston pointed to a workbench below, where an oblong mass of squashed metal about a cubic foot in size rested.

'Good God, is that all that's left?' Klein blurted.

The solid metal cube reminded him of the shapes of scrap metal he'd seen in automobile wrecking yards after cars had been compacted by enormous pressure between the jaws of a powerful hydraulic vice. He could see the black-knobbed throttle levers rammed through the slotted gates and driven into the pedestal structure. Other levers looked like fossils embedded in some primeval, silvery stone. Bits of automatic pilot control panel stuck out of the centre of the sharp-spiked hunk of metal.

'That's not going to tell us much about the position of the throttles at the time of flameout,' he said to Qand.

'What about the flight data recorder, Mr Klein?'

'Zero power, from thirty-one thousand feet to impact,' Liss said positively.

Klein leaned inside the nose opening of the new aircraft. It smelled of fresh paint and the characteristic odour given off by the delicate electronic gear mounted on slide-out racks. Electric cables poked through airtight connectors on the pressure bulkhead. It would be easy enough for a fire in the nose cone to engulf all the gear, set fire to the plastic insulating material of the cables, and race back to the bulkhead. If the metal connectors at the bulkhead face resisted the fire, it was likely that the flames had been contained at that point: in other words, no fire aft of the pressure bulkhead; ergo, no collapse of the bulkhead and *no* depressurisation. It checked out with the CVR, but not conclusively.

He backed out of the nose and examined the cone hinges, slowly swinging the cone to observe the action. 'Bradley looked at this?' he asked Liss.

'We both have. What about the bit stolen by souvenir hunters?'

Klein shook his head. 'Forget it.' He turned to Pelrine. 'I'm no expert on how the collision avoidance gear works. Let's go on the flight deck and you can explain it.'

Nostalgia hit Klein as soon as he stepped into the flight deck – the warm, leathery aroma of the upholstery, the antiseptic odour of plastic interior furnishings, the smell of brightly polished metal parts and new paint. He lowered himself into the captain's seat, gripped the control yoke with his left hand, and looked through the windshield. For a fleeting moment the roof girders in the hangar dissolved into a clear blue sky. He glanced down at the rows of flight and power instruments. When he looked up he saw only ugly girders.

Liss sat in the co-pilot's seat, and the others crowded around, Pelrine at the front. 'Start from the beginning, Mr Pelrine,' Klein said. 'Pretend I know nothing about it – which isn't far from the truth.' He grinned.

'As you know,' Pelrine began, 'collision avoidance equipment became mandatory under the new FAA regulations for all new civil aircraft with an all-up weight of one hundred and fifty thousand pounds and over. The CA-100 Caravan is the first production aircraft affected by the new requirements –'

'Stop right there,' Klein interjected. 'What about *automatic* collision avoidance? Didn't the FAA update that requirement recently?'

'You're right, Mr Klein. They now demand automatic collision avoidance gear.'

'After our Bureau recommended it,' Liss said sarcastically.

'The automatic gear is tied in with the auto-pilot. The older type simply flashed a light on the instrument panel when another aircraft came within five hundred feet of the aircraft, warning the pilot to take evasive action. The new equipment automatically manoeuvres the aircraft away from the other aeroplane, through being tied into the auto-pilot.'

'And the Caravan is the first aircraft to be fitted with the automatic gear, is that correct?'

'Right, sir.'

'What type of system is it?'

'Infra-red optics.'

'Not a radar system?' Klein asked, surprised.

'Requires less power to operate,' Liss said.

Pelrine nodded. 'More accurate than radar and a faster response. The backscatter power's improved too.'

'Backscatter? A reflection? Explain, please.'

'The scanner in the nose cone, which continually scans at high speed up and down and to each side of the aircraft, sends out a narrow infra-red beam. Infra-red, as you know, reacts to heat from the engine jet nozzles of other aircraft. Backscatter is the term we use to describe the heat reflection that comes back from the other aircraft's engine to the scanner. These signals are fed into the auto-pilot. The auto-pilot then manoeuvres the aircraft away from the other aeroplane approaching it.'

'What about piston-engined aircraft? Does the equipment react to them too?' asked Klein.

'It's very sensitive. It'll even pick up heat generated by the small engine of a Piper Cub.'

'Pretty sophisticated equipment,' Liss said.

Pelrine smiled with the pride of a man who knew he worked for a successful company. 'It's taken us five years to research and develop. On tests at Ames it won out over four competing systems. FAA approval followed very quickly.'

Klein remembered that Dave Jacobs had told him the ATC tapes had shown the nearest aircraft to the crashed aircraft before it fell from the sky was twenty miles away. Now he worked backwards from the second officer's remark about the high temperature, the captain's feeling heat near the front of the pedestal. He came up with a theory: the heat sensor was triggered, and switched on the fire warning bell. Work backward from there: fire warning bell, heat sensor signal to set off the bell, the sensor having responded to an over-temperature. But where the hell from? The cables, burning like a pyrotechnic snake at a fireworks display, set aflame by the burning collision avoidance gear? But what in hell's name set *that* on fire? And what would cause the mirror-like steel scanner of the collision avoidance gear to be exposed to such tremendous heat that it melted? Hugh Turney had confirmed that in his lab tests.

There was also the question: did the over-temperature interfere with the wires going to the auto-throttle? He took his hand off the yoke, picked up his right wrist with his left hand, and placed it on the throttle levers, feeling the black knobs cool to the touch. He couldn't push the levers forward because he had no strength in that arm.

'Swap seats,' he ordered Liss, standing up.

'The bigger they build these birds the smaller they make the driver's compartment,' Liss grumbled, lifting his gangly leg over the pedestal.

'Let's face it,' said Houston. 'The airlines reckon the crew ain't fare-paying passengers. They just go along for the ride.'

'I think you're right, Bill,' Klein said, lowering himself into the right-hand seat. He checked that the ignition switches were Off, and pushed the throttles forward.

'Smooth action,' he observed. 'Er – is this the auto-throttle master switch?'

'Right, sir,' replied Qand.

'Is Mr Alvarez back there somewhere?' Klein asked, twisting around.

'Somebody call me?' Alvarez pushed his way to the front.

'Where's the fire detector sensor? There's supposed

to be one someplace near the front of the pedestal.'

'Here, sir,' Alvarez replied, painfully arching his barrel body over the pedestal and reaching down with his arm. Klein caught a whiff of after-shave scent mixed with the pungent odour of hair cream. He bent forward to examine the spot Alvarez indicated.

'On the front of the pedestal box? Near the floor?'

'Yes, sir.' Alvarez got up and smiled benignly.

'Who's here from Astral Aircraft's engineering department?'

'A whole team, Mr Klein. Headed by Mr Darrard, the chief designer.'

'Would you please fetch Mr Darrard to the flight deck?'

'Certainly, sir.'

Darrard was a tall, skinny man with a sad face who averted his eyes like a socially awkward schoolboy who always came top in the maths class and felt guilty about it.

'We installed the detector as an extra,' he said.

Klein thought about this for a few seconds. 'Did you have any reason to suspect a potential fire hazard, Mr Darrard?'

Darrard stared at the black knobs on the throttle levers, sucking the insides of his cheeks until his face looked skeletal. He ran bony fingers through grey hair and said in the thin voice that matched his features, 'No reason whatever.'

This character's wrapped up in theory, Klein thought, living in a world of computerised design printouts, stress calculations, and abstruse aerodynamic data. Yet his thinking processes were flexible enough to include a flight deck fire detector, not normal practice, and nobody could deny that he'd produced a fine aircraft.

'Have you discovered anything yet?' Darrard went on. He glanced at Klein, and Klein recognised the look of a haunted man. And no wonder. This man's creation, two years on the drawing board, one year to produce the prototype, rigorously tested each step of the way through the production process, finally and proudly rolled out to the accompaniment of public relations ballyhoo, its first flight, the lengthy test flying to meet FAA's tough approval requirements for its Certificate of Airworthiness, the much heralded entry into airline service – blasted to nothing in a few seconds owing to an as yet unknown cause, exterminating in the process four hundred and six human beings, for which he must feel responsible.

'Too early to suggest a probable cause, Mr Darrard. You know the nose cone detached before impact and was burned to hell on the inside?'

'Your Mr Bradley told me.' Darrard paused and sucked his lip. 'Have you got the printouts from the data recorders?'

Klein told him briefly what the recorders had yielded. 'Copies have been sent to you, Mr Darrard.'

'So you think the fire spread from the collision avoidance equipment to the auto-throttle?' Darrard asked. 'Causing simultaneous flameouts on three engines?' He caressed the black knobs with the tips of three fingers.

'Only theory, nothing more.'

Darrard straightened up, hefting his shoulders. 'Surprising the crew didn't react faster when they heard the fire bell,' he observed. 'Does the bell come through on the CVR?'

Klein nodded. 'Come on up to Washington and Jeff Liss will arrange for you to hear the tape. We think the crew reacted very fast. There wasn't a hell of a lot of time between the bell sounding and the dutch roll, and they lost height fast.' He wiped the perspiration from his forehead: it was warm in the cramped, overcrowded flight deck. 'I've gotta take a look at the crash reassembly.'

There was a general shuffle as the men moved back into the cabin, talking in small groups. Klein stalked down the platform steps and looked across at the reassembly. Bradley appeared, holding a chunk of earth-caked metal, a tag dangling from it.

'Bit of the nosewheel door,' he said nonchalantly.

Klein stood with his left arm on his hip, right hand hanging loosely, slowly running his eye along the length of the partly reassembled fuselage. 'Looks like we can rule out the sabotage theory, from this side at least. What's it like on the right side?'

'Same. No bomb pattern.' Decreasing size of the fuselage skin fragments in any direction indicated an in-flight bomb explosion, the pieces being smaller nearer the point where a bomb had gone off. 'And no odour,' Bradley added. 'Bombs always leave a faint smell of nitrate.'

Klein climbed into the reassembly and stood, with Bradley, balancing on pieces of metal floor planking that had been recovered. Circular frames giving the fuselage its shape were suspended from the hangar ceiling girders, a quick and easy way to place major components in their correct position when gaps in the structure showed that parts were missing. Scores of shapeless seats, trailing ripped, bloodstained upholstery, were braced by wooden supports, and someone had laid scraps of gaily patterned carpet on the floor. Klein cautiously stepped along the aisle, lit with naked work lamps, and knelt to inspect the floor-support beams. They were, he noted, of the specially strengthened type, indicating that the CA-100 was a class of civil transport included in the United States Air Force's Civil Air Reserve Fleet. In case of war, hundreds of DC-10s, Boeing 747s, Lockheed TriStars, and other aircraft on the civil registry, including the Caravans already in airline service, could be commandeered by the military to transport army tanks, missile launchers, and other heavy equipment to a war zone.

'Has your group come up with anything tangible, Howard?'

'We've about ruled out structural failure. There's nothing in the flight data recorder printout showing anything structural. And Jeff played the CVR tape to us.'

Bradley paused reflectively. 'Everything goes back to that goddamned fire.'

'Any theories on how *that* started?'

Bradley pointed to a crack in the hunk of metal he was holding. 'Ask me what caused this crack, ask me the yield strength of a bit of aluminium the size of a pin-head and I can answer you. But a fire in the nose cone –' He shook his head and smiled wryly.

'What's your reaction to a fire caused by a source *external* to the aircraft?'

A puzzled look creased Bradley's oval face. 'External cause? How d'you mean, Steve?'

'Suppose the aircraft ran into an extremely high intensity energy source. A spurious beam from a micro-wave transmitting station, for instance.'

'You're not – er, serious?'

Klein had hoped Bradley would be more receptive to the idea. He'd suggested it to Bradley because the structures expert had only a slight knowledge of electronics and would be an objective person to sound out. 'Purely hypothetical,' he replied, disappointed.

Bradley stood with one foot crossed over the other, swinging the piece of debris in his hand. 'What sort of high-energy source did you have in mind, Steve?'

Encouraged, Klein said, 'Very high frequency radio waves, infra-red rays, for example. They're all invisible to the human eye. I thought –'

Bradley shook his head again. 'Death-ray stuff. Nobody'll go for that.'

Klein moved a step closer. 'But supposing – just supposing – a Russian spy satellite during one of its over-passes across the United States sent out spurts of high radiation energy.'

'And started a fire in the CA-100's nose cone?'

Klein anxiously studied Bradley's face for his reaction. A look of incredulity passed over Bradley's features.

'I'd say it's a no-no, Steve.' He saw the look on Klein's face and hurriedly added, 'The board members would think you're crazy.'

Would Harrilyn? Klein wondered. She was a down-to-earth type and had a reputation for possessing a receptive mind. The rest of the board members? He mentally envisaged himself explaining his hunch to the other four members. They were all men. As each passed through his mind, he realised that Bradley was right: not one of them, experts in judging the veracity of air accident reports before adding their signatures to what became public documents, would consider such a far-out idea. Yet he'd persuaded Malik to request a grounding of in-service CA-100s for four weeks. 'Oh, hell. It was just a crazy hunch,' he said offhandedly.

A gruff male voice boomed through the PA speakers in the hangar, echoing between the girders. 'Calling Mr Klein, Investigator-in-Charge. Please come to the office.'

He strode across the floor towards the lighted glass-enclosed office. 'Klein here,' he said into the phone.

'It's Ray Malik. You're out of luck, Steve. Grewson refuses to issue a grounding directive.'

Klein suddenly felt hollow inside.

'I don't mind telling you, Steve, I had my doubts – about your hunch, I mean.' Like everyone else, Klein thought. But Malik deserved credit: he'd been sceptical, but he'd tried. 'Grewson thought I was joking. When I told him I was dead serious, he laughed out loud.'

'He has a reputation for having an open mind,' Klein said sarcastically.

'What's happening up there, Steve?'

'We've not been incinerated by spurious electromagnetic waves.'

'Steve, for Christ's sake, don't go sour because of Grewson.'

Klein collected his thoughts. 'They've done a good job on the reassembly. Except for the nose fuselage, as you'd expect. Just a pile of bits in the corner. One thing's certain. It wasn't a sabotage job.'

'Fragmentation pattern's regular?'

'And no nitrate odour. Houston's already checked the engines on site and at the labs for bomb damage. Wings are clean too. I expect the FBI boys will confirm it.'

'Okay. My secretary's waving at me. I've got visitors. S'long.'

Klein replaced the receiver slowly. He stood for a long moment, his hand resting on the telephone. It rang again, and instinctively he picked it up. 'Klein here. Excuse me. It's the –'

'Oh, Steve.' He recognised Downey's soft voice.

'Yes, George. What's up?'

'I've got the official pathologists' report on the lactate profiles of the flight crew. The captain was definitely flying it. The lactate level in his arm muscles shows he was straining back on the yoke. The first officer's profile shows a lesser lactate level. Looks like he was helping on his yoke in the final seconds before it ploughed in.'

Another loose end tied up, Klein reflected. 'What progress with the passengers' bodies?'

'I've called in Interpol to help identify some of the foreign passengers. The manifest shows Italian, German, and Arab names, people who'd interconnected from overseas flights with Flight One-Three-Seven at O'Hare.'

'Any cases of smoke inhalation, George?'

'None. Not even the flight crew.'

A fire in the nose cone that sent no smoke into the flight deck, just heat. And caused three flameouts. Another confirmation of the CVR.

'Thought I'd give you a verbal interim report, Steve. How's the reassembly going?'

'Surprisingly good. But no clues. We're working on the theory that the fire in the nose cone was started by the collision avoidance equipment and spread through the electric cables to the throttles, shutting them and causing flameouts.'

There was silence on the line for several seconds. 'You still there, George?'

'I'm thinking about what you just said. Sounds a bit like the domino theory. Knock one down and the rest fall. We're dealing with a very complex set of circumstances. Aeroplanes don't drop from a CAVU sky. I've been trying to think up reasons for it these last few nights. Helps take my mind off cadavers.'

'Come up with any theories?'

'I saw Liss's printouts on the FDR and heard the CVR when I flew up to Washington day before yesterday to make my report to the Surgeon General. But I'm lost. My figuring is that we're dealing with something extraordinary.'

Should he try out his theory on him? It was tempting. George was easygoing, as far as his grim work allowed him to be, and never ventured a definitive opinion until he'd carefully considered the facts. The facts. He had no facts. Only a theory, a hunch. He decided against it.

'If you get any firm ideas, you know I need them. Thanks for letting me know about the flight crew.'

'Sure, see you later, Steve.'

Klein replaced the receiver. Incredibly, the telephone immediately rang again. 'Mr Klein, Investigator-in-Charge?' The voice was familiar. A dull, plodding, clear voice that Steve had learned to fear.

'Klein speaking.'

'It's Derrigan, sir. Duty Officer. Albuquerque ATC have this moment relayed a signal through the FAA office and asked me to pass it on to you.'

'What is it?' God, did the man have to speak like a damned robot?

'Albuquerque reports another CA-100 Caravan has had simultaneous flameouts on all engines, sir.'

'Yes – yes – '

'Re-ignition was successful. The aircraft landed safely at Albuquerque Airport a few minutes ago.'

TWELVE

'A second CA-100 with an all-engine flameout, for God's sake.'

'I just got the teletype from the FAA.' Malik's voice was strangely subdued.

Klein pressed the telephone receiver closer to his ear, recalling his earlier conversation with Malik. *On this flimsy evidence?* Despite the knot of frustration in his stomach, he resisted yelling into the mouthpiece. *See, I told you! It's happened to a second Caravan.* Air accident investigators were supposed to be patient and forebearing, he reminded himself.

'The teletype doesn't give details more'n re-ignition was successful and the aircraft landed safely.' Malik went on.

'In God's name, if Grewson doesn't ground those damned aeroplanes we must go to higher authority,' Klein blurted out.

'It's not possible under the legislation.'

'To hell with legislation. There's something screwy about CA-100 flameouts, and we've *got* to have them grounded.' The Bureau could only *recommend* to the FAA, he reflected bitterly. While aeroplanes fall out of the sky, the FAA sits on its ass.

'You *are* going to ask him again?' he continued.

'We've got a valid argument now.' Malik sounded really convinced at last. 'Hold a moment, Steve. Here's another teletype.'

Klein heard paper rustling in the background. 'It was a CA-100 belonging to American Overland Airlines

Flight Four-Five-Five. Hell, the aircraft was on Route Six, from O'Hare to L.A.'

'Say that again!'

'I said the flight was from O'Hare to L.A. On Route Six.' Malik paused. When he spoke again, his voice was pitched high. 'Steve, you may be on to something. Your idea of high-energy radiation – microwaves or – '

'Satellite-propagated?'

'Satellite-propagated,' Malik admitted grudgingly.

'What else does the teletype say?'

'Confirms three simultaneous flameouts, successful re-ignition, and safe landing at Albuquerque.'

'The aircraft's still there with the flight crew?'

'Yes.'

'I'm going right over.'

'I'll get on to Grewson. Good luck, Steve.'

Klein threw the receiver on the cradle and made for the door.

Klein sat in the front seat of the small cabin of the Avianjet he'd hurriedly hired from Skyway Charters, reflecting on the coincidence of his travelling on a type of aircraft currently under investigation. During the take-off he made a point of watching the pilot's hands dance over the levers with a confidence born of training and experience. He remembered what he'd written: *There are three possible explanations for the catastrophe resulting from one of the engines in reverse thrust at take-off*... and he wondered if Malik had taken up the redrafted report with General Counsel. The airspeed indicator needle moved around the dial as the pilot pushed forward the throttles of the twin-engined executive jet. At seven thousand feet the voice of the en-route controller came through the overhead speaker. 'Avianjet Four-Three-Three, turn on course. You are cleared for flight level two-seven-zero. Make next position report to Albuquerque Centre.'

Although he couldn't hear the pilot's voice, he saw him speak into the stick microphone attached to his headset. He slackened his seat belt, reclined the seat to a comfortable position, and leaned back. Houston, in the seat across the aisle, did the same thing. Liss, behind Houston, had his head down, reading an avionics technical journal. Across from Liss, directly behind Klein, sat Qand, his baby-pink face immersed in a newspaper. The aircraft climbed rapidly, and in a few minutes they were at cruising height. The pilot, who had introduced himself as Saul Collins, was a dark-haired slim man with angular features, who reminded Klein of a ferret. He swung aside the microphone and turned around.

'Here's a bar, gentlemen, inside this.' He put a bony finger on the cover of a hand-polished walnut cabinet built behind the open partition between the tiny flight deck and the cabin. 'Glasses are on the side.'

Klein shook his head. 'Thanks, no.'

'They're on the house. Part of Skyway's service.'

'Let's face it, I deserve it,' Houston said, smiling broadly. He turned around to the others. 'Anybody join me?'

Both Liss and Qand shook their heads. Houston opened the cabinet, surveyed the contents, reached for a bottle of Kentucky corn whiskey, critically examined the label, and poured himself a generous portion. He took a sip and smacked his lips. A grin spread from ear to ear. 'Alcohol works faster at altitude – and I'm not driving.'

Klein smiled and lay back on the embroidered headrest cover. It was about seven hundred air miles between Kansas City and Albuquerque. He looked up and glanced at the air-speed indicator: it showed 550 knots.

'What's your ETA for Albuquerque?' he asked Collins.

'Flight plan calls for eighteen hundred hours, sir. But we've got a twenty-five knot tail wind. If it keeps up, we should cut that by thirty minutes.'

'Can I borrow your nav chart a moment?'

'Sure can.'

Klein spread the chart on his knees. Route Six was

shown by a thick line, with intermediate airports between Kansas City and Albuquerque indicated by black triangles inside circles – Salina, Garden City, and Las Vegas. The Avianjet's course would take them over a large sector of Kansas, through a slice of Oklahoma, and into New Mexico. On impulse he asked Collins, 'Did you pick up Notams for this flight, Mr Collins?'

Collins pointed a finger at Ken Toye, the first officer, who took several sheets of paper from a shelf behind his seat and handed them to Collins.

'Four, sir,' Collins said.

'May I see them?'

'Sure. Help yourself.'

The first Notam was dated March 1, and referred to the prohibition on landing floatplanes at Lake McMillan in New Mexico. The next was concerned with restricted air space that covered a section of Kansas and limited all flights to below ten thousand feet. The third was for the radiosonde balloons from the unnamed Air Force base in Nevada. The fourth, the most recently dated Notam, was a warning to pilots to watch out for construction work at the end of a runway at Dodge City: the runway was being extended and would be closed at the hours specified.

He handed the Notams back to Collins. 'Any idea what this restricted air space is about, Mr Collins?'

Collins shrugged. 'Haven't a clue. Probably top-secret Air Force stuff.' He grinned. 'The way they're going, they'll soon have all the United States covered with restricted air space.'

Klein turned to Houston who had replaced the empty glass in the cabinet. 'Ackerman says there was a Notam issued to the captain of Flight One-Three-Seven about a restricted air space over Kansas. Issued by the Department of Defense. It's directly north of here, so wouldn't affect Route Six traffic. Got any idea what it might be?'

Houston reflected before replying. 'Could be anything, Steve. Rocket tests, airborne missle firing. Anything.'

'It's a hell of a big area. I traced the latitude and longitude co-ordinates on a nav chart.

'Couldn't you find out from the FAA?'

'It's top secret. So even the FAA don't know. Defense Department instructed them to issue the Notam and ask no questions.'

'Democracy, let's face it,' Houston commented.

Klein thought about the autocratic rulings of the Department of Defense. Off California a huge air space south of Los Angeles extending far out over the Pacific had been reserved for testing of undisclosed airborne equipment by the department, over objections by the FAA. Another massive block of air space had been restricted to all aircraft, except military aeroplanes on special assignments, off the Alaskan coast. He'd heard that the area was constantly patrolled by Airborne Warning and Control System aircraft, modified Boeing 707s, each with a garage-size streamlined disc mounted on pylons on the rear fuselage filled with highly sophisticated radar scanning devices. The aircraft cruised on zigzag courses as close to Chinese and Russian air space as was legally possible to pick up Communist aircraft targets and electronic signals. The recorded data the aircraft brought back to base were carefully sifted by electronic-countermeasures experts in Defense. The deciphered information was run through computers, processed, evaluated, and considered by scientists for new methods of jamming potential enemy radar defences. New Defense contracts were let to the military-industrial firms to design and produce updated countermeasures devices. By the time they went into service, the Russians and Chinese had improved their own silent, secret electronic warfare gear. In the meantime, fresh data were brought back by the patrolling United States aircraft, and the whole process started over again.

His thoughts were interrupted by Liss. 'Did you see this, Steve? Got it from Charlie Reynolds.' He handed

Klein a recent copy of the New York *Times*. 'THE CARAVAN CRASH: LAWSUITS PILE UP,' ran the headline.

Many hundreds of relatives of those killed in the CA-100 Caravan crash near Topeka, Kansas, in which four hundred and six passengers and crew lost their lives, have instituted suits against the aircraft's manufacturer, Astral Aircraft Corporation, California, and against American Constitution Airlines, operators of the aeroplane.

So far no official report on the cause of the disaster has been released.

The legal procedure is complicated by the fact that many of the dead passengers were foreign nationals. Astral Aircraft Corporation applied to a Los Angeles court for a motion to prevent these foreign citizens from bringing action against the company in California. Astral claimed that these cases should be tried in the country of the victim's nationality to prevent what in legal jargon is known as 'forum shopping' – picking a place for their suit to be tried where damage awards, if any, would be much bigger than if the case were tried in their own country.

The motion by Astral Aircraft Corporation was denied by Judge Andrew F. Thompson. Yesterday, counsel for the aircraft manufacturer cited a legal doctrine known as *forum non conveniens* – meaning that the place where the trial is to be held, namely California, is not suitable for the manufacturer. Counsel chose as its test case the action by a French woman widowed by the crash.

The motion denial now means that all foreign relatives of the crash victims may proceed with legal actions and have their cases heard in California. There are at least ninety foreign nationals involved, the *Times* learned from a source close to Washington. Dispositions are expected to start on July 15.

American Constitution Airlines, operators of the ill-fated aircraft, has filed a $50 million suit for damages against Astral Aircraft Corporation. The central claim is that the crash was caused by negligence on the part of the aeroplane manufacturer.

Klein snorted. The lawyers were already baring their teeth, like sharks nearing a carcass. He handed the newspaper back to Liss, who gave it to Houston. After he'd read it, he said, 'Turkish Airlines slapped a twenty-five-million-dollar lawsuit for damages against McDonnell-Douglas for negligence and recklessness.'

'The DC-10 case?'

Houston nodded.

Klein said, 'I seem to recollect the airline's lawyers brought action after studying charges that the FAA may have bowed to industry pressure and ignored our recommendations to correct the defects in the rear cargo door.'

Houston opened his great palms in a helpless gesture. 'Let's face it, the Bureau of Aviation Safety can't win 'em all.'

At a little after five-thirty the small jet began to lose height, and soon airport buildings, a runway, and taxi strips were in sight. In a few moments they were on the ground and taxiing towards the terminal building.

'There it is,' Klein said, pointing to a Caravan parked a hundred yards away from the terminal building. A portable fence had been rigged up around the aircraft, and several policemen stood guard.

Nobody spoke as they climbed out of the Avianjet and hurried across the asphalt. A beefy man in a grey suit came running to meet them, and several other men were grouped in the background.

'Mr Klein?'

Klein nodded.

'I'm Jerry Segraves, Airport Manager.'

A young man hurried up. 'Jim Bartino, Mr Klein.'

'You're the new man at Albuquerque Regional. I don't think we've met.' Klein shook his hand.

'I've impounded the CVR. It's in my office safe,' Bartino said with the self-conscious authority of a newly promoted official. 'I also asked the flight crew to stay until you arrived.'

'Where are they?'

'In my office. This way, sir.'

Captain Peter Haskett was tall and powerfully built.

Klein recognised that paradoxical easiness of manner that could be relied on to change to lightning-quick, controlled action in an emergency. He had cool, alert eyes set deep in an all-weather face, and a full thatch of grey hair. The four bars of gold braid on his epaulettes caught the sunlight slanting into the room. He was writing in the Aircraft Journey Log Book, smoke curling up from a cigarette held between lean fingers.

Haskett got up and introduced First Officer Ted Byers and Second Officer Don Felske. Felske was ascetic-looking and, of the three, looked the most worried. Which wasn't surprising, Klein reflected, since he had been responsible for the power output of the engines that had flamed out.

Bartino had chairs brought from another office and arranged around the table.

'Captain – ' Klein said. He nodded at Byers and Felske, who had pulled up chairs. 'I believe Mr Bartino told you why we're here.'

'Because we're the only surviving crew members of three simultaneous flameouts,' Captain Haskett said in a deep, self-assured voice.

'There have been other instances,' Klein said. 'What's happened to your passengers? Anybody hurt?'

'Just shaken up. They're waiting in the terminal. The airline's dispatching another aircraft to continue the flight to L.A.'

'A CA-100?'

Haskett shook his head. 'A Lockheed TriStar.'

Smart move by the airline's public relations department, Klein thought. If I'd been on Flight 455, I sure as hell wouldn't climb aboard another CA-100.

'What happened, Captain?' Klein asked.

Haskett pulled his chair closer to the table and studied his notes for a full minute before speaking. 'I'll take you back to our en-route clearance from Kansas City Centre. We were at thirty-five thousand feet, on autopilot, and ' – he opened the log book and turned the pages – 'at five-five-zero true airspeed. Course was two-

two-five. We were estimating L.A. a little earlier than our original ETA on account of a twenty-five-knot tail wind. He looked up, and Klein nodded appreciatively.

'Kansas City Centre informed us that no further position reports were necessary until we came under Albuquerque ATC. The flight was normal, just like any other day. We'd just entered Albuquerque's control area when I smelled something burning.' Haskett stopped reflectively and picked his front teeth with his thumbnail before consulting his notes again.

'Smelled?' Klein queried.

'It wasn't exactly a *smell*. More like warm air coming from the floor in front of the pedestal. I immediately asked Don' – he nodded at his second officer – 'to check the inside temperature on his panel gauge. He reported seventy-two degrees. Normal. Then we had flameouts, on all engines.' He looked up, surprised. 'Just like that. No warning, no nothing.'

'Did the fire warning bell go off?'

'Simultaneously with the flameouts. The aircraft rolled steeply, a dutch roll, and we began to lose height in a hurry. I snapped off auto-throttle and called to Ted to help control the roll. We were lucky. I ordered Don to re-ignite all engines simultaneously; otherwise we'd get asymmetrical power. They re-ignited right away. By that time we'd lost seventeen thousand feet. At eighteen thousand feet I levelled off and requested clearance to land at Albuquerque.'

The room fell silent. Klein sensed that the three crew members were mentally reliving the experience.

'Two questions, Captain. You said you were on auto-pilot. Were you also on auto-throttle?'

'Yes, sir. Don kicked it off when he re-ignited.'

Klein turned to Felske. 'In what position were the throttle levers when you re-ignited?'

'The damned things had slammed shut.' Felske scratched a bald spot on his head, looking puzzled. 'I don't understand it.'

'The other question, Captain. You were at flight level three-five-zero, thirty-five thousand feet. When it started to roll, you put the nose down to pick up speed. Can you remember your rate of descent?'

'We went down at four thousand feet a minute.'

'Is there anything else you think may be relevant, Captain? That might help pinpoint what went wrong on the other CA-100?'

Haskett checked his notes again, and the log. 'I think that's it,' he said conclusively.

'No further trouble with the engines between re-ignition and landing, for instance?'

'They behaved themselves,' Haskett said. 'Normal functioning to the moment of shutdown.'

Klein turned to Bartino. 'Let's inspect the aircraft.'

'We can walk over. It's not far.'

'Coming, Captain?' Klein said, his glance taking in the other crew members. 'I think you'll find this interesting.'

Haskett looked mystified. He picked up his notes and the aircraft's log book and put them in his brainbag, the capacious square leather bag pilots carry, so called because it contains the all-important navigation maps and airport runway layouts. They followed Bartino down a flight of steps and through a door that led to the asphalt. The policeman let them through the barrier, and Klein turned to Bartino. 'We'll need a platform to open the nose cone. Will you arrange it, please?'

'The nose cone? Aren't you going to check the flight deck, sir?'

'Later.'

The mobile platform drove up and was positioned near the aircraft's nose. Klein mounted the steps two at a time. Houston, Liss, Qand, and the flight crew gathered around him. He swivelled and twisted the recessed catches securing the nose cone, and Liss helped ease the cone on its hinges away from the front of the aircraft. An acrid odour of burned plastic material and electric cables wafted out on the cool evening air.

'Jesus!' Felske exclaimed.

'A goddamned fire?' Haskett asked.

Klein and Liss exchanged glances. 'Yes, Captain. That's the cause of the warm air you felt,' Klein said.

Haskett bent to peer into the interior of the nose fuselage. 'Weather radar? No, collision avoidance gear by the look of it. The scanner looks like it's been hit by a blowtorch. And those cables. Christ! Crisped to a cinder.'

'How in hell's name would that shut down the auto-throttle, sir?' Felske asked.

Klein knelt on the platform. 'You see that junction box for the cables?'

'The big one way back? Where the power comes off the main supply?' Felske asked.

'There's a bunch of cables passing up through the pressure bulkhead. See it?'

'Yes.'

'It goes through the flight deck floor, into the pedestal, carrying cables for the collision avoidance gear and the auto-throttle. If you look closely, you can see the cables are burned.'

'Why didn't we get a depressurisation?' Haskett asked.

'There's an airtight electrical connector at the bulkhead,' Klein explained.

'But the higher pressure inside the aircraft would slowly leak outward when the cables burned through the connector,' Felske protested.

He knows his job and his theory, Klein thought. 'That's right. But the cables burned into the connector. Despite the slight leak of air pressure, you'd smell burning on the flight deck.'

Byers scratched the top of his head. 'But what caused the fire, sir?'

'That's what we're trying to find out,' Klein replied.

'Is this how the crashed CA-100 looked?' asked Captain Haskett. 'What remained of it?'

Klein nodded. 'As near as we can make out from the

reassembly of the bits. Was there any traffic near you when you first noticed the heat, Captain?'

'Nothing within fifteen miles, as far as I recall. ATC will know for sure.'

'We'll check later. What was the weather?'

'CAVU.'

Klein examined the collision avoidance scanner. The formerly mirror surface was blackened, with rainbow colours at the edges. He scratched the surface with his nail and smelled it. 'Carbonised,' he said to Liss.

'Very high temperature,' Liss said. He shook his head. 'Beats all logic.'

Klein reflected uneasily: completely illogical and so far inexplicable. But, he vowed, he was *not* going to write into the final report, 'Conclusion: *This accident has no determinable cause.*' He turned away and descended the steps. Bartino closed the nose cone, locked it, and followed the others down.

They entered the flight deck, and body odours were noticeable in the crammed un-air-conditioned space. Haskett demonstrated how the throttle levers had moved from their Cruise position to Closed. After further questioning Byers and Felske, Klein said, 'Thank you, gentlemen,' and stomped down the steps with a frown on his face.

'Where's the nearest phone?' he demanded of Bartino.

'In my office, sir.'

Inside the office he spun the telephone dial.

'Hello, Malik speaking.'

'It's Steve. We're still clueless. But the collision avoidance gear is burned to a frazzle, just like the first aircraft. And the cables to the pedestal are burned, and the auto-throttle slammed shut from Cruise. For God's sake, is Grewson going to ground all these goddamned aircraft or isn't he?'

'He still refuses.'

Klein was stunned. Finally he became sarcastic. 'Whose pocket is he in, the airline's or Capitol Hill's?'

'You know better than that.'

'I sure do, Ray.' Klein stuck out his jaw defiantly. 'If we don't get an FAA directive immediately grounding every CA-100, the airlines *and* Capitol Hill will be on our necks.'

A long sigh came over the line. 'When are you coming back to Washington?'

'Right away.'

'Report to me when you arrive. I may have some good news.'

Like hell. Grewson's not going to ground those aircraft. But I think I know who will. Klein tossed the telephone on the cradle and fished in his pocket for the Go-Team roster he'd ripped from the notice board in his office. He looked down the list of telephone and Bellboy numbers, lifted the receiver, and dialled. A female voice answered, 'Mrs Harrilyn's office. May I help you?'

Part V
Simulation

THIRTEEN

Klein stalked past Shaw's vacant desk, hung his jacket on the coat rack, and lay flat on his back in the middle of his office. He drew in several deep abdominal breaths, releasing the air in long, controlled, audible sighs. Slowing his breathing and allowing it to take care of itself, he directed his concentration to his legs and trunk, and slowly lifted his legs high into the air and backwards over his head until he attained the Pose of Tranquillity, with only his left hand supporting his ankles. He stayed in this position for five minutes and then, with perfect control, allowed his legs to slowly return to the carpet until his body was once more in a straight line. He bent forward until he was sitting cross-legged in the Easy Pose.

'OM . . . OM . . . OM . . . ' He let the sound vibrate in his chest. It reverberated around the small room.

'Shanti . . . peace . . . shalom . . . '

He remained in the Easy Pose for some minutes, enjoying the quietness that suffused his whole being, before slowly getting to his feet and moving to the chair behind the desk.

There was a neat pile of correspondence that Shaw had prepared for his signature, but he ignored it and reached for a familiar blue-covered report. It was from Liss's Systems Group. He opened it and read rapidly, so quickly that an observer might have thought he was merely glancing at the typescript as he flipped the pages. But Klein was reading every word, weighing up the significance of Liss's findings, automatically correlating each fact with the reports of the other group chairmen, which had begun to arrive on his desk.

Under 'Conclusions', page fifteen, Liss had written: *After exhaustive laboratory tests with the remains of the wiring and debris recovered from the wreckage, and in close association with the Powerplant Group, Chairman William P. Houston, and the manufacturers of the auto-throttle equipment and of the collision avoidance equipment, we believe that the auto-throttle limit switches failed due to an overheat condition. Electrical failure of the auto-throttle control resulted, causing simultaneous flameouts on all engines. The cause of the fire in the nose cone is unknown.*

He read the draft reports that had come in from other group chairmen, eventually to be incorporated into the over-all accident report he would have to write. Houston's was headed 'Preliminary', and so was Downey's. Bradley's Conclusion was definite: *We conclude that no primary structural failure of the aircraft occurred in flight; the exception is the non-load-bearing nose cone. Trajectory analysis indicates this component separated from the aircraft four seconds before impact.*

Regional's report, signed by Armstrong, confirmed Klein's suspicion that the stolen hinge fitting would not be returned by the souvenir hunter, and there were no other witnesses who could add anything of value. Len Davies' report on the weather, taken from the meteorological data filed for Flight 137 at O'Hare, confirmed CAVU for the whole of the flight's projected course, from Chicago to Los Angeles. He searched for a report from Dave Jacobs, chairman of the Air Traffic Control Group, but couldn't find one.

He shoved the reports aside. Everything came back to the cause of the fire: not the fire itself, but the *cause*, he reflected. There was a movement outside the door. 'Is that you, Shaw?'

'Oh, you're back, Steve.' She came in, studying his face to gauge the progress of the accident investigation. From what she saw, the CA-100 case was going badly.

'I can't find Dave Jacobs' report here, Shaw.' He leaned towards the Investigations-in-Progress chart on the wall, checking the plastic strips. 'It's not marked.'

'He hasn't sent it along yet.'

'Probably waiting to check the dummy radarscope. Has Kansas City sent it up?'

'I checked the labs yesterday. It's coming this morning.'

She saw the worry in his eyes and the deep lines running from his nostrils to the corners of his mouth. The beneficial effects of his yoga relaxation had already dissipated. She sat in the chair and lit a cigarette.

'I've never seen you like this before, Steve. Is it *that* bad?'

Klein felt a surge of self-pity. He pointed to the blue reports. 'Everything's so goddamned negative. And three weeks of a four-week grounding directive already gone.'

'Steve, don't give up on your hunch. You've always been right in the past.'

He leaned back, twiddling the handle of the letter opener. 'I've just been lucky, Shaw.'

'Stop feeling sorry for yourself, and stick to your guns. You made Malik and Grewson ground the aircraft on a theory based on your hunch. Don't give up now.'

'Grewson didn't ground the Caravans on my hunch, you gotta believe. I went over Malik's head and Grewson's bureaucracy and asked Mrs Harrilyn to intervene. She contacted Congressional Liaison and had senatorial pressure put on Grewson.'

'Hell, he must *love* you.'

'He doesn't know yet. But he'll figure it out eventually.' He looked out of the window. 'God, I wish I had a firm clue.'

'You haven't exhausted all leads, Steve. You're going to run through the flight simulator tests today, remember?'

He brightened and pointed to the letters waiting to be signed. 'What's in here, Shaw?'

'Routine stuff.' She sifted several reports and letters. 'This covers the disposition of the Lockheed TriStar case, and here's the final on the DC-10 that missed the approach at Logan and hit the seawall. The rest are light aircraft Minors.'

'I'll take them home tonight and you can distribute them tomorrow. Please phone the labs again and see if the dummy scope has arrived. If it has, ask Dave to meet me there in five minutes. Then get us two seats on the earliest scheduled flight to Chicago. O'Hare. We'll take the tapes and play them through the simulator.'

Shaw rose and went to her telephone outside, and he wondered if it was possible to hook up the flight data recorder tape to the flight simulator in addition to the ATC tapes. That way they'd get the closest simulation of what went on in the cockpit of Flight 137. He dialled the phone.

'Jeff Liss, Systems.'

'It's Steve. Can you hook the FDR tape up to a CA-100 flight simulator? That way the simulator will manoeuvre like the actual aircraft before it crashed.'

Liss hesitated. 'I guess it could be done. It'll take a bit of cooking to get it synchronised.'

'Dave and I are going to O'Hare to play back the ATC tapes in the simulator. You free?'

'Yes.'

'I'll give you a shout in thirty minutes.' He put down the receiver. Shaw entered.

'The radarscope's arrived. Dave is on his way to the lab now.'

'Thanks, Shaw. Book *three* tickets for O'Hare. Jeff's coming too.'

Dave Jacobs was waiting at the foot of the stairs in front of the laboratories. He was a stocky little man of about forty, nattily dressed in a well-tailored dark suit but wearing a shirt half a collar size too small. As a result, he had a perpetual roll of fat at the back of his pink neck that exaggerated his stoutness.

'You still got the tapes locked up, Dave?'

Jacobs ran a pudgy finger around the inside of his collar. 'In the safe.' Veins wriggled at his temples when he spoke.

They walked smartly along the corridor, past Turney's laboratory, and entered a small room. Electronic equipment stood on a bench, and power transformers lined one wall. A television set with a round picture tube rested on a table in the middle of the room. It was in fact an exact replica of the radarscope used by air traffic controllers to guide aircraft along airways.

Jacobs crossed to the transformers and yanked down a massive lever. In a few seconds the radarscope flickered into life; Jacobs switched off the room light, and the two men stood for half a minute in front of the scope, waiting for the green translucent light to stabilise. Except for the absence of the radial finger of light that swept around a real working radarscope every four seconds, the scope showed an exact reproduction of the position of all air traffic within a two-hundred-mile radius of Kansas City Airport at the moment the controller on duty responsible for 'working' Flight 137 reported that the flight's blip had vanished. Klein studied the blips on the scope and their relationship to the concentric circles representing twenty-five-mile distances from the airport.

'I froze it at Zulu 10.52.37,' Jacobs explained. 'That's the time the en-route controller estimated Flight 137's blip disappeared. Corresponds with the CVR too.' He put his finger on the glass. 'About one hundred and fifty miles southwest of Kansas City ATC Centre.' He moved his finger to another blip. 'Up here we have an Air Canada DC-8 swinging on to Air Route Six. This is TWA's flight from O'Hare to San Francisco via Denver. Here's Continental's flight from L.A. bound for O'Hare, and this is Delta's flight coming out of Springfield.' He stabbed the scope near the top. 'North West Airlines milk run from Milwaukee. Goes through the Midwest every morning regular as clockwork. In the middle here's a Cessna 172 under visual flight rules on the approach to Kansas City.' The woman pilot requesting landing clearance, Klein told himself; the woman the first officer on Flight 137 had rudely remarked about.

'Does the Cessna's landing request come through on the tapes, Dave?'

'A bit blurred. She got clearance immediately, from three thousand feet.'

'What's this?' Klein pointed to a cluster of fluorescent dots in the southern sector of the radarscope.

Jacobs produced an envelope from his pocket. He extracted several strips of paper eight inches long and an inch wide: the Flight Progress Strips used by air traffic controllers to check flights through their sectors. Each strip was inserted in a plastic holder and put in the controller's console tray at the appropriate flight level representing the aircraft's altitude. As the aircraft's blip crept across his radarscope, the controller scribbled remarks on the aircraft's heading, requests by its captain for clearance to another flight level, and the time the flight entered and left his sector.

'This is an SAS overflight from Copenhagen to L.A. at flight level three-niner-zero,' Jacobs said, handing Klein a paper strip. He pointed to the edge of the scope. 'He's way up here, northwest. And here's a Seaboard World freighter on an overflight from Honolulu bound for New York, taking advantage of Great Circle and a forty-knot tail wind.'

'What've we got down here?' Klein asked, tapping the glass at the bunch of blips at bottom scope.

'General Aviation inward bound to Washington.' Jacobs shuffled the strips. 'A Learjet here and an Avianjet over here. This is light stuff below two thousand feet, from the Dodge City flying club.'

'Indian country,' Klein remarked appreciatively, airline pilots' jargon for the Cheyennes, Apaches, Cherokees, and Navajos, light planes that rose in flocks from flying clubs all over the United States any fine spring day, especially week-ends. With the Learjets, Avianjets, and other executive aircraft, they comprised the category of aviation known as General Aviation, representing more than 98 per cent of all civil aircraft on the United States registry: the commercial airlines combined represented less than 2 per cent of the total aircraft in the United States. The number of accidents to General Aviation aircraft far exceeded those of scheduled airlines: more than five thousand a year for General Aviation compared with about a hundred for aircraft operated by airlines. These statistics included minor accidents as well as the major catastrophes: a bent undercarriage, a slight collision on the ground, a wing tip shaved on a hangar door.

Klein stepped back and studied the scope from a distance. 'There's nothing close to Flight 137,' he said.

'The Continental flight is nearest. Twenty miles away. At twenty-nine thousand feet.'

Klein rubbed his chin thoughtfully. Obviously the collision avoidance system could not pick up a target that far away. Pelrine had explained it was set for a range of five hundred feet. Jacobs handed him another strip. 'Flight 137,' he said dryly, digging his fingertip under his shirt collar.

Klein took the paper. It was an awesome feeling to hold a strip of paper representing the last tangible link with four hundred and six human beings thirty-five seconds before their lives had been snuffed out. He read the controller's annotation. 'Fl. 137 reported at flight level 310. Zulu 10.40.40.' He turned to Jacobs. 'Does the Zulu check with the ATC tapes?'

'Exactly.'

Klein was silent for several seconds. 'How's the controller?'

Jacobs made a birdlike stretching gesture with his neck, freeing it from his collar. 'Grim. He's on compassionate leave. The supervisor asked me if I wanted to interview him. I didn't, of course.'

Klein moved away from the scope. 'Turn it off, Dave.' He handed the Flight Progress Strip back to Jacobs.

'Lock it in the safe with the others. Evidence for the public inquiry. You've made copies?'

Jacobs nodded and switched off the power supply. The fluorescent light faded from the scope.

'I've asked Jeff to come to O'Hare. He thinks he can play back the FDR in the simulator with your ATC tapes.' Klein looked at his watch. 'I'll see you at the airport. Check Shaw for the flight number.'

'The airline's vice-president of operations has cleared Captain Haskett and his crew to run through the tests,' Liss said.

'Good work,' Klein said appreciatively.

'They'll be along any moment.'

Klein looked up at the exterior of the CA-100 flight simulator, where technicians made last-minute adjustments. It reminded him of a giant's shoe supported on hydraulic struts. The toe part of the shoe was a replica of the nose of a CA-100, except that the windshield and side windows were covered with panels extending several inches away from where the glass would be. The panels contained flat television-like screens that, from inside the simulator flight deck, portrayed the exact scene that the crew would see when they 'flew' the simulator. The heel contained masses of electronic gear and a console and seat for the check pilot. Every three months, according to FAA regulations, an airline's flight crew were retested in the appropriate simulator by a tough FAA check pilot. If a crew member failed the examination, he was given a week or two to relearn the complex procedures and then be rechecked. In some cases a check pilot might insist that the crew member fly an actual aircraft, with the check pilot in the jump seat. Airlines hated having to haul one of their fleet out of service for testing aircrew: airliners were costly to operate, not to mention the loss of revenue. Klein recalled the figures an airline vice-president of operations had once quoted: it cost $2,200 an hour to fly a Lockheed TriStar and $240 an hour to operate a TriStar simulator.

He strode up the stairs that took him to a landing on a level with the entrance to the simulator. A bank of computers was against the wall, with cables meandering across the floor to switchgear at the back of the simulator. The simulator was separated from the concrete landing by a short bridge, which was pulled up after the crew entered to allow the simulator freedom of action as it nosed up for take-off, banked at steep angles, and dived as the man at the controls worked the yoke and rudder pedals.

'Quite something, eh?' Jacobs remarked.

'At three million bucks a throw, it should be. Ah – here's Captain Haskett and crew,' Klein said. He nodded as the three men entered from a door at the other end of the landing. 'Everything hooked up?' he asked Liss.

'Yes.'

'The ATC tapes are lined up,' Jacobs confirmed.

Klein turned to Captain Haskett and pointed to the brainbags he and his crew carried.

Haskett grinned. 'Failure point number one. Anybody who forgets to take his brainbag aboard.'

'Here're copies of the CVR printout, Captain,' Klein said, handing a sheaf of papers to each crew member. 'Please look at the legend in the front. I want each of you to speak the words the actual crew of Flight One-Three-Seven spoke. I'll speak the stewardess's lines. We've cut the speech out of the tape, but left the engine and other noises. When we come to asterisks, just say "unintelligible word". The same for the other symbols – just speak them. And pause if you see a long dash. Everybody got it?'

'It's clear to me,' Haskett said. 'Let's go aboard.' He seemed anxious to get it over.

Liss fiddled with equipment he had set up on a trolley on the landing, gave precise instructions to one of the technicians, and stepped across the bridge. Felske was the last to board, pulling up the bridge to isolate the simulator from the concrete landing.

Captain Haskett lowered his massive frame into the

left-hand seat, taking care to avoid the three throttle levers, switches, and knobs sprouting from the pedestal. Byers got into the right-hand seat, and Felske sat in the second officer's chair facing the huge panel on the right-hand wall. He studied the maze of dials, switches, and fuel flow charts, turned, and pulled a switch at the back of the simulator. From his position in the jump seat behind Haskett, Klein saw the simulated runway with its white dashed centre line, green grass at the sides, and the Chicago skyline in the distance, as if he were looking out of a real CA-100 lined up for take-off on a real runway, an illusion created by videotape. He passed his eyes over the instrument panel, the ceiling with its emergency fire bottle pull handles, switches, and levers. Even the ashtray at the crew positions and recessed holders on the windowsill for coffee cups had been included in the simulator. On the floor was Haskett's brainbag, filled with maps, Standard Instrument Departure and Approach plates, his pipe and tobacco pouch. Klein found it difficult to remember that he was not actually on the flight deck of a real aeroplane.

Haskett, as an automatic reaction to his hours of training, reached for his shoulder harness and fastened it. Byers and Felske did the same. 'Do you want us to go through the emergency fire and other drills we do before take-off, sir? I dummied up a mock flight plan.' Haskett pulled a sheet of paper from his brainbag. 'From O'Hare to L.A.' He grinned. 'I'm an optimist by nature.'

Klein had intended to use the simulator to duplicate Flight 137's last half hour of flight. But Haskett had a point. Why not duplicate the complete flight from take-off to the proposed destination? That way they'd be sure to cover everything. On the other hand, duplicating the complete take-off procedure and the climb to cruising altitude was unnecessary. The unknown critical thing that had occurred on board Flight 137 had taken place in the few minutes after the aircraft overflew Kansas City.

'It's a good suggestion, Captain. But not necessary.

Let's start at the point where Flight One-Three-Seven approaches Kansas City.'

Haskett put down the flight plan and picked up the CVR printout. 'Where the Kansas City en-route controller picks him up?'

'Yes. Have you got the ATC chatter?'

Haskett examined the first sheet. 'Yes. It's been added to the front of this.' He turned to Felske. 'Start *all* engines simultaneously and shove us up to flight level three-one-zero at a true airspeed of four-niner-five knots.'

Felske pulled switches on the back panel, and a high-pitched slipstream whine overlaid with the distant rumble of three jet engines shattered the flight deck. The airspeed indicator needles on Haskett's and Byers' panels jumped to 495 knots, the altimeter readout soared to 31,000 feet, and the engine power gauges suddenly flipped to their Cruise positions. The runway had vanished. Klein now saw the pleasant Kansas countryside, hazy under the morning mist, and miles of open wheatfields and green pastureland sliding under the aircraft's nose. Klein knew that if he'd called for turbulence to be simulated, Felske could flip the appropriate switch and the simulator's flight deck would pitch and roll on its telescopic support struts, actuated by signals from the computer outside.

'Quick blast-off,' Haskett dryly commented, examining his instruments.

They went through the simulation, speaking from the text ending with the simulator tilted nose down at the extremity of its limit and the instruments and visual displays frozen at the point of impact. Liss wrote down all the instrument readings to compare later with the FDR printout. But the test was a disappointment – in no way did it allow a 'post-mortem' to be made – and Haskett and his crew sat in silence, slouched forward in the sloping machine.

Klein was utterly dejected, his hopes dashed. There was nothing else left: they had gone through every standard test and followed through with all conceivable experiments, from metallurgical testing to flight simulation. Nothing – not a solid clue.

He looked at the crew. It was clear that they had detested going through the pantomime. Pilots rarely talked about crashes, much less simulated them. But he wasn't satisfied, and talked them into a second try. Again, nothing.

'That's enough of that,' he exclaimed. He followed them out of the simulator, feeling strange suddenly passing from the world of a simulated flight deck to the dusty concrete landing where a cleaner pushed a wide broom across the floor. Klein shook hands with Captain Haskett and the others and thanked them again. When they had gone, he stood in the middle of the landing with Liss and Jacobs, chewing his tongue thoughtfully. The others, sensing his need to be left alone, walked on. Klein suddenly jerked his head and ran after the others.

'There's another test!' he called out. 'A final, conclusive test. The last resort if we want to clear up this goddamned mystery before the grounding directive expires next week.' Liss recognised the tone of voice Klein used when he'd come to a decision from which nothing would deflect him.

'What's that, Steve?'

'Run a *real* flight of a CA-100 from O'Hare to L.A. duplicating everything exactly as it took place on the deck of Flight One-Three-Seven. I want to see for myself what the hell went on thirty miles southwest of Topeka. For *real*, at thirty-one thousand feet.' He cast a contemptuous glance back at the flight simulator. 'Not what a bunch of your electronic wizardry shows on a make-believe flight deck.'

Part VI
Re-Enactment

FOURTEEN

'Where's George?' Klein asked, looking around his office, where the Go-Team occupied seats or stood against the walls.

'Here he is,' Houston said, putting a cup of coffee on the edge of Klein's desk and sinking his teeth into an enormous apple. Downey's slouched form appeared in the doorway. He nodded at Steve, shuffled to the back of the room, and squeezed between Ackerman and Bradley.

Klein picked up the letter opener and tapped it on the desk. He felt drained. 'I've been through all your reports,' he said in a dry voice. 'And we've done simulator trials and drawn a big zero.'

He tossed aside the letter opener and stabbed a button on his desk. Shaw's face appeared around the door.

'When did you say the public inquiry's gonna start?' he asked.

'July seventh.'

'God – *that* close. Where the hell does the time go?'

'I always ask myself the same question, Steve.' She smiled at the others and withdrew.

Klein checked his calendar. 'That gives us seven days to come up with a probable cause – if not *the* cause – and twenty-one days to prepare a final report and get it okayed by the board,' he said. 'Everybody's got a finger in it now – the Air Transport Association, Civil Aeronautics Board, ALPA of course, and the Aerospace Industries Association. And we can expect observers from the Senate Subcommittee on Aviation Safety. Just our luck they set it up two months ago,' he said caustically.

He picked up a letter with the FBI imprint. 'The FBI confirms our findings on the sabotage question. No bomb,' he said. 'They've researched the backgrounds of three hundred and thirty passengers and cleared them. When they have the others they'll let us know.'

'That's quick work,' Davies remarked. 'What did they say about the Zionist guy on board – the fellow you mentioned at last week's meeting?'

'He was included in the check, so the no-sabotage conclusion automatically rules that out.'

There was a general buzz of consent. Bradley summed it up in one word. 'Agreed.'

'And here's your report on Weight and Balance, Don,' Klein went on, nodding at Ackerman. 'The aircraft was properly loaded before take-off. The centre of gravity was within the specified limits.' He looked around the room. 'Anybody got anything new to report?'

'The press hounds are on my neck again,' Charlie Reynolds said ruefully. 'There's been a dozen calls since yesterday.'

Klein pointed a finger at him, his eyes hardening as he thought of the way some newsmen had behaved at the wreckage site. 'We're not holding another press conference until we get at least a probable cause.'

Liss, sitting near Klein's desk, asked diffidently, 'And how are we going to get that?'

'Re-enact the flight,' Klein replied, looking up sharply.

'How d'you mean?' Howard Bradley asked, knowing exactly what Klein had in mind.

'Re-enact Flight One-Three-Seven's trip from O'Hare to the Point of Inevitability –'

'But all CA-100s are grounded,' Houston interrupted, slurping coffee.

'So we'll put one back in service,' Klein said implacably. The mantle of depression that had descended after a sleepless night had begun to lift with the prospect of action.

'Ray Malik won't go for that,' Len Davies said.

Liss put a hand on Klein's arm. 'I'd like to come along, Steve,' he said quietly.

'Let's face it. You're gonna need a powerplant expert aboard. I'm coming too,' Houston said determinedly.

'You'll need someone to monitor the ATC,' Jacobs said, jerking his neck.

Klein was overcome. He'd never been consciously aware of the loyalty of his staff. They'd always worked well together, but he hadn't realised before that they regarded him with a special sort of respect. The telephone rang, together they went to a crash site, sifted through the wreckage, each man doing what he had been trained to do; they held meetings like this, and debated what they'd discovered, argued theories, called in outside experts, and wrote their reports. Now they were insisting that they accompany him on a flight that was likely to be hazardous: in the eyes of some, he guessed, highly dangerous. He stared at the chart on the wall for a moment, collecting his thoughts.

'The way I figured it,' he said slowly, looking around the room, 'the only guy needed on the flight deck besides the crew is the IIC.'

'Like hell, Steve,' Houston exclaimed. 'You're gonna need somebody to watch those throttle levers and power settings.' He glanced at Liss. 'And someone to check out the electronics and –'

'I've worked on aircraft for ten years, and I'm telling you that practically every system in a modern aeroplane is controlled by electronics or electrics and all electronics and electrics can fail, as we've seen,' Liss said breathlessly.

The room fell silent, then everybody laughed at the vision of a flight deck crowded with so many of the Go-Team. When the laughter subsided, Downey asked, 'Can you get a crew, Steve?'

'I'm sure,' Klein replied, thinking of Haskett, Byers, and Felske.

'You're – uh – sure – you want to go through with it?' Downey said.

'My mind's made up. Hell, it's a chance to solve the unsolvable.'

'What if nothing happens?' Downey asked. He knew what Klein's answer would be.

'We'll backtrack and try again.'

'To the Point of Inevitability?' Downey leaned forward.

'If necessary.'

Downey made a sound like a bear sighing and stepped back against the wall. From long association with Klein he knew it was useless to argue.

'Jesus, Steve. It's a hell of a risk,' Houston said.

'It's the only way. In a week's time the airlines will be flying Caravans again.'

'Is this based on your idea that the fire was caused by high-intensity energy?' Bradley asked. 'The external source you mentioned the other day?'

'That's what I want to discuss,' Klein said. He leaned back in the chair. 'I've already talked about my theory – hunch, if you like – with Ray Malik. He was only half sold on the idea. Briefly, I believe the fire was caused by an external agency. High-intensity energy from an electronic source like microwave scanning radiation or extremely high frequency radio-wave propagation, in the upper part of the radio spectrum.'

Klein went on, ignoring the look of incredulity on Bradley's face. Houston, eyebrows raised, munched his apple. 'I'm not thinking of ground-based electronic equipment, but propagation from a satellite overflying the United States. Specifically Russian spy overflights – '

'The newsboys would really go to town on that,' Reynolds interrupted. 'I can see the three-inch headlines.'

'It's way out, Steve – ' Davies muttered.

'So was high-frequency metal fatigue that blew up British Comet airliners years ago. Nobody, but nobody, dreamed of that despite the tough testing. Have you guys forgotten what happened when the Lockheed

Electras went into airline service? God, we had enough of *them* to investigate. Who'd have thought wings would snap off due to vibration?'

'But satellites, Steve?' Downey said appealingly.

'You've given me an idea,' Liss said slowly. 'Frankly, I don't think energy from a passing satellite would be strong enough to cause a fire of that intensity. There'd have to be neat bundles of energy in a very narrow wave band.' He shook his head. 'Unless the Russians have developed something entirely new to pinpoint our electronic defence signals. But you've given me an idea. What about the missile counter-measures gear Defense is developing?'

'How d'you mean?' asked Len Davies.

'Defense is doing top-secret experiments to detect oncoming enemy missiles so that they can be destroyed before they land. The Air Force avionics labs and their flight dynamics labs are working on it. They've got a test evaluation centre at Randolph Air Force Base in Texas, and they're working on optical transmission wave bands at the Naval Air Development Center in Warminster, Pennsylvania.' He looked up thoughtfully. 'And the Air Force avionics labs are doing voice-jamming experiments under contract with the Pentagon's Office of the Director of Telecommunications and Command and Control Systems.'

'How in hell's name do you know all this?' Reynolds demanded. 'Who's the press information guy around here anyway?'

'Let's face it, our Jeff's a regular spy,' Houston remarked, grinning.

'It's all in the *Electronic Engineer's Quarterly Journal*,' Liss replied modestly. 'General unclassified information.'

Klein felt relieved. He'd expected to be laughed down. Now Liss, good old reliable Liss, had come to his aid.

'Got any details about these experiments, Jeff?' he asked.

Liss shook his head. 'No more than I've told you. But there's a lot going on in different fields. I heard that NASA's Marshall Space Flight Center is in on this anti-missile work.'

'If it's to do with satellites, you *may* have something, Steve,' Houston said. But Klein saw by the set of his lips that he was only half convinced.

'Let's suppose, just suppose,' Klein said, turning to Liss, 'that spurious radiation leaked from some of this gear they're using. Would it have enough energy to set fire to electric cables and distort a steel scanner in an aircraft flying at thirty-one thousand feet?'

'Depends on the power source. But I suspect the military are using energy sources up in the tens of thousands of watts range.' He cocked his head reflectively. 'If the range was fairly short, say a few miles, there'd be enough energy to set fire to wires. The nose cone is transparent to radar waves, as you know, so it wouldn't act like a protective shield.'

'Then we may be on to something, eh?' Klein purposely stressed the 'we'.

'*You* may think you're on to something, Steve,' Houston said, tossing an apple core into Klein's wastepaper container.

'I'm just sounding everybody out. I think we've got a consensus. Nobody's really opposed the idea, at least.'

'We're supposed to be open-minded in this business,' Bradley said doubtfully.

'It's settled. I'll arrange a re-enactment of the flight. And thanks for volunteering, but it's a one-man show. Meeting's over. No – ' He held up his hand as Houston opened his mouth to protest, and turned to Liss. 'I've got a job for you to do.'

The men slowly dispersed. When Downey, the last to leave, quietly closed the door, Klein sighed.

'I knew they'd give me a hard time. Thanks for coming to my rescue, Jeff.'

'I didn't do anything.'

'You made out a convincing case.'

'Me?' Liss exclaimed.

'Sure. I know about the experiments you mentioned, but if I'd said anything, everybody would've thought I was loading the case.'

'You *do* know?'

'Made it my business to find out. About this job I want you to do while I'm away. I've got security clearance for you to see Dr Bruce D. Lowrie, director of Defense Research and Engineering at the Pentagon. Your job is to tabulate all secret Defense countermeasure projects. Some of the information is readily available from the published testimony when Lowrie outlined some unclassified projects before the House Armed Services Research and Development subcommittee. He gave only general information, naturally. But he'll go through the computer retrieval printout with you on a top-security basis. You've been cleared. Your job is to evaluate *anything* that the computer kicks out that may show that a spurious high-energy source could home in on something like a collision avoidance scanner at thirty-one thousand feet and set it on fire.'

'Jesus – I never thought – ' Liss exclaimed. He scratched the nape of his neck thoughtfully. 'Where do I find this Dr Lowrie?'

Klein opened his desk drawer, pulled out a sheet of paper, and showed it to Liss. 'Here's his office number at the Pentagon. Park your car in the north parking area. Security Guard Number 17359 will be on duty. He'll phone for an escort officer to take you to Dr Lowrie. It's all arranged. You're to be there at thirteen hundred hours. Better be on your way.' As Liss rose, Klein added, 'Don't get lost in the Pentagon. It's a maze.'

Liss held up two crossed fingers and grinned. 'I promise not to get lost.' He took up the paper, carefully folded it, and inserted it in a pocket of his billfold, marvelling at Klein's efficiency. On the way to his car he wondered how Klein had persuaded Malik and the FAA to release a CA-100 aircraft for the test flight, especially since he'd been the person who'd asked for the grounding in the first place. But to Liss Mrs Harrilyn was just one of the NTSB's board members: he'd hardly exchanged greetings with her.

Dr Bruce D. Lowrie reminded Liss of a character he knew at MIT, a professor with the fragile body of a gnat and a penchant for covering it with outsize clothes. Lowrie was five feet three, he estimated as he strode with gangling steps towards the figure extending a welcoming hand from behind a huge glass-topped desk. The size of the desk, like the other furniture in the room, emphasised Lowrie's diminutive figure. With the exception of a crystal ashtray and a marble-based pen set, the desk was clear. The sign of a busy man, Liss reflected: busy men knew how to delegate work.

'You didn't get lost, then,' Lowrie said cordially.

'Your escort knew his way, sir.'

'Probably an old hand. Some of the new staff still get lost,' Lowrie remarked, his serious face suddenly warm. He motioned Liss to a chair and sat behind the desk. 'When they made me director of Defense Research whatnot and shoved me in this place, I had to use an escort for two weeks to find my office. After that I relied on a compass and chalk marks I surreptitiously dashed on the corridor intersections. It worked well until the cleaners rubbed them off.'

He looked at Liss with shrewd, appraising eyes. Lowrie, Liss suspected, examining the bland face and thinning grey hair, was that rare combination: a top-notch scientist *and* an efficient administrator. The man in charge of research and development for future United States defence projects could be no less.

'I expect you want to get your hands on these data, Mr Liss. I'll take you along to the Military Preparedness Room for Future Scientific Projects.' Again his face relented and he smiled warmly. 'That's something else I learned about this place. They dream up the most long-winded names.' He opened a desk drawer, withdrew a security badge bearing a coloured photograph of himself, his name, and number, and pinned it on the wide, loose lapel of his jacket. 'Hate being tagged like a refugee,' he remarked. 'Ah, I see they gave you a red one. If you try to get out of this prison after five o'clock with a visitor's badge, they'll likely lock you up for the night until someone comes back in the morning to re-identify you.'

'You serious, Doctor?' Liss asked anxiously.

Lowrie grinned as he came around the desk, and stretched up to put an avuncular hand on Liss's shoulder. 'Don't worry, we'll have you out by five.'

He accompanied Dr Lowrie along a corridor and entered a small room. There was no furniture in the room, only a television monitor on the wall, a small camera, and a console of buttons and switches.

'This is simply another precaution in the security arrangements,' Lowrie said apologetically. 'Post-entry-reception identification. It's to confirm what we already know about you. Please stand in front of the camera.'

Liss stepped forward, and Lowrie pressed a switch on the panel. Instantly a white light flickered across the monitor screen. Lowrie moved to a computer terminal and punched buttons. Liss's face appeared in colour on the screen.

'You're photogenic,' Lowrie said, chuckling like an elf. Liss had the impression he had said it before. Lowrie flicked a switch and Liss's face vanished. The words LISS, JEFFREY appeared.

'I feel sort of naked,' Liss remarked.

'Just a couple more things,' Lowrie said, pushing buttons. The screen dissolved and filled with several lines of blocked-out words: AGE 37 EYES GREEN HAIR BLACK OCC. CHAIRMAN SYSTEMS GROUP NTSB BUREAU OF AVIATION SAFETY.

'One more thing,' Lowrie said, picking up a microphone from a bracket and holding it in front of Liss's mouth. 'Say a few words for the record, please.'

'Words?'

'Anything that comes into your mind. Sing a song, or tell a dirty joke.'

'The machine identifies voice patterns electronically?'

'That'll do. See.' Lowrie pointed at the screen.

IDENTITY CONFIRMED SUBJECT MAY PROCEED TO TOP SECURITY CENTRE UNDER ESCORT.

Lowrie replaced the microphone and switched off the monitor. 'Let's go.'

Liss was surprised at the small size of the Military Preparedness Room for Future Scientific Projects. He'd expected to find himself in a large room filled with scientists and researchers quietly working at desks and drafting tables. Instead, he was in a room no bigger than his bachelor apartment. In the centre was a computer terminal and printout machine, and against the far wall a bank of computer cabinets. The only occupants of the room were two young women and an older woman, obviously the supervisor, to whom Dr Lowrie introduced Liss as 'an accredited party with security clearance.' The woman smiled, nodded, and went about her work, examining large sheets of paper printed with computer-coded symbols that she passed along to the other women.

Lowrie drew up a chair for Liss in front of the computer terminal. 'I understand from higher authority that you want all classified and non-classified projects dealing with ultra-high-energy outputs. Correct?' he asked quietly, climbing on to the seat beside Liss.

Liss nodded. 'Ground-based and from satellite overflights, basically. But I'm not tied to those.'

'Let's see what the Air Force is up to first.' Lowrie studied the keyboard for several seconds, yanked up his shirtsleeves through the armholes of his jacket, and pressed buttons. Lights lit up the console behind the keyboard. The printout burst into life, and a paper roll unwound from a slot. When the clatter ended, Lowrie stretched forward and tore off the paper. He put it on the keyboard where they both could read it.

'This is the electronic proposal for the new B-1 strategic bomber,' Lowrie said, pointing.

ELECTRONIC WARFARE USE: RADIO FREQUENCY SURVEILLANCE AND ELECTRONIC COUNTERMEASURES. CONTRACTORS: CUTLER HAMMER CORP. & HALLICRAFTERS CORP. COMPUTER: LITTON INDUSTRIES

'It doesn't involve very high energy sources, Mr Liss. It's semi-classified now, by the way. I'll pull out the top-secret projects.' He poised his tiny hand over the keys expectantly, then struck them vigorously. He tore off the paper that rolled out of the machine.

HARASSMENT VEHICLES WITH AUTOMATIC SENSORS, PRIME CONTRACTOR: SPACEPROBE CORP. JOINT USAF/DEFENCE ADVANCED RESEARCH PROJECTS AGENCY. USE: EXPERIMENTAL AERIAL VEHICLES FOR HARASSING HOSTILE GROUND-BASED AIR DEFENCES

'The vehicles would be shipped to an overseas theatre of war?' Liss asked.

Lowrie ignored the question, and Liss felt chastened. 'The experiments use high-power energy, Mr Liss. The work's being done at Randolph. Nowhere near Kansas.' Obviously Klein had briefed him, Liss told himself.

'But I thought Randolph was purely a flight dynamics lab. For test evaluation of flight characteristics of new aircraft,' Liss remarked.

Again Lowrie avoided answering. He changed the subject. 'The Tactical Air Command of the Air Force is working on remotely piloted vehicles – we call them RPVs. They come equipped with interchangeable noses for specific missions such as bomb delivery to a target, photographic reconnaissance, or electronic warfare, and are carried aloft by Lockheed DC-130 command transports. There's an on-board Univac computer that controls many RPVs simultaneously.'

'Where are these experiments going on?'

'Off the California coast. There's been a restricted air space for the past three weeks that will stay restricted for four months. You're interested in satellite energy propagation? Let's see what NASA's doing.'

Liss dug his heels in. 'Doctor, can you retrieve from the computer memory experiments going on just in restricted air spaces?' He visualised Steve and the flight crew stepping aboard the CA-100 at O'Hare in preparation for take-off.

'Easily,' Lowrie replied. His hands danced over the buttons again, and the printout disgorged more paper. The two men studied the symbols, discussed them, and finally rejected them all.

Liss scratched his head and said, 'At the Bureau we wondered about the possibility of *Russian* satellite overflights beaming high-intensity energy in a narrow band over United States territory. Is it possible for that to go undetected, Doctor?'

'Yes, if they discharge energy in random spurts. We've intercepted microwave and heat-sensing propagation from Soviet spy satellites, but it's impossible to monitor everything. Their sweeps over the United States take in huge chunks of territory, and the on-board equipment is remotely switched on and off by command from their operations base near Moscow.' Lowrie paused and looked at Liss. 'You think microwave energy or something on those lines homed in on the Caravan, is that it?'

'It's my boss's idea.'

'Burned out the collision avoidance equipment,' Lowrie continued. 'Beamed in and locked on the scanner and caused the fire.' It was now absolutely clear that Lowrie knew all about Klein's theory. The little man shook his head. 'They'd have to use a power source up in the tens of thousands of watts range to do that.'

He folded his arms and stared thoughtfully at the ceiling. A half minute passed before he stirred.

'Margaret, bring me the air navigation maps for the mid-west states, please,' he called to the supervisor.

She disappeared into an antechamber. A few minutes later she came back with several folded charts. Lowrie studied the titles of the charts until he found the one he wanted, and unfolded it on the keyboard. 'Missouri, Kansas, and Colorado. This should give it.'

Liss said, 'There was a Notam issued for all traffic over Kansas, Doctor. Restricted air space above ten thousand feet.'

'That area's well north of Air Route Six. But I was just wondering – ' The little man shoved the map aside and attacked the keyboard with such fury that Liss thought he would damage the mechanism. He suddenly stopped pounding, waited for the machine to cease making its internal clicking sounds, and tore off the printout. He read it to himself before handing it to Liss. As Liss read, his eyes widened.

AIRBORNE OPTICALLY-HOMING WEAPON SYSTEM USING RPVS AS EXPERIMENTAL TARGETS. HIGH-POWERED BLUE-GREEN LASERS ON NARROW BEAMS. FOR DESTROYING INCOMING MISSILE TARGETS. PRIME CONTRACTOR: LASBEAM CORP. SUB-CONTRACTOR: SPACEPROBE WEAPONS, INC. IN CONJUNCTION WITH USAF WEAPONS LABS AND NASA. SECURITY CLASSIFICATION: TOP SECRET.

'Lasers!' Liss exclaimed.

Dr Lowrie nodded, and picked up the map.

'Jesus,' Liss said excitedly. 'Lasers have enough energy to bore a hole in a battleship.' He thought about the laser demonstrations he'd seen at the last meeting of the Institute of Electrical and Electronic Engineers in New York. The narrow-beam light waves had burned a hole in a half-inch toughened steel plate in seconds.

Lowrie checked the printout again. 'These are the details,' he said, his voice subdued so that the women could not hear. 'A specially converted Boeing 747 of the Air Force is doing random daily practice runs in that restricted air space above ten thousand feet. On board is a generator supplying power for high-energy laser beams. The lasers seek out the remotely piloted vehicles – radio-controlled pilotless planes – which act as enemy targets. The laser homes in on an optical scanning device fitted to the targets, and the Boeing has a device that measures the backscatter from the scanner. As soon as the backscatter is detected by the Boeing's equipment, the target's scanner is saturated with energy, enough to set fire to the plane and burn it up. A timing device on board the target opens a parachute when the fire's burned itself out and harmlessly brings what's left to earth.'

'But why Kansas? Why not over the Pacific or Atlantic?'

'Because Kansas is approximately at the geographical centre of the United States. Time is of the essence in these experiments: the enemy keeps abreast of us, Mr Liss, and we need to do the experiments over what is the ultimate target of an enemy – the land mass of the United States. The eventual idea is to place the laser generators in bombproof underground silos, able to scan the atmosphere for incoming nuclear-tipped missiles and burn them out of the sky.'

Liss pondered this information. 'But the CA-100 was well outside the restricted air space. Bang on Air Route Six.'

'It might well have been,' said Lowrie quietly. 'It might well have been.' He hefted his jacket shoulders uncomfortably.

'What are you suggesting, Doctor?'

'The laser beams from the Boeing 747 are the most powerful airborne lasers ever developed. I'm suggesting a spurious beam homed in on the collision avoidance scanner of your aircraft and –'

'My God!' Liss exclaimed, his stomach turning over.

FIFTEEN

'Flight One-Three-Seven requests engine start-up clearance.' Captain Peter Haskett spoke quietly into the microphone.

'One-Three-Seven cleared for start up.' The voice of the O'Hare terminal air traffic controller broke from the overhead speaker.

Klein adjusted his shoulder harness. He was sitting in the jump seat directly behind Haskett. At his right Felske turned towards the huge console on the side of the flight deck, consulting his rows of dials. Byers was in the right-hand seat.

Haskett reached to the overhead panel, held down a switch, and looked at Felske. 'Start Two,' he said tersely, glancing at the engine power dials on the front instrument panel. 'Fuel flowing, rotation, I have a light on Two,' he called.

'Twenty-one per cent power,' Felske said over his shoulder, rapidly following with 'thirty per cent, forty-six per cent.'

'Number Two normal,' Haskett announced. Klein heard the distant rumble of the rear engine and felt a tremor under his feet. He glanced behind. They had forgotten to close the flight deck door and he could see row after row of empty first-class seats and, past the archway in the bulkhead, more rows of vacant seats in the economy-class cabins. Too bad: he wasn't going to unstrap himself to close it.

Haskett called for start-ups on engines One and Three, the wing engines. Felske called out the power percentages as the engines speeded up.

'Flight One-Three-Seven. Give the transponder a kick, willya?' the unseen controller asked.

Byers' hand shot up to the ceiling panel and pushed a button. 'Thanks. Gotcha now, One-Three-Seven. You weren't showing up on the scope.'

A new voice came through the speaker, the tower controller's. 'Flight One-Three-Seven. Cleared for take-off on runway two-seven left. Proceed to holding bay. The altimeter reads twenty-niner-niner-two, the wind is southwest at four knots. Have a good flight.'

Have a good flight! And at Kansas City Air Traffic Control Center they must be waiting anxiously for the first sign of Flight 137's blip to appear on their radar-scopes.

The aircraft glided backward, pushed by the ground tug, and the terminal buildings receded.

'Cleared to climb to ten thousand feet. Contact en-route controller at Joliet one-one-two-three.'

'Climb to ten thousand and contact en-route controller on Joliet one-one-two-three,' Haskett repeated. He moved a small lever, a little larger than a car window handle, at his side. The lever controlled the computerised steering system of the twelve main wheels a hundred feet behind where he sat, each turing at a different angle to accommodate its varying angle of turn. In three minutes he had skilfully manoeuvred the huge aircraft to the holding bay at the runway's end. He waited for a Delta Air Lines Boeing 727 to take-off.

'Pre-take-off checks,' Haskett called. Twenty levers and switches were checked, the three men touching each control as they recited the litany and responses.

'Flight One-Three-Seven. You are cleared for take-off.'

Haskett's right hand moved to the black knobs of the throttle levers. Felske, who had moved his electrically propelled seat forward on rails until he faced the front, repositioned a small card he had placed on the pedestal.

It showed V1, the speed along the runway at which the aircraft would be committed to flight, as 135 knots, and VR, when Haskett would pull back on the yoke to rotate the aircraft about its main wheels, as 141 knots. Klein thought the speeds were high for an empty aircraft. But then, he considered, the CA-100 was the latest design of the fast aircraft breed, the newer generation of wide-body jets with high manoeuvreability for quick climb-outs and steep flare-outs on landing. It was a heavy aircraft in relation to the area of its sharply swept-back wings.

The view through the windshield reminded him of the panorama from the simulator: an empty highway two miles long with white dotted lines along the centre line stretching into the distance, the Chicago skyline in the near distance, a cloudless sky above, and the greensward at the side of the runway.

'Lined up on the runway, turn up the taps to a hundred and ten to test, and away we go,' Haskett said quietly, releasing the toe brakes. Klein gave a hurried, extra tug on his harness straps.

The engine sound changed to a growl, a roar as Haskett steadily advanced the throttles. The dotted lines on the runway moved backward faster, blurred into a solid white line.

'Vee-one,' Byers called, his eyes glued to his airspeed indicator. Three seconds later he said, 'Rotate.' Haskett eased back the yoke, the remaining unused portion of the runway dipped as the nose pointed upwards, and the rumble of wheels on concrete ended. Flight 137 was airborne, climbing into a clear blue sky.

Byers watched the needle sweep around the altimeter dial as the aircraft soared upwards, his eye on the tiny white plastic button – air crew call them bugs – he'd slid around the rim of the instrument to 10,000 feet. Inside a little window behind the glass the numbers of the digital readout whirled: 8,000 . . . 8,120 . . . 8,140. At 10,000 a chime sounded.

'Flight One-Three-Seven at Joliet at ten thousand,'

Haskett said into his microphone. 'Proceeding on heading two-two-five to Bradford.'

'Have you at Joliet,' said a deep voice. 'Proceed on course. Cleared to flight level two-zero-zero at Bradford. Report on Bradford frequency one-one-four-seven.'

Haskett repeated the instruction. Klein loosened his harness and leaned forward. 'You're on auto-pilot *and* auto-throttle, Captain?'

Haskett nodded without taking his eyes off the instruments. Klein looked out of the side window where the Chicago suburbs sprawled below. Ahead lay the open countryside, with here and there a town linked by the arrow-straight line of a highway. A TWA TriStar inward-bound on the approach to O'Hare passed them four thousand feet below.

'Flight One-Three-Seven reporting position to Bradford. Flight level two-zero-zero. True airspeed three-niner-five knots,' Haskett said into his microphone.

'Roger, Flight One-Three-Seven,' said a voice through the overhead speaker. The en-route controller repeated the Caravan's altitude of twenty thousand feet, and the airspeed.

Byers consulted the computerised figures on the flight plan lying on the pedestal between them, and reset his altimeter bug to thirty-one thousand feet. Haskett did the same with his altimeter. Felske reached for the Aircraft Journey Log Book, opened it, consulted his dials, and entered the engine power setting and fuel figures in the little squares on the printed sheets. He did this for the three engines and glanced at the hundreds of little circuit-breaker knobs above his head. Two had popped out. He quickly read the labels beneath them, flicked a switch on his control panel, and called out, 'Galley cooker for cabin three inoperative, Captain. Also ceiling light in number three first-class toilet.'

Haskett nodded. Felske opened the drawer of his little desk and took out a narrow roll of yellow self-adhesive tape, printed on one side with the words 'Non-Operative' in a repeat pattern. He ripped off two lengths of tape and wound them around the two circuit-breaker knobs, silently cursing when the paper stuck to his fingers. The stickers would tell ground maintenance mechanics that the galley cooker and toilet light needed fixing. At that moment the altitude chime sounded, and the en-route controller's voice came through the speaker.

'Flight One-Three-Seven. What is your altitude?'

'Flight level three-one-zero,' Haskett replied.

'Roger. Contact Kansas City one-one-two decimal six and report flight level three-one-zero. Good day.' Klein recognised the familiar words from the CVR printout, and his throat tightened.

'Contact Kansas City one-one-two decimal six and report flight level three-one-zero,' Haskett repeated calmly. Klein pushed the voices of the dead crew out of his mind with difficulty. He glanced at Byers, whose face was immobile but whose eyes darted from instrument to instrument between quick looks out of the windshield. Glancing below, Klein recognised the outline of a Boeing 747 swinging into the descent pattern into O'Hare, followed at a higher altitude by a Lockheed TriStar.

Haskett again spoke into his microphone. 'Kansas City Center. Flight One-Three-Seven. At flight level three-one-zero.'

'Hello, One-Three-Seven,' replied a friendly voice. 'Check you at three-one-zero. Squawk ident on two-one-zero-zero.' Was it the same voice that greeted Flight 137 on May 16? Klein wondered.

Haskett pushed a button on the ceiling and waited. A few seconds later the voice said, 'Roger. Radar contact. No further position reports required – er – correction on that. Report your position at Wichita on one-one-three-eight as instructed for your special flight. Read back please.'

'Report position Wichita one-one-three-eight.'

'Roger. Your readback is correct.'

The tension on the flight deck mounted. Haskett

looked straight ahead, and Klein peered over the captain's shoulder to check the engine power indicators. The needles were rock steady. Nobody spoke. The flight deck, a deceptively solid-looking cubicle six feet wide and eight feet long, filled with instrument dials, levers, scores of switches, and green, red, and orange lights, hung as if suspended by an invisible thread; only the backward-moving countryside as it slid slowly under the nose indicated that the aircraft was moving. The cords on the back of Haskett's neck stood out like a veined rock. Klein looked up into the dark blue sky. Somewhere out there was the answer to the question: why did the collision avoidance gear scanner burn up? As the seconds passed, he began to wonder. Was there *really* something out there with the power to do that? Maybe Malik was right after all, and he was all wet. Haskett consulted the map he'd opened on the shelf.

'Topeka coming up,' he announced evenly, jerking his thumb downward.

The Caravan would swallow the next thirty miles in less than three minutes. That would put them exactly over the spot where the crash had occurred. Klein glanced at the clock set to local time. It showed 10.48.00. He had the printout in his briefcase but couldn't force himself to take it out to read it. He tried to recall. Wasn't that somewhere about the point where First Officer Roberts was telling the story about the taxi plane that had crashed in the mountains and they'd found all those bodies with lots of money? He saw Haskett's head move from side to side, checking instruments, touching each glass as he absorbed each reading, left hand lightly resting on the control yoke, despite the fact that the aircraft was on auto-pilot. Felske's eyes were on his engine gauges. The remote roar of the engines and the high-pitched sound of the slipstream zipping past the nose of the aircraft were reassuring. Byers stared straight ahead into empty space, a muscle working under his jaw. Haskett called out, 'Thirty miles southwest of Topeka.' Now he braced his hands around the yoke. Klein felt his heart thumping wildly as the seconds crawled by and he stole a glance at the inside air temperature gauge on Felske's panel. It showed seventy-two degrees. Normal.

'Report our position to Wichita, Ted,' Haskett said.

'Flight One-Three-Seven giving air position report. Estimated position thirty-five miles southwest Topeka. Heading two-two-two.'

'Roger. Report to Garden City on one-three-zero decimal four-five.'

Byers repeated the instruction. He looked relieved. Haskett slackened his harness and turned to Klein. 'We can carry on to L.A. as arranged, sir. Or head back and try again.'

Klein was glad that Haskett had volunteered for another attempt. He'd wondered how the captain would have reacted if he'd had to ask him.

'What about you other fellas?' Klein's flashing eyes took in Byers and Felske.

Byers nodded. 'I never said I'd pull the chicken switch if it didn't work the first time around, sir.'

'It's okay with me,' Felske said. But still Klein had a vague feeling Byers and Felske wouldn't mind if he called off the test at this point.

A bell chimed. 'Huh-huh. The company wants us,' Haskett said, switching the radio selector to the airline's SelCal frequency.

'This is Everett, duty officer at American Constitution's dispatch at O'Hare,' said a gruff voice. 'There's a special call from Washington for Mr Klein.'

'Put the Washington caller on,' Haskett replied.

'It's Jeff Liss of the NTSB. Can I speak to Mr Klein privately?'

'Sure. We can give him a set of earphones and we'll switch to another frequency.' Haskett handed Klein a headset and plugged the jack at the end of the cable into a socket.

Klein adjusted the headpiece and swung the stick microphone into position. 'Steve speaking. What's up, Jeff?'

'I think we know what hit the other CA-100s. Laser beams.'

'Laser beams! My God. Why didn't I think of that? From a satellite?'

'No. An airborne source.' Liss sounded strangely elated. 'Remember that Notam about the restricted air space north of Air Route Six? For traffic above ten thousand feet?'

'I remember. I never got an answer from Defense. Goddamned bureaucrats.'

'The Air Force's experimenting with high-power lasers on narrow beams to burn up incoming hostile missiles. That's the ultimate aim. At the moment they're incinerating remotely piloted vehicles in the air to test the system before they try it at higher altitudes and for longer distances. It's an optically scanning system – '

'That homed in on the collision avoidance scanner,' Klein exclaimed. 'There's enough energy in a narrow laser to set a whole goddamned aeroplane on fire.'

Byers and Felske were staring at Klein, utterly mystified.

'Jeff, is there any reason why these guys up here can't be told?'

'It's classified top secret.'

'But for God's sake. These fellas are taking the risks. We've just passed the point where the crash occurred, but we're still in the area where the second aircraft flamed out and they're the guys who flew it.' Klein's eyes were drawn involuntarily towards the throttle levers, the black knobs gleaming silver from the sunlight pouring through the windows. He suddenly experienced cold fear, expecting the levers to slip back and cut off power. 'They're entitled to know what's going on. I'll take full responsibility. Hold on a moment.'

'Captain,' Klein said, 'switch on the speaker.'

Haskett pressed a button. 'Okay, Jeff, tell 'em.'

Liss repeated what he'd told Klein but left out the purpose of the experiment. 'The airborne source is on a 747 cruising inside the air space at various flight levels above ten thousand feet. The laser beams shoot out at random periods to seek out the optical scanners on the RPVs. The instrumentation on board the 747 detects the backscatter and saturates the target with very high energy. Burns them up. What's left comes down on a parachute in a fireproof container.'

'The lasers can only home in on CA-100s?' Haskett asked, his face aghast.

'Yes, Captain. The Caravan's the first aircraft with an optically scanning collision avoidance system. The scanner's in the nose cone. When the 747 detects backscatter from your scanner, even forty miles away, it shoots out a narrow laser beam that saturates your scanner with heat.'

'Jesus Christ. Goddamned death rays,' Byers exclaimed incredulously.

'Now that we know the cause of the crash, why don't we get the Air Force to call off the tests?' Felske asked, a trifle anxiously.

Klein was in an awkward position. There were two things he could do: ask the Air Force to discontinue the experiments for a limited period and have the grounding directive for the CA-100s lifted. If there were no further accidents, it would mean that the probable cause of the crash and the flameouts on the second aircraft had been spurious laser beams homing in on them. On the other hand, he could ask the crew to turn around and try again, hoping that a stray laser homed in. Only *that* would give conclusive proof, an *actual* rather than a probable cause. He turned to Felske. 'We could ask them to do that, but it defeats the purpose of this test,' he said bluntly, but feeling scared inside.

Felske cocked his head, considering. He was in his late thirties, Klein estimated, with a wife and a couple of kids depending on his twenty-five grand a year. But, like the others, Felske had readily agreed to do the test flight, expecting an emergency en-route. Now that they had overflown the suspected danger area, he was having second thoughts. Hell, I can't lose this chance to prove my theory, Klein reflected. And it was, he reminded himself, still only theory. Here was an irretrievable chance to test it.

'We don't know for sure whether a stray laser caused the crash,' he said. 'We can probably get the Air Force to cancel their tests and get the CA-100s flying again. But we'll never be *sure* that it was the cause. We may be jeopardising hundreds of lives. On the other hand, knowing the 747 is cruising around shooting out lasers at remotely piloted targets, we could run through the danger area again, possibly catching an eyeful of laser on the collision avoidance scanner. Only that way will we know definitely.' He appealed to their sense of responsibility as commercial pilots. 'I put it to you.'

'Oh, hell,' Byers said offhandedly. 'We expected to catch a package of trouble the first time around.'

Felske considered this for several seconds. He was about to speak when a light flashed on Haskett's radio panel. He switched the frequency.

'Flight One-Three-Seven. Report flight level and position to Garden City.'

'Flight level three-one-zero. Position five miles southeast of Garden City.'

'Roger.' The controller at Garden City repeated Haskett's flight level position. 'Next reporting position Albuquerque. Report flight level three-one-zero.'

'Roger.' Haskett looked around at Felske. 'Make up your goddamned mind. We'll soon be in L.A.'

'Count me in,' Felske said conclusively.

Klein spoke into his microphone. 'Jeff, we're going around again to pick up from Kansas City Center handoff. Maybe this time we'll have something positive to report.'

'In a way I hope you don't. For God's sake, take care, Steve.'

Klein removed his headset and hung it on a hook. Haskett gripped the yoke and pushed the button to disconnect the auto-pilot. A hooter whoop-whooped and died to remind him that he was flying the aeroplane manually.

'Kansas City Center. Flight One-Three-Seven requests one-hundred-and-eighty-degree turn to repeat en-route course on Air Route Six.'

The Kansas City Center reply was immediate. 'Request granted.'

Haskett turned the yoke and the aircraft banked steeply. The compass swiftly rotated as the Caravan came around in a wide, graceful sweep, heading back to Kansas City.

Over the city he readjusted the heading and contacted the en-route controller. Then he switched on auto-pilot and auto-throttle, and retightened his harness. They flew on a south-westerly course for fifteen miles in silence.

'Temp's up, Captain,' Felske called abruptly.

Klein suddenly remembered to note the time. He looked at his watch and checked it with the instrument panel clock. They coincided. 'Remember the time,' he told himself, releasing his harness and bending over the pedestal, searching with his left hand.

'Feel anything?' Haskett asked.

'Nope.'

'Circuit breaker for the collision avoidance system's popped,' Felske said in a tight voice.

'Outside temp's normal,' Byers said.

'I kinda smell something burn – ' Haskett said. The clangour of the fire bell cut him off.

'Throttles!' Klein yelled.

He was too late. The throttles slammed shut and the engine roar ceased, emphasising the high-pitched whine of the slipstream above the clamour of the jangling fire bell. The off-key noise of the horn indicating that the undercarriage was up with throttles closed added to the racket. Haskett shoved the throttles forward a notch, his left hand struggling with the violently swinging yoke.

'Re-ignition. Start Two,' he shouted.

Byers' hand shot to the ceiling panel, heavy thumb slamming down a switch. 'Can't get a light. Fuel flowing. *No* light,' he yelled.

The green and red lights on the instrument and ceiling panels had gone out. When engines flame out, the electrical generators stop operating, although a wind-driven generator inside the nacelle of the Caravan's rear engine was supposed to cut in automatically. For some reason it hadn't. Haskett pushed the yoke forward to establish the aircraft in a glide descent. The aeroplane pitched forward as if a giant's hand had punched up the tail. Klein, his harness unbuckled, was hurled against the windshield. He caught a vision of yellow and brown fields swivelling from left to right. Then the fields began to swing the other way as the huge aeroplane was gripped in a dutch roll. With each rotation the fields swept faster past Klein's eyes. He remembered the aerodynamics course at Dulles: when the right wing dipped it retreated as the aircraft swung sideways, losing lift and increasing the speed of the roll; at the same time the rising and advancing left wing, thrusting higher against the sky, gained lift, pushing the fuselage over even farther. If the roll was allowed to speed up, the aircraft would flip over on its back and dive vertically into the ground.

His body was in the grip of massive alternating centrifugal forces, pinning it with enormous pressure against the windshield and instrument panel, crushing his left arm, while his useless right arm hung below Byers' panel. He felt he was inside a colossal pinball machine, with blinking green and red warning lights – the emergency generator had started up – and howling horns, plinking chimes, and the clanging fire bell sounding above the rising shriek of the slipstream. He focused his eyes on the altimeter at the side of his face, and watched thunderstruck as the white figures whirled down the scale at frightening speed: 20,000 . . . 19,000 . . . 17,600 . . . 16,400 . . . the vertical speed increasing as the aeroplane started its spiral earthward, metal parts rattling and screeching. All loose objects in the flight deck crashed against the windshield and instrument panels as the angle of dive increased. Felske's brainbag narrowly missed the back of his head, a shower of ball-points and a circular slide rule cracked against the windshield, followed by a wad of maps, uniform jackets, caps, and coat hangers from the crew's coat rack at the back of the flight deck. The altimeter figures became a blur, impossible to read.

He wriggled and heaved, but gravity and the high acceleration forces glued him in position. The blood in his brain, forced upwards, drew a veil over his eyes until the yellow and brown fields racing towards him at ever-increasing speed merged into a muddy-coloured mat. He felt himself slipping away, the noises subsided, and in a detached, dreamlike vision he saw himself lying on the beach with Sarah, the sun warm on his chest, and Sarah facing away from him, gently rubbing suntan lotion on her shoulders, brown, supple skin glinting with the oil . . . 'Opposite rudder, give it opposite rudder!' he heard Haskett's voice yelling. *'Opposite rudder! Now!'*

An excruciating pain gripped the fingertips of his right hand. Byers was standing up on the left rudder pedal as far as his harness would allow, exerting the full weight of his sturdy body, magnified by the enormous gravitational forces, on the metal pedal, and the fingers of Klein's right hand were squeezed between Byers' shoe and the pedal. Klein screamed in agony and the action brought him back to reality. Then, magically, the pressure on his cranium slackened, and he was conscious of a warm, sticky wetness around his fingers. The altimeter figures appeared through a haze: 7,800 . . . 7,600 . . . 7,500 . . .

'Easy on opposite rudder,' Haskett's voice boomed. 'She's coming out. You lovely bastard, you're coming out.'

Klein felt the pressure on his body ease. By gripping Haskett's armrest with his good hand, he managed to get his legs over the pedestal. A shower of loose articles fell from the ceiling as the aircraft slowed its violent rolling descent and levelled off at seven thousand feet. Jackets and caps lay in a pile on the floor.

'Jesus Christ, sir. I didn't know your hand – ' Byers blurted.

'What about dousing the fire in the nose cone, sir?' Haskett demanded.

Klein braced his body into the back of the seat, fighting nausea. He looked down at his fingertips, splayed chunks of meat, with fragments of white bone poking through the flattened flesh. 'There's no fire bottle in the cone,' he said weakly, binding a handkerchief around the bloody mess.

'Start Two,' Haskett called above the cacophony of the horn and bell.

Byers pressed the switch for the rear engine. 'No light,' he gasped.

'Try One.'

'Gotta light – fuel flowing – rotation,' Byers stammered.

'Twenty per cent,' Felske shouted. The raucous noise of the Undercarriage Up warning horn suddenly ended.

'Hard left rudder,' Haskett said, his voice kept under control by an iron will. He clamped his feet hard on the pedals to compensate for the surge of power from the wing engine, tending to swing the aircraft to the right.

'Thirty per cent . . . forty-six per cent . . . '

'Hold the rudder, Ted. Start Three.'

'A light – fuel flowing – rotation.' The whine of the wing engines changed to a roar.

'Let's get this thing back on the ground,' Haskett called. He scanned his shattered instruments. 'Where the hell are we?' he said to Byers, thumping the fire-bell cutoff button on the pedestal. The bell stopped instantly. Byers searched for the correct map.

'Flight One-Three-Seven at seven thousand feet on two outer engines,' Haskett said into the microphone. 'Heading – er – ' He saw that the horizontal situation indicator was undamaged. 'Heading ninety.' Quickly he checked the airspeed indicator. The dial glass was smashed, but the little window beside it was intact. 'True airspeed two-one-zero. We have a fire in the nose cone.' He glanced down at the throttle levers as if expecting them to be hot. 'Power response uncertain. Request landing clearance at – hold it –'

'Great Bend,' Byers said. 'It's an emergency airport.'

'Get that map off the windshield. I can't see a goddamned thing,' Haskett shouted. A map had unfolded and flattened against the glass. Byers tore it away, and turned his attention to Klein.

'Get the first aid kit,' he said. 'It's at the rear bulkhead.' Klein tried to get up, but his knees buckled.

Haskett spoke into his microphone, quieter now. 'Request emergency services on standby.'

'Flight One-Three-Seven. Cleared to land at Great Bend. Emergency services alerted.'

Haskett called over his shoulder. 'What'll happen to that fire, sir?'

'If the nose cone stays on, it may burn itself out.' Klein thought about the softened hinges and what would happen if the streamlined nose of the aircraft suddenly blunted. Turbulent air would burble over the front end of the aircraft and buffet the nosewheel when they lowered the undercarriage, probably tear off the nosewheel doors.

'How far's Great Bend, Ted?'

'About sixty miles.' Byers flipped the pages of the approach plates in his ringed binder. 'We can do a straight approach on runway one-one. It's eight thousand and sixty feet long. Airport elevation is one-eight-niner-zero.'

Haskett clicked his microphone switch. 'Flight One-Three-Seven requests approach and landing on runway one-one.'

'Roger. You are cleared for landing runway one-one,' replied a slow, reassuring voice.

'Smoke!' Byers shouted.

'Extinguisher,' Haskett called.

Felske released his harness, jumped up, and grabbed the hand fire extinguisher from a bracket at the back of the flight deck, near the fire axe. He stood behind the pedestal, pointing the red canister.

Haskett held up his hand. 'Hold it. Can't smell anything now. Stand by.' He turned to Byers. 'What's the landing bug speed?'

Byers picked up a fresh card from a clip on Felske's console and retrieved the relevant flight instruction book from the floor. He jotted down the landing speed on the card. Haskett glanced at it and set the button on the edge of the airspeed indicator to 121 knots. 'It'll be a nice slow landing without passengers,' he commented.

Klein looked through the side window. They were flying over open countryside, and he could see the early wheat bending as the wind rippled across the fields. Here and there a farmhouse stood out in brilliant white under the bright sunshine, and the earth suddenly seemed very dear to him. His hand ached, and the pain crept upwards until his arm throbbed. He glanced at the altimeter figures to take his mind off the pain. They were at 6,400 feet, in a steady descent.

Haskett jerked his head about, sniffing loudly. 'Still seems okay, but get ready with smoke goggles.' He twisted around. 'Yours are by the side of your seat, sir. If I call "smoke goggles," yank them clean over your head, like putting on a cap. Twist the bottom button if you're not getting oxygen. Can you manage with one hand?'

'Sure,' Klein said, taking the goggles from the shelf. Two steel rods extended backwards from the heavy eyepieces to connect with an adjustable band. He checked the oxygen button at the bottom, where it attached to a rubber hose. At that moment a pillar of dense black smoke swirled up from the base of the pedestal.

'Extinguisher,' Haskett shouted.

Felske squirted and the smoke dissipated.

Klein glanced at the altimeter. It showed three thousand feet. 'The fire's coming through the pressure bulkhead electrical connectors, Captain,' he said. Now that they were flying low, the air pressure inside and outside the aircraft was almost equal. As they got lower, the fire would work its way with growing ease through the cracks and spaces that separated the floor from the structure beneath. He struggled against the gnawing pain in his arm to recall all the flammable things in the understructure. Farther aft were fuel tanks in the belly of the aircraft.

'Captain, the fire will work itself aft the lower we get. Suggest you isolate the fuselage tanks and dump the fuel.'

Haskett called over his shoulder, 'Don, work the cross-feeds to feed the engines from the wing tanks only. Then jettison all fuel in the fuselage tanks.'

Felske rapidly flipped switches. 'Wing tanks to engines,' he announced. Then he lifted a red panel and jammed his fingers on two buttons. Klein peered out of the side window, looking back at the wing tip. For several seconds nothing happened. Then a spray of kerosene streamed from the pipe extending from the wing tip, and vanished as the fuel vaporised.

'Fuselage tanks empty,' Felske said.

Haskett turned to Klein. 'Sir, go aft and grab all the fire extinguishers. There's one in the aft flight attendant's position near the rear door, one in each of the three galleys, and another in the first-class cabin, behind the bulkhead. Hurry.'

Klein rose cautiously. He felt stronger now and made his way down the left aisle, past the hundreds of empty seats. As he re-entered the flight deck, smoke billowed behind the centre instrument panel.

'It's through the pressure bulkhead.' Felske grabbed an extinguisher from Klein and directed a steady stream of fluid under the instrument panel. The smoke died, leaving a pungent odour.

'Stinks like hydraulic fluid,' Haskett said. 'Nosewheel hydraulics?'

'Could be,' Klein replied uncertainly. He hadn't realised, when he'd studied the CA-100's systems, that he'd have to remember their layout under these circumstances.

'It *must* be hydraulics,' Felske said. 'The pressure's down.' He appealed to Haskett. 'What if it affects the flight control systems?'

'It hasn't yet,' snapped Haskett. 'And we'll be on final approach in a few minutes.' Too much theory, he told himself, more to steady his nerve than to criticise Felske.

'Hey – I smell rubber burning,' Klein reported.

'Wire insulation?'

Klein sniffed and shook his head. 'That's *solid* rubber. Nosewheel tyre,' he replied with hesitation.

'Maybe we can blow the fire out if we lower the gear.'

'Try it. How far are we from Great Bend?'

'Straight ahead,' Byers said, pointing.

In the distance the low buildings of a small farming town stuck out of the flat countryside. Several miles the other side of the town were tall, slim buildings, grain elevators, and the glint of a curving river.

Byers consulted his map. 'That's Pawnee Rock and the Arkansas River,' he said. 'Great Bend is fifteen miles farther east.'

Haskett looked at the instruments. 'My artificial horizon's kaput. How's yours?'

'Okay,' Byers replied. 'But my altimeter's dubious.'

'Mine's A-okay.' Haskett touched the instrument and the two outer throttles for reassurance. He glanced at the airspeed indicator and called, 'Gear down.'

It occurred to Klein that Felske might be right: if they were losing hydraulic fluid, the pipes leading to the under-carriage actuators might be empty. He held his breath as Byers moved a lever.

For five seconds nothing happened. Then, with relief, he heard a clump as the wheel-well doors opened and the hydraulic actuator thrust the twin nosewheels out into the slipstream.

'Three greens,' said Byers.

For several minutes they flew on in silence before the speaker suddenly became alive. 'Flight One-Three-Seven,' a midwest voice drawled, 'looks like you gotta nosewheel fire.'

'Yeah,' Haskett said calmly. 'How come you can see us?'

'We got you in our binoculars.'

'Tell me if the fire blows out when I open up the throttles.'

'Don't take the wheels off.'

Haskett thrust the throttles forward and watched the airspeed indicator. Maximum speed for flying the CA-100 with wheels down was 155 knots. If he exceeded that, the slipstream would seriously strain the undercarriage structure, and upset the balance of the aircraft. At 155 knots he asked the controller, 'What's doing?'

'You're trailing fire and smoke like a black comet. Christ – there go your wheel doors.'

Haskett quickly yanked back the throttles. Two semi-molten doors fluttered earthward like autumn leaves and landed on U.S. Highway 56, one narrowly missing a speeding oil tanker truck filled with gasoline it had picked up at the Great Bend oil refinery.

'Fire!' Byers shouted, pointing to the floor below the instrument panels. Tongues of flame licked through the space where the rudder pedals swivelled. Felske aimed a stream of fluid from an extinguisher. Byers grabbed another extinguisher and sprayed the flames at his feet.

'Wires,' he yelled, changing the aim of his extinguisher to direct the fluid to scorched, blackened cables dangling beneath the panel. They put the fire out, but fumes and dense smoke continued to swirl behind the panels.

'Smoke goggles,' Haskett called, yanking the heavy

fabric over his head. Klein pulled his on, twisting his left hand around to the right side of his head to position the headband. He rotated the button and took a breath. Oxygen was flowing. Felske had trouble with his hose: it snagged the armrest and kinked, cutting off his oxygen supply. He struggled to untangle it, straightened the hose, and breathed deeply.

The aircraft was down to eighteen hundred feet, passing directly over the little farming community of Pawnee Rock. Klein saw the upturned faces of workers in the fields, and caught a glimpse of a man on a tractor driving along a lane, staring up as he drove. Then they were over the houses and their view was cut off by a haze filling the flight deck. He peered through the windshield, but the smoke had reduced forward visibility to a few hundred yards. Haskett adjusted his headset and spoke to Felske through the microphone attached to his mask. 'Turn the equipment cooler on full blast. It might help.'

Felske rotated a switch for the fan that cooled the electronic equipment, and opened panel shutters. The smoke partially cleared. Klein's oxygen hose was long enough to allow him to go back to open the flight deck door. The smoke was instantly sucked rearward into the passenger cabin, but fumes continued to eddy through apertures in the instrument panels.

'I think the structure inside your nosewheel well's on fire,' announced the laconic voice on the speaker. 'Must be leaking burning hydraulic fluid over it.'

Klein cautiously lifted a corner of the mask and sniffed. For several seconds he couldn't identify the faintly sweet smell. Then he remembered Bradley had told him the wheel-well structure was built of a new magnesium alloy metal with a low ignition point. The goddamned structure was on fire!

'Captain!' he yelled. Realising the mask muffled his voice, he banged Haskett's shoulder. 'The inside of the nosewheel's made of magnesium alloy – it burns,' he said, and quickly shoved the mask back in place. At that moment the aircraft's nose started to sway around like a porpoise diving and resurfacing. A tumultuous whistling noise buffeted the windshield and a sound like a colossal fist hammered the flight deck roof.

'Grab her,' Haskett called to Byers, gripping the pounding yoke until the sinews in his wrists ached. The aeroplane continued to buck and sway. Haskett, mystified, glanced over his instruments. The altimeter was at 1,600 feet and the airspeed had dropped to 140 knots. He shot a glance at Byers, questioning the peculiar change in the aerodynamics of the aircraft. The answer came through the speaker. 'You've lost your nose cone.'

'For Christ's sake,' Haskett said, holding the swaying yoke. 'What's happening to the fire?'

'Spreading aft.'

'You got those fire trucks standing by?'

'At the ready. Engines running. They'll follow you down the runway.'

'Give me the landing dope.'

'The altimeter is two-niner-zero. The wind on the surface is from zero-one-four at a steady eight knots.'

'Roger.' No crosswind at least, Haskett thought.

Klein peered over the captain's shoulder. The Arkansas River was now directly below, with a barge chugging upstream, barely rippling the water. Several miles ahead he saw an airport building with two aircraft parked near it. The runway was foreshortened by the angle of their descent and looked narrower than a main-line airport's runways.

'Flaps,' Haskett called.

Byers grasped a lever on the pedestal, pulled it back with a deliberate movement, and waited for the flap indicator needle to move. Behind the goggles his eyes opened wide in astonishment. The needle wouldn't budge. He pressed hard on the lever to make sure it was locked down.

'No flaps,' he shouted.

'Hydraulic pressure's dropped. Almost zero,' Felske called.

'Good thing we got the gear down,' Haskett said with a deliberately calm voice.

'If we've got no pressure, we've got no wheel brakes,' Felske said self-righteously.

'I'm more concerned about elevator control right now. It's gone heavy,' Haskett replied, cautiously moving the yoke fore and aft to test the response in the flight controls, operated by hydraulics. Darrard, Caravan's designer, had taken advantage of the latest techniques used in the supersonic transports, where the conventional steel cables connecting the control column and rudder pedals to the control surfaces were used merely as a standby in case of hydraulic failure. With almost zero hydraulic pressure, Haskett was controlling the big aeroplane only by the mechanical cables now.

'Great Bend,' he said into the microphone, 'we got real trouble. Hydraulic pressure's near zero. It's affecting the flight controls and I – er – guess we'll have no brakes on landing. The pressure in the backup systems has gone low on us too.'

For several seconds the ceiling speaker was silent. Klein heard voices in the background as a discussion took place between the controllers in the tower.

'What's your landing run if you had all services operating, Captain?' the tower controller asked at last.

Haskett glanced at the landing card, wreathed in smoke spiralling through the slots in which the throttle levers worked. 'Four thousand two hundred feet. We've got no payload.'

'You got eight thousand and sixty, Captain. What's your bug speed?'

'One-two-one knots.'

'You'll make it.' The voice was confident, almost offhand.

The black paint at the edges of the throttle slots had begun to blister, like the scorched surface of a barbecue grill. Haskett, preoccupied with keeping the aircraft flying as it continued to buck and weave about the sky, was not sure what damage the fire was doing below the floor.

But Klein, knowing the structure most intimately, guessed exactly what was happening.

Driven by hurricane-force wind into the exposed wheel well, the flames seized hungrily on the magnesium alloy structure. Copper pipes containing hydraulic fluid, clipped to the collapsing structure, burst and showered flaming fluid over interior parts of the aircraft directly below the flight deck. What he didn't know was that bits of igneous material were dropping off and leaving a trail of little pyres across a cornfield.

The once smooth airflow over the nose was now a fiery maelstrom of twisted energy that screamed and pummelled the thin bulkhead at the aft end of the wheel well. A lock washer securing a bolt attaching a heavy strut for the retraction gear softened and collapsed under the tremendous heat, loosening the bolt. The strut slammed through the weakened bulkhead with the force of a cannon shell, smashing frames and ribs, and exposing the forward freight hold to the elements.

'Christ, what in God's name was that?' Byers exclaimed.

'Sounded like a bomb,' Felske said. The skin on his face had acquired a bluish pallor.

Haskett stiffened but said nothing. Perhaps he's more familiar with the aircraft structure than I believed, Klein told himself, wondering how far back the fire had worked. It was impossible for either man to know that the flaming liquid had tunnelled through the ragged hole in the bulkhead, setting fire to everything that could burn: rubber hoses, electric wires, padded fabric for noise absorption, and plastic lining.

Steve glanced at the altimeter. It showed exactly 1,000 feet. The haze on the flight deck coloured the buildings of Great Bend, population twenty thousand, a browny hue, and the tall steel towers and girders of the oil refinery this side of town looked like vague spidery structures. Beyond the refinery and the city was the runway, about five miles distant. Suddenly, all the runway lights lit up. Somebody down there was damn smart. Klein felt a surge of gratitude.

In the freight hold rubber insulating material sizzled, cooked, and burst into flames. The heavily reinforced floor sagged and collapsed as the beams supporting it expanded under the blowtorch heat in the confined space, and the sharp, raw edges of the floor began to fray the tensed elevator cables in their channels directly below, the cables moving backward and forward as Haskett tried to keep the shuddering aircraft on an even keel. The crumpling floor pressed steadily downward. During one of Haskett's violent yoke movements, the cables snapped.

'Elevator control's gone – ' he shouted, feeling the yoke go slack. Instinctively his hand shot to the throttle levers, pushing them forward to maintain flying speed. At that moment the controller said, 'Flight One-Three-Seven. You are cleared to land.'

'Yeah,' Haskett replied dryly. 'We've just lost elevator control.'

'Jes – er, Captain. You still got two engines?'

'Sure. I'll use the throttles to lose speed and trust to God she'll lose height. We'll have to make it first time. There's no chance of a go-around with the condition of this crate.'

He adjusted the throttles. The airspeed indicator dropped to 130 knots, and the altimeter, Klein noted with relief, sank to 700 feet. He glanced over the side and saw the shadow of the aircraft sliding swiftly across a highway, with several cars pulled over to the shoulder, their occupants staring up as the big aeroplane lumbered over them, trailing a half-mile-long cloud of black smoke behind it.

Degree by degree Haskett edged the throttle levers back through the smoking slots. The altimeter showed 620 feet . . . 600 . . . 580. The airspeed steadied on 128 knots.

A sudden upsurge of hot air struck Klein's face. He slackened his harness and put his hand to the carpet.

The floor was hot. To himself he said, You gotta believe, Captain – if you don't get this thing on the ground in five minutes, we're going to fall through the goddamned floor, or be incinerated.

'Flight One-Three-Seven. You are holding nicely on course and your angle of descent to the threshold looks good,' the tower controller said. It was the man on the ground's way of instilling confidence in a crew under duress. That tenuous link of communication had made the difference between disaster and a safe landing thousands of times.

'You're a bit high for the threshold,' said the voice.

'I got no elevators,' Haskett replied testily. 'Remember? And no flaps.' On sudden impulse he reiterated, 'And we got no brakes once we're down.'

'You'll make it down the runway okay. You've got nearly twice as much length as you need. Just thank Jesus you ain't got passengers aboard, Captain.'

'I am,' Haskett replied, thinking how much heavier the aircraft would be, as well as getting the passengers safely down and out of the burning aircraft. 'What's doing with the fire?'

'Er, it's looking sorta red in your nosewheel well. And looks like you've lost your nosewheel tyre.' The controller could not see in his binoculars the huge hole in the underbelly because streaming smoke covered it.

'What about the wheel?'

'Can't really tell. It's sorta black with no rubber left.'

'I'll drop her down on the main gear.'

Klein checked the altimeter. Four hundred feet. The aircraft was descending evenly, but not quickly enough. They were over houses and about a mile from the threshold. Treetops came up and vanished as the nose of the aircraft jerked about as if caught in turbulent air, and the floor grew steadily warmer under his feet. He wondered why Felske, sitting opposite, hadn't noticed.

Haskett moved the throttles. The airspeed fell to 125 knots. He was cutting it fine: only four knots above touchdown speed and still nearly a mile to the threshold.

On one of its circular lurches the nose of the aircraft stayed up, cutting off Klein's view of the runway. They were stalling – then the runway reappeared and they were descending at a steeper angle. God, this guy Haskett knew how to fly. The altimeter sagged to 300 feet.

'Quarter mile to threshold,' announced the voice from the ground.

'Roger,' Haskett said, the veins on the back of his hand standing out as he gripped the throttle levers for the outer engines. For some inexplicable reason the smoke had stopped curling through the slots but was pouring from the base of the pedestal in a sheet that flowed backward, hugging the floor and scorching the carpet. The air in the flight deck had cleared as the fire had taken hold farther aft inside the belly of the aircraft.

'Runway in sight,' Byers announced, in accordance with the rules. 'Decision height.' The altimeter quivered on 200 feet.

The white lines on the end of the runway slipped beneath the aircraft. Klein waited for the bump of the main wheels, but nothing came. They were overshooting. He glanced at the airspeed indicator. They were flying down the runway at 121 knots, fifty feet above it. Get down, you bastard. Haskett eased back the levers. Too far.

The airspeed fell to 117 knots. Obeying a law of physics, the aeroplane stalled and gravity took over. The main wheels fell upon the runway with a shattering crash that shook every rivet in the aircraft, telescoping the main wheel shock struts to their limits, driving up and bending the heavy fittings where they were bolted to the structure. The shock struts rebounded, and again Klein felt the aeroplane floating above the runway. When it struck the second time, Haskett rammed the yoke forward, hoping that some last remnant of pressure in the hydraulic system would move the elevators down. This time the aircraft stayed on the ground, main wheel tyres screeching like pigs being slaughtered, leaving twelve smears of melting rubber a hundred yards long on the concrete as the Caravan raced at one hundred and twenty miles an hour towards the far end of the runway.

'Reverse thrust,' Haskett shouted.

Felske pulled the levers through the gate with a powerful movement. But the aircraft still sped out of control towards the end of the runway.

Haskett yanked back the yoke until it hit his belly, an instinctive movement to keep the nosewheel off the runway as long as possible. But he knew it was useless. Slowly, ever so slowly, the nose tipped forward as the airspeed indicator dropped to 70 knots and the wings lost all lift. He pressed the brake toe pedals, but they simply clumped forward under his feet. The twin nosewheels struck the concrete, screaming and glowing with heat, bare aluminium discs spinning crazily, hurling chunks of white-hot metal outward like a catherine wheel that pierced the softened underbelly of the fuselage, and smaller bits that pinged and ricocheted backward along the runway. In five seconds the wheels were consumed in a puff of smoke, and the shock strut, without the support of the strut now lodged in the freight hold, gouged a deep furrow in the concrete before collapsing. The blunted nose of the fuselage struck the runway with a tearing sound, pitching Klein and the others hard against their harnesses as the aircraft slid along the runway with its tail high in the air. Showers of crimson sparks shot past the windows. The din was deafening as tons of metal forward of the main wheels exerted their full weight on the nose, grinding the front structure into hot shreds of twisted aluminium that spiralled off and bounced and tinkled along the runway behind the machine. The airspeed dropped to sixty.

Klein shoved his hand on the back of Haskett's seat with all his strength. The white lines at the end of the runway were clearly in sight, and beyond it, to one side, a line of trees. The left main wheel shock strut, weakened by the terrific punishment it had endured on first contact with the runway, buckled. Klein had a glimpse of a red fire truck racing to get out of their way, and saw Felske's hand straining back on the reverse thrust levers. There was a loud bang as the aircraft slewed off the runway and hit the grass. The line of trees spun wildly, the left engine pod dug into the ground and ripped off, spewing streams of kerosene from severed fuel lines. The airport buildings whirled past the windshield, followed by the line of trees, and then Klein's head stopped spinning and he found himself looking at the buildings again. But this time they were stationary.

For several seconds there was a silence such as he'd not heard before. Then his numbed brain registered the gurgling of fuel splashing from broken wing tanks, the crackling of flames and the agonised sound of metal tearing and bending as the aircraft settled deeper into the soft earth. The rise and fall of a screaming siren and Haskett's booming voice jerked him into action.

'Through the escape hatch!' Haskett snapped his harness loose, tore away his goggles, pointed at Klein, and commanded, 'You first.'

Klein twisted his harness release and stood up, forgetting that his goggles were still attached by the oxygen hose to the airframe. His head yanked sideways. Felske leaned over, ripped off Klein's goggles, and looked up at the roof. The floor at the back of Klein's seat suddenly buckled and collapsed, the flames shot into the flight deck. Felske jumped on his console and grabbed a handle that secured the crew escape hatch. With a practised twist he rotated the handle and threw the hatch clear.

'Grab this, sir,' he shouted, thrusting a wooden handle into Klein's hand. Designed for the crew to escape in a ground crash when they could not exit from the aircraft by the front passenger door, the escape gear consisted of a handle like a water skier's tow bar attached to a reel of rope in the ceiling. The idea was to lower oneself outside the aircraft after climbing through the hatch. But Felske had forgotten about Klein's useless right arm.

Byers came to the rescue. Springing over his seat, he pushed Klein on to the console and shoved him upwards until his head stuck through the hole in the roof. Klein realised that lowering himself down the side of the burning aircraft might land him directly in the flames. But escape through the passenger cabin was impossible: flames bursting through the collapsing floor cut them off. Heat and acrid fumes seared his lungs. Then strong arms grasped him under the shoulders and he felt Byers' burly form leaning heavily on him, and his shoes scraping and clanging over metal. A shower of sparks flared and cool air wafted over his face. His knees banged solid ground.

'You okay, sir?' asked Byers anxiously.

'Yeah – thanks,' he gasped. 'Where's the second officer and the captain?'

'Right here, sir. Now run, for Christ's sake, run. She'll blow any moment.'

Klein glanced back at the flames skyrocketing through the hatch, and ran with the others for a couple of hundred yards before sinking to the grass. The din was terrible, sirens and the yelling of men as the fire trucks drove up and directed streams of foam and chemicals that spluttered and sizzled against the aircraft. But their efforts were useless. An explosion tore off the tilted wing, hurling bits of smouldering metal high into the air. The right engine pod dropped off and rolled over, spinning flames into the grass.

In less than three minutes it was all over. The fiery skeletal hulk slowly settled on the blackened earth, and the burning fuel, running over the metal surfaces, seized on some yet undiscovered flammable material: passenger seats, seat belts, life jackets, plastic decor material, electric cables, and pockets of trapped fuel. The rear fuselage, gawkily pointing at the sky and untouched by flames, sagged for a second or two before the complete tail section, rudder and tail plane, drooped and slumped to the ground. The rear engine thudded on the earth with the finality of an elephant felled by a high-velocity bullet.

Klein looked at the pillar of smoke slanting upwards into the blue sky. He took a deep breath, smelling the sweet fragrance of early clover borne on the breeze from distant pastureland, dimly conscious of a nagging pain in his right hand.

'It *was* an external cause. It goddamned *was*,' he croaked. But the others couldn't hear him above the awesome noises of collapsing metal and the shouting of the fire fighters.

SIXTEEN

The morning of the public inquiry was one of those rare Washington July days when the air was sparklingly clean and the temperature hovered in the low eighties.

Klein stood behind his desk, a smile on his face. Shaw entered as he was in the act of picking up a ninety-page type-written report in a blue binder.

'What, no yoga this morning?' she teased.

They laughed happily. 'Look at that, Shaw.' He held up the report and read aloud from the cover. 'Aircraft Accident Report Number DCA 77-A-22 . . . FINAL.' He patted it affectionately and slipped it into the scuffed leather brainbag he'd kept since the Constellation crash. 'See what hunches do.'

'We must thank the Air Force, too. They confirmed the 747 shot out a laser on a target outside the restricted air space. Good thing they had begun to monitor every strike.'

'You mean it's a good thing you had the presence of mind to remember the time it zeroed in on Captain Haskett's aircraft.' She looked at the sling supporting his right arm. 'Oh, Steve, you can't present your report looking like that.' She put down her cigarette holder and tucked in the loose ends of the sling fabric.

'Thanks, Shaw. I don't know what the hell I'd do without you.'

'You sound like a broken record.' She pushed his shoulder. 'Better be moving. Bill and Jeff are waiting downstairs.'

He picked up the bag with his left hand, thinking of

the presses rolling in the government agency, running off the printed version of the final report for publication.

'Good luck, Steve,' Shaw called after him.

He made his way downstairs. The others were waiting in a taxi at the kerb.

'Hey, come on, Steve,' Houston shouted, pointing to his watch. 'We've got time for a coffee and a coupla sandwiches.'

'Can't you forget your stomach for once?' said Liss. 'Let's go the long way round. Up Independence Avenue and down Constitution. Just for the drive.'

'Good idea,' Klein agreed. 'It's a beautiful morning – and I *mean* beautiful.'

'Oh, for Christ's sake,' Houston grumbled. 'What are we supposed to be? Goddamned tourists?'

'For ten minutes.' Klein grinned. He gave instructions to the driver, and the taxi swung away from the kerb, made an illegal left turn, and sped up Independence Avenue. A few minutes later it turned right at the expansive green lawn in front of the White House. They cruised past the Washington Monument, where guides stood lecturing to groups of early-morning tourists. Farther on the White House shone brilliantly, then disappeared from sight as the vehicle turned right and went down Constitution Avenue. It drew up outside the Senate Office Building. Ray Malik, Mrs Harrilyn, and the other board members were standing on the sidewalk, talking animatedly. Klein got out of the taxi as another drew up behind, and Christopher Grewson and other FAA officials climbed out.

Mrs Harrilyn spotted Klein and hurried over. 'How's your hand, Mr Klein?'

'The doctor says it's going to be A-okay, thanks.'

She patted a stray brown curl into position under her graceful, wide-brimmed straw hat. 'You took a hell of a risk re-enacting the flight.' She looked again at the sling. 'You're a very brave and dedicated man.' Then she pretended to be stern. 'You know it's against the rules for investigators to do that sort of thing.'

Klein saw the dimples in her cheeks deepen as she tried to maintain her composure. 'Yes, madam. I'll try not to do it again.'

They both laughed, and Grewson and the others approached. Grewson looked reprovingly at Klein and Harrilyn joking together. Had he discovered who had exerted government pressure to get him to issue a grounding directive for the CA-100s? Klein wondered.

'Hello, Steve. I read your report,' he said patronisingly. He nodded at the group of lawyers and aviation legal experts walking up the steps of the Senate Building, carrying attaché cases. Klein recognised a few faces from the Air Transportation Association and ALPA. 'We'll see what some of these fellows say, eh, before we concur?'

'I guess *you* will,' Klein said coldly. He turned to Mrs Harrilyn. 'Shall we go in?' He offered his good arm.

At the top of the steps Malik called Klein aside. 'Don't say anything to Jeff Liss,' he said in a confidential tone. 'I've put his name down as an IIC when the next promotions come through, probably in the fall. But he'll have to take structures seminars at Dulles.'

'He'll jump at the opportunity.'

Malik opened the door for them all. 'One other thing, Steve. I had it out with Legal's chief counsel about the Avianjet case. It now looks certain they're coming around to your viewpoint. They're going to take the pilot off the hook. The poor guy didn't stand a chance.'

Glossary

ALPA. Air Line Pilots Association, the commercial pilots' union.

ATC. Air Traffic Control. The system of tracking and directing aircraft by ground controllers using radar and radio. In the United States the ATC system is administered and operated by the FAA.

Auto-throttles. A device connected to the auto-pilot that automatically sets the throttle levers to the best position for power requirements and fuel economy.

Backscatter. A reflecting, or scattering back to the original source, of a beam of energy; like reflecting a flashlight's beam from a distant mirror back into one's eyes.

Black box. *See* FDR (Flight data recorder).

CB. Circuit breaker. An electric fuse that can be reset.

Collision avoidance equipment. Electronic equipment that warns of the too close approach of another aircraft, or of an obstruction such as a mountain.

CVR. Cockpit voice recorder. A tape recorder in a crash-proof case that records the conversation between members of a flight crew, and between the flight crew and the air traffic controllers.

DME. Distance measuring equipment. An electronic navigation aid. The pilot presses a button and his exact distance in miles to the next ground station shows up in a little window on the instrument panel.

Dutch roll. The rolling of an aircraft from side to side. A divergent dutch roll increases in magnitude. If not quickly corrected, the aircraft may become uncontrollable, flip over on its back, and dive vertically. Some aircraft with sharply swept-back wings are particularly susceptible to dutch rolls in the event of engine failure.

ETA. Estimated time of arrival.

FAA. Federal Aviation Administration. The U.S. government organisation responsible for setting airworthiness standards for civil aircraft, including requirements for the design, manufacture, and performance of aircraft. It issues Certificates of Airworthiness for aircraft, and a 'type certificate' must be obtained for every new transport before any individual aircraft of a new class can be operated by an airline. The FAA also specifies when aircraft have to be inspected, maintained, and overhauled.

FDR. Flight data recorder. Sometimes called the 'black box'. It is a tape or wire recorder in an insulated thick steel sphere – crashproof, fireproof, and waterproof – mounted in the back of an airliner. It automatically records the positions of all movable wing and tail surfaces, the time to a half second when they are moved, and the engine power settings and other critical information. It records how the aircraft is flown, from take-off and climb-out, through cruising flight, to approach and landing, and shows if a pilot strains the structure by making too violent a manoeuvre.

Flameout. The sudden unintentional stopping of a jet engine.

Flight simulator. A ground-based copy of the flight deck of a particular type of aircraft, supported on hydraulic jacks. Through a computer linked to the control levers and switches on the exactly duplicated flight deck, it is capable of simulating all the sensations of movement of the real aircraft. It is used for training and checking pilots.

G. Acceleration due to gravity.

Nose cone. The streamlined conical cap at the front of the fuselage. It is usually made of fibreglass or other plastic material, and houses the weather tracking radar and collision avoidance equipment.

NTSB. National Transportation Safety Board. The U.S. federal agency that investigates, through its Bureau of Aviation Safety, the cause of air accidents. It makes recommendations to the FAA for changes in design or manufacture of aircraft, or on flight procedures or other factors affecting flight safety, depending on its findings. (New recent legislation now gives the NTSB broader powers.)

SelCal. Selective calling. The radio aboard an airliner on which the airline flight operations office or a ground controller may privately call the pilot.

CLIVE CUSSLER

PACIFIC VORTEX!

Fully armed and with all hands on board, the nuclear submarine *Starbuck* sailed into the calm Pacific Ocean for sea trials – and vanished. No wreckage, no signals, no survivors – nothing, until ace maritime troubleshooter Dirk Pitt finds a single, chilling clue in the shark-torn surf off Hawaii – the log of the *Starbuck*. 'Do not search for us, it can only end in vain . . .' A crazed journal of madness and death is all that remains.

The search for the *Starbuck* plunges Dirk Pitt into his most shattering assignment yet – a whirlpool of deep-sea mystery and terror.

ADVENTURE/THRILLER 0 7221 2753 7 £1.95

the trade

william h. hallahan

'Puts William Hallahan up above Le Carré, Deighton and Co.'
The Bookseller

Journalist Bernie Parker didn't make a lot of sense that day. His words needed a bit of explanation. But Bernie is in no position to do that right now because he's just stopped several bullets outside a Paris metro. Bernie is dead. And no one knows what his last words mean.

The least Colin Thomas owes his late friend is a reason. As an international arms dealer scoring off the hotter edges of the cold war he has contacts. Contacts that lead him back to a ruthless and uninhibited woman and to the centre of a devastating plan to change the face of Europe – even if it means starting World War 3 – even if it means starting the countdown to doomsday . . .

ADVENTURE THRILLER 0 7221 4215 3 £1.75

From the author of RAISE THE TITANIC!

CLIVE CUSSLER

NIGHT PROBE!

May 1914. Two top diplomats hurry home by sea and rail, each carrying a document of world-changing importance. Then the liner *Empress of Ireland* is sunk in a collision, and the 'Manhattan-Line' express plunges from a shattered bridge – both dragging their VIP passengers to watery oblivion. *Tragic coincidence – or conspiracy*?

Three-quarters of a century later a chance revelation re-opens the question. In the energy-starved, fear-torn 1980s, those long-lost papers could destroy whole nations – and Dirk Pitt, the man who raised the *Titanic*, confronts his biggest challenge yet. Racing against time, against the hired killers of enemies and allies alike – and the horrors of the sea bed – he launches his revolutionary deep-sea search craft in the hunt for the documents. 'Night Probe' has begun . . .

ADVENTURE/THRILLER 0 7221 2746 4 £1.95

Enjoy!

Rai x

Penrith
2015

CUT
- & -
CRUSHED